DEAD MIDNIGHT

Sharon McCone Mysteries
By Marcia Muller

Dead Midnight
Listen to the Silence
A Walk Through the Fire
While Other People Sleep
Both Ends of the Night
The Broken Promise Land
A Wild and Lonely Place
Till the Butchers Cut Him Down
Wolf in the Shadows
Pennies on a Dead Woman's Eyes
Where Echoes Live
Trophies and Dead Things
The Shape of Dread
There's Something in a Sunday
Eye of the Storm
There's Nothing to be Afraid Of
Double (with Bill Pronzini)
Leave a Message for Willie
Games to Keep the Dark Away
The Cheshire Cat's Eye
Ask the Cards a Question
Edwin of the Iron Shoes

Non-Series

Point Deception

#-AM 7/14

RAVES FOR MARCIA MULLER'S *DEAD MIDNIGHT*

"A well-laid plot...high-tech gloss on a tricky case."

—Marilyn Stasio, *New York Times Book Review*

"Muller packs plot, personality, and lots of life's messiness into the continuing saga of the San Francisco private investigator....Highly recommended."

—*Library Journal* (starred review)

"Her cases continue to be complex and chilling....This book is a good one."

—*Sunday Oklahoman*

"McCone remains one of the most popular of hard-boiled female private eyes....You don't have to be a card-carrying McCone fan, however, to appreciate the tightness of plot and wealth of intriguing background in her latest adventure."

—*Booklist*

"DEAD MIDNIGHT is superb, above and beyond Muller's past work....Muller is one in a million and so is McCone."

—*Denton Record Chronicle* (TX)

"A totally satisfying series....DEAD MIDNIGHT is a wonderful mystery."

—Ilovemysterynewsletter.com

"A fun who-done-it for those readers who want a story line faster than a world class 100 yard dash."

—*Midwest Book Review*

"Another guaranteed hit for a master of the craft."

—*Anniston Star* (AL)

more...

"Marcia Muller helped pioneer the female P. I. genre....DEAD MIDNIGHT proves timely indeed as Sharon plunges into the post-dot.com-bust world...a neatly plotted and smoothly written story."

—***Sentinel Book Critic***

"Solid characterization, strong plotting, good writing, and...real detective work. Muller and McCone should be required reading for all those wishing to write a hard-boiled female P. I. series."

—***I Love a Mystery***

"A setting all too real in today's world. This is a timely novel that will please Muller's many fans."

—**NewMysteryReader.com**

PRAISE FOR MARCIA MULLER'S OTHER SHARON McCONE NOVELS

LISTEN TO THE SILENCE

"A series best."

—***Los Angeles Times***

"Engrossing...quite possibly this talented author's best effort to date."

—***San Diego Union-Tribune***

"Especially satisfying."

—***Orlando Sentinel***

"Muller realistically unravels this intriguing tale, weaving Indian culture to enrich the plot. A very satisfying mystery."

—***San Francisco Examiner***

"Fans of this long series will enjoy seeing a more vulnerable side of McCone here. Newcomers will be pleased to be along for the ride."

—***San Francisco Chronicle***

A WALK THROUGH THE FIRE

"Incandescent characters and descriptions of Kauai...one of America's finest writers of any genre."

—Cleveland Plain Dealer

"An enjoyably convoluted plot and a real sense of the trials, techniques, and tribulations of true-life gumshoeing."

—San Francisco Examiner & Chronicle

"Muller, as usual, deftly combines an intriguing mystery with a persuasive romance." ***—San Diego Union-Tribune***

"Muller is 'must' reading for all mystery fans. Start with this one, then go back and enjoy the others."

—Cleveland Plain Dealer

WHILE OTHER PEOPLE SLEEP

"An excellent tale...by a master."

—San Francisco Examiner & Chronicle

"Intriguing and unpredictable....One of the most consistently satisfying series in whodunit history."

—San Diego Union-Tribune

"A tense and enthralling story."

—Detroit News and Free Press

"A rip-roaring conclusion." ***—Washington Post Book World***

"A fascinating novel that goes far beyond the range of most detective tales....Muller has been turning out engrossing novels featuring an intelligent, maturing detective for two decades and shows no signs of slowing down."

—Dallas Morning News

more . . .

BOTH ENDS OF THE NIGHT

"Profoundly entertaining...amazing...another winner from Muller."

—***Washington Post Book World***

"Terrific...tightly plotted....McCone is way up."

—**Marilyn Stasio, *New York Times Book Review***

"Evocative....One of the treasures of the genre."

—***Chicago Tribune***

"Muller's novels are models of thoughtful plotting and rich characterization....A superior tale."

—***Seattle Times***

"Muller is in top form....The tale is ripe with the best of Muller's traits—strong dialogue, authentic characters, and a good mystery....[McCone is] one of the first of her ilk and still one of the best."

—***Minneapolis Star Tribune***

"Reading the McCone novels in order, one can track the astounding literary growth of author Marcia Muller as she hones her skills to scalpel sharpness....A prime example of just how good the noir novel can be."

—***Cleveland Plain Dealer***

DEAD MIDNIGHT

MARCIA MULLER

An AOL Time Warner Company

This book is a work of fiction. Names, characters, places, and incidents are the product of the author's imagination or are used fictiously. Any resemblance to actual events, locales, or persons, living or dead, is coincidental.

If you purchase this book without a cover you should be aware that this book may have been stolen property and reported as "unsold and destroyed" to the publisher. In such case neither the author nor the publisher has received any payment for this "stripped book."

WARNER BOOKS EDITION

Cover design and art by Tony Greco

Warner Books, Inc.
1271 Avenue of the Americas
New York, NY 10020

Visit our Web site at www.twbookmark.com

 An AOL Time Warner Company

Printed in the United States of America

Originally published in hardcover by The Mysterious Press
First Paperback Printing: July 2003

10 9 8 7 6 5 4 3 2 1

For Susan Richman,
One of my finest partners in crime

Many thanks to:
Suzette Lalime Davidson, for her dot-com expertise
Jim Moen, for his tale of intrigue among the venture capitalists
Mark Terry, for luring me into the twenty-first century
Michael Terry, for getting me set up for samc
And, of course, the in-house editor and Title Master

O coward conscience, how dost thou afflict me!
The lights burn blue, it is now dead midnight.
Cold fearful drops stand on my trembling flesh;
What do I fear? Myself?

Shakespeare, *Richard III*

Monday

•

APRIL 9

At one time or another, it happens to everyone. A call comes late at night, bringing news of the death of someone close, and with it a nightmarish sense of unreality. You entertain selfish thoughts: Why is this happening to me? Then you immediately feel ashamed because tragedy has not actually struck you. You, after all, are still alive, healthy, and reasonably sane.

Practicalities intrude, because they are a way of keeping the pain at bay. To whom to break the news, and how? What arrangements must be made? How badly will your life be disrupted? But in the end it all boils down to loss and finality—in my case, loss and finality heaped upon recent losses and betrayals.

My call came at eleven-twenty P.M., from a deputy sheriff in Humboldt County, some two hundred and seventy miles north of San Francisco. Deputy Steve Brouillette. I'd spoken with him several times over the past six months, but he'd never had any news for me. Now he did, and it was bad.

My brother Joey was dead at age forty-five. By his own hand.

Friday

•

APRIL 13

"I'd hate to think we're going to be making a habit of this."

My brother John's remark, I knew, was intended to provide comic relief but, given the nature of the situation, it was destined to fail. I looked up at him, shielding my eyes against the afternoon sun, and saw his snub-nosed face was etched with pain. He slouched under the high wing of the Cessna 170B, one hand resting on its strut, his longish hair blowing in the breeze. With surprise I noted strands of white interwoven with the blond of his sideburns. Surely they hadn't been there at Christmas time?

"Sorry," he said, "but it's a thought that must've occurred to you too."

My gaze shifted across San Diego's Lindbergh Field to the west, where we'd earlier scattered Joey's ashes at sea. Joey, the family clown. Joey, whom we'd assumed had never entertained a somber thought in his life. The dumb but much loved one; the wanderer who was sorely missed at family gatherings; the worker who more often than not was fired from his low-end jobs but still managed to land on his feet.

Joey, a suicide.

"Yes," I said, "it's occurred to me. First Pa, now this."

"And Ma and Melvin aren't getting any younger."

"Who is?" I moved away and began walking around the plane. A red taildragger with jaunty blue trim, Two-five-two-seven-Tango was my prize possession, co-owned with my longtime love, Hy Ripinsky. I ran my hand over the fuselage, checked the elevators and rudder—preflighting, because I felt a sudden urge to be away from there.

John followed me. "I keep trying to figure out why he did it."

I went along the other side of the plane without responding.

As he gave me a boost up so I could check the fuel level in the left tank, he added, "What could've gone that wrong with his life? That he'd kill himself?"

"I don't know."

John hadn't wanted to talk about Joey when I'd arrived last night, and he'd been mostly silent on today's flight over the Pacific and later at lunch in the terminal restaurant. Now, in the visitor tie-downs, he seemed determined to initiate a weighty discussion.

"I mean, he had a lot going for himself when he disappeared. A good job, a nice woman—"

"And a crappy trailer filled with empty booze and pill bottles." I eased off the strut and continued my checks. "From what Humboldt County told me when they called, the shack where he offed himself had the same decor."

John grunted; my harsh words had shocked him. Shocked me, too, because up till now I hadn't been aware of how much anger I felt toward Joey.

I opened the engine cowling and stared blankly inside. One of those strange lapses, like walking into a room and not knowing what you went there for. Jesus, McCone, I thought, get a grip. I reached in to check the oil, distracted by memories of my search for Joey.

When Pa died early in the previous September, we hadn't been able to reach Joey at his last address, and it wasn't till the end of the month that John traced him to a run-down trailer park near the Mendocino County hamlet of Anchor Bay. By then he'd disappeared again, leaving behind all his possessions and a brokenhearted girlfriend. I immediately began a trace of my own, but gave up after two fruitless months, assuming that—in typical Joey fashion—he'd resurface when he was good and ready. Then, this past Monday, the call from Deputy Brouillette. Joey had been found dead of an alcohol-and-barbiturate overdose in a shabby rental house in Samoa, a mill town northwest of Eureka. His handwritten note simply said, "I'm sorry."

I shut the cowling and climbed up to check the right fuel tank. I was replacing its cap when John spoke again. "Shar, haven't you wondered? Why he did it?"

"Of course I have." I twisted the cap—hard, and not just for safety's sake—and lowered myself to the ground. Why was he doing this now, when he knew I wanted to leave?

"We should've realized something was wrong. There must've been signs. We could've helped him."

I wiped my oil-slick fingers on my jeans. "John, there was no way we could've known."

"But we should've. He was our brother."

"Look, you and I lived with Joey for what was actually a very short time. He was five years older than I, and for the most part we went our separate ways. I doubt I ever had a real conversation with him. And as far as I know, all the two of you ever did together was stick your noses under the hoods of cars, drink beer, and get in trouble with the cops.

During the past fifteen years, Ma's the only one who got so much as a card or a call from him. Half the time we didn't know where he was living or what he was doing. So you tell me how we could've seen signs and known he needed help."

John sighed, giving up the illusion. "I guess that's what makes it so hard to deal with."

"Yeah, it is."

I took the keys to the plane from my pocket, and his eyes moved to them. "So where're you headed?"

"Hy's ranch for the Easter weekend, then back to San Francisco. I've got a new hire to bring up to speed at the agency, and a Monday lunch with an attorney who throws a lot of business my way."

"Gonna keep yourself busy, keep your mind off Joey."

"Is that so bad?"

He shook his head.

Not so bad to try to forget that sometimes people we love commit self-destructive acts that are enough to temporarily turn that love to hatred.

Monday

•

APRIL 16

Glenn Solomon, San Francisco's most prominent criminal-defense attorney, and I were braving traffic—angling from Momo's restaurant where we'd just had lunch toward the city's handsome new baseball stadium. Pacific Bell Park struck me as a perfect combination of the old and new: red brick, with the form and intimate atmosphere of early urban ballparks, yet comfortable and equipped with every modern amenity. And, most important in this car-infested city, easily accessible by public transportation.

"You been to a game there yet?" Glenn asked me.

"Of course I've been to a game. You let me use your season tickets last June."

"Ah, yes. Hottest temperatures for that day in the city's history. You and your friends in the sun right behind third base. You greased up with SPF thirty, poured bottled water on your heads till it boiled, and left after the third inning. And to make matters worse, that game was the first time the Giants played well in the new park. You'll never stop reminding me, will you?"

"Not till I get another crack at those great seats."

"Mmm." Glenn nodded noncommittally, his mind already having strayed from baseball.

Like the ballpark, Glenn Solomon was a perfect blend of old and new San Francisco. Over an unhurried lunch, his cell phone turned off, he'd wined and dined me without a word about business. As waiters hovered, eager to please a cornerstone of the local legal establishment, he'd flattered me by asking about Hy, about the home we'd recently had built on our Mendocino Coast property, about some recent startling developments in my personal life. But now his focus had shifted into high gear, and soon he would trot out all his persuasive skills in order to interest me in taking on a job that I gathered, from his reticence so far, was one I'd surely want to turn down.

But he wasn't ready yet, and I walked along the Embarcadero beside him, content to enjoy the view of Treasure Island and the sailboats on the bay. When we reached Miranda's, my favorite waterfront diner, and he still hadn't spoken, I frowned and glanced at him. Glenn was a big man, silver-haired, rotund in a prosperous fashion, with a clean-shaven chin that looked strange to me because he'd worn a full beard the whole time I'd known him. In spite of his bulk he handled himself gracefully, and he cut an imposing figure, attracting many glances as we strolled along.

Glenn was known as a genial fellow among his golf and tennis partners; a kind and generous employer to his staff; a respected litigator among his fellow bar association members; a bulwark of strength to both clients and friends in need. And to his wife of twenty years, Bette Silver, he was a pussycat with a lion's roar. But Glenn could also be devious and sly. His quick mind, sharp tongue, and caustic wit demolished those who opposed him; his attack mode both in and out of the courtroom was formidable. I'd stood up to some tough characters in my years as an investigator, but I'd long ago decided I would never want to get on the wrong side of Glenn Solomon.

He noticed me studying him and touched my elbow. "Let's sit awhile."

There was a bench in front of Miranda's, flanked by planter boxes where tulips and daffodils bloomed. The flowers were evidence of the gentle side of the café's owner, an often brusque former longshoreman nicknamed Carmen Miranda from his days offloading banana boats at China Basin. Glenn and I sat there, but only after he—with great ceremony—dusted it off with his crisp white handkerchief.

We were facing the waterfront boulevard, as wide as the average city lot, with a median strip where stately palms grew and vintage streetcars rattled along. A red one passed, its bell clanging. Directly opposite us was the condominium complex where my nephew and operative, Mick Savage, lived with another of my staff, Charlotte Keim. The condos were built of white stucco incorporating a great deal of glass block and chrome, and to either side of them were other complexes, with shops, delis, and restaurants on the street level—all evidence of the revitalization of our waterfront.

In 1989 this area was at the bottom of a steeply descending curve. Years before most of the shipping industry had fled to Oakland or other West Coast ports; factories and warehouses stood abandoned; many piers were vacant, run-down, and rat-infested; the torching of buildings for insurance money was not uncommon. Then, on October 17, the tectonic plates along the Loma Prieta

Fault shifted, the earth heaved, and one of the ugliest structures in the city, the Embarcadero Freeway, crumbled. When its ruins were razed, bay vistas that hadn't been seen for over thirty years were revealed, and we all realized that San Francisco could have a beautiful waterfront.

Now, with the redevelopment still continuing, the heart of the city has gradually moved from such traditional places as the financial district and Union Square to the water's edge, where it pumps lifeblood into long moribund areas. New buildings rise, and old structures are being converted to offices or live-work lofts. Technology-related firms have relocated to the South of Market, and close on their heels have followed the upscale restaurants, clubs, and boutiques that their owners and employees require. Even the crash of the hot tech market hasn't put too much of a damper on the vibrant ambience of South Beach, SoMa, and Mission Bay, and the future looks bright there. Of course, all change comes with its price, and in San Francisco's case, it has been costly.

As if he knew what I was thinking, Glenn said, "Too much, too fast."

"The changes in the city? Yes."

"I don't mind most of them. The Mission Bay complex, for instance, that's exciting: six thousand more badly needed apartments, the new UCSF campus, all the open space. It's good development. No, it's the divisiveness that bothers me. The haves versus the have-nots. The old people who can't afford to remain in the neighborhoods where they were born. Young families and working-class people who are being forced out by the high cost of living. The black community shrinking. It changes the face of the city, makes it a playground for rich people. What's the average rent on a two-bedroom apartment in a decent neighborhood these days?"

"I'm not sure. I paid well under a hundred thousand for my house, but last year a smaller one down the street sold for five hundred to a couple from Silicon Valley—and it was advertised as a fixer-upper. Office rents're coming down since the dot-com companies started failing; I've been watching them in case the Port Commission doesn't renew my agency's lease on the pier next year. But they were astronomical to begin with."

Glenn waved to a man in blue spandex who was jogging by. "One of my young associates," he said. "Top talent out of Columbia. I had to pony up a hundred and twenty-five thousand to get him. All these baby nouveaux throwing money around as if it were confetti. If the dot-com fire hadn't fizzled, we'd be ass-deep in them by now." He sighed. "Don't misunderstand me, my friend. I don't begrudge those who've earned it. And I like the new vitality in the city, even if we do have the worst political machine west of Chicago. But I wish . . ."

"You wish the bucks were spread around more evenly. Or that the haves exercised some old-fashioned concern and charity."

"Exactly. This isn't an abstract conversation, you know. It's leading up to the reason I asked to meet with you today."

At last he was getting around to the matter at hand. I glanced at him, expecting to see the crafty expression—what he called his "wolf look"—that always accompanied his efforts to enlist my aid in a near impossible case. But instead I saw only deep melancholy.

He said, "I am about to ask a very personal favor of you."

The matter he wanted me to investigate, Glenn explained, was atypical for his practice. A civil case, which he almost never took on. A wrongful-death suit against an online magazine called InSite.

InSite's market niche was chronicling the new and the hip in the Bay Area: whatever restaurant the hordes were about to flock to; hot artists, authors, and celebrities; trendy products and fashions. In short, a *W* of the local wired set. I myself had visited their site a few times: to check out good shops for unusual Christmas presents; to read an interview with Mick's father, Ricky Savage, whom they'd described as a "country-and-western icon"; to see what subjects my reporter friend, J.D. Smith, was currently delving into. The writing was lively and informative; the content changed frequently. *InSite* and a handful of other quality online publications such as *Salon* had survived the recent economic downturn.

I asked Glenn, "What's the personal angle?"

"The suing family are people I count among my closest friends. The *InSite* employee who died was my godson."

"And how was the company at fault?" Working at a magazine didn't sound like particularly hazardous duty.

"Have you heard of *karoshi*?"

I shook my head.

"The word is Japanese. Literally it means to die of overwork. A common phenomenon in that country—

responsible, they estimate, for between one thousand and ten thousand deaths per year."

"What kind of deaths? Heart attacks? Strokes? Pure exhaustion?"

"All of those, and more. Until recently the majority of such deaths seldom resulted in litigation, but last year the family of one victim successfully sued a large Tokyo advertising agency. My clients, who are of Japanese descent, knew of the case and decided to see if the same could be accomplished in the U.S. courts."

"And you need my agency to document that the employer was liable for your godson's death."

"Yes. And I want you, Sharon, not one of your operatives."

"Of course." The concept was intriguing. Why had Glenn felt he needed to ply me with expensive food and wine in order to interest me? I pulled my mini-cassette recorder from my bag and said, "I'll need some particulars now, so I can open a file. And I'll need copies of your files on the case as well. What's the family's name?"

"Nagasawa."

"That sounds familiar."

"You've probably seen the name in the paper. They're patrons of the arts and supporters of a number of local charities. I went to college with Daniel Nagasawa. He's an eye surgeon and owns one of those clinics that do corrective laser treatment. His wife, Margaret, has a small press that publishes quality children's books. They have—had—three sons. Harry, the oldest, is twenty-nine and a resident in cardiac surgery at U.C. Medical Center. Roger, my godson, was twenty-six when he died, the middle child. Eddie's twenty and still down at Stanford, studying a combination of physics and computer science, top of his class."

"From their given names, I judge the family has been in this country awhile."

"Four generations. Daniel's grandfather came over from Osaka to work on a truck farm in the Central Valley, and ended up owning his own farm near Fresno. He left his son a going concern that earned enough to put Daniel through college and medical school. The Nagasawas are worth many millions now."

"Okay, what about Roger? What was he like?"

Glenn's face grew more melancholy. "An underachiever in a family of overachievers. Had a degree in journalism from the University of Michigan—the only one of the boys who ever lived far from home. Personally, I think he chose Michigan in order to escape the family pressures. After graduation, he drifted from one reporting job to another, moving west with each change. A year and a half ago he returned to San Francisco, and a friend recommended him for a staff position at *InSite*. Roger saw it as an opportunity to excel, eventually exercise promised stock options, and measure up to the rest of the family."

"He told you that?"

"Yes. We were close. But apparently not as close as I thought."

"What does that mean?"

Glenn ignored the question. "The atmosphere at *InSite* was brutal. Sixteen, twenty-hour days, seven days a week, and no comp time. Low pay, and their promises of stock options went unfulfilled. The editor and publisher, Max Engstrom, is an egomaniac who delights in abusing and humiliating his subordinates. Stupid stuff, reminiscent of hazing in college fraternities, but it cuts to the core when a person's sleep-deprived and unsure as to whether he'll have a job the next day. And particularly hard to take for a sensitive young man who's desperate to win his family's love and approval."

"So what happened? Did Roger die because the hazing went too far?"

Glenn's mouth twitched and his eyes grew liquid. "You could say that. Two months ago, on Valentine's Day, Roger committed suicide. Stopped his car on the Bay Bridge, climbed over the railing, and jumped. Beforehand he mailed a letter to his parents in which he apologized for being a failure."

I'm sorry.

Joey's note. God, the parallels were so obvious! A man who drifted from job to job. An underachiever in a family of overachievers.

A man who killed himself.

Suddenly I felt lightheaded. I touched my fingers to my forehead. It was damp, and the too-heavy lunch I'd eaten now lay like a brick in my stomach.

"Sharon?" Glenn said.

I pressed the stop button on my recorder. "I'm okay," I said after a moment. "But I can't take this case. There's no way I can take it."

And there was no way I was going to discuss Joey's suicide with Glenn. Too much of my private life had been the subject of conversations over the past six months. Bad enough that I was repeatedly forced to explain—as I just had at lunch—that when the man whom I'd thought to be my father died in September, I'd discovered that I had a birth father living on the Flathead Indian Reservation in

Montana. That while I had a family in California, I also had a birth mother, a half sister, and a half brother in Boise, Idaho.

No, I couldn't take this case, but I'd find some way of explaining why that didn't involve Joey. Or so I told myself until Glenn spoke again.

"I know about your brother," he said. "Hank told me."

Hank Zahn, my closest male friend since college, had betrayed a confidence.

"The subject came up because of Roger," Glenn added.

"And you, like a typical lawyer, saw a way to capitalize on it."

"That's not fair."

"No, what's not fair is you asking me to do this. Why would you want me to take on a case that would continually remind me—"

"Perhaps you need to be reminded, and to deal with it."

"What're you saying? That you're offering me the job for its therapeutic value?"

Glenn stood, put both hands on my shoulders, and looked into my eyes. "Yes, for its therapeutic value—for you, me, and the Nagasawas."

"Sorry, the answer is no."

He studied me for a moment longer, then straightened, smiling faintly. "I'll have copies of my files messengered over to you by close of business."

"So that's how it is. You understand why I've got to tell Glenn I can't take the case."

Curled up on my sofa, a cat draped across the back with its paws dangling onto my head, another purring on my feet, I was sipping a glass of wine and talking on the phone with my birth father, Elwood Farmer. Elwood was one of the few people I knew whom I could find wide awake and eager for conversation at eleven-thirty P.M.—the hour I'd finished reading Glenn's files on Roger Nagasawa's death.

"I understand why you *think* you can't take it," he said.

I could picture him seated in his padded rocker in front of the woodstove in his small log house in Montana. He'd be wearing a plaid wool shirt and jeans, his gray hair unkempt and touching his shoulders, a cigarette clamped in the corner of his mouth, its smoke making him squint. We'd taken to talking every couple of weeks, feeling our way toward a comfortable father-daughter relationship. Unfortunately, the conversations were not always amicable, because I harbored a resentment toward him for having suspected my existence my whole life but making no effort to find me, and he was plainly bewildered at how to be a parent to a forty-one-year-old stranger.

"What?" I said. "You think I *should* accept a job that's going to make me dwell on Joey's suicide?"

"I didn't say that."

"Well, *do* you?"

"What I think isn't important."

"Come on, Elwood. Be a father for once. Give me some advice."

"I'm only learning to be a father. And I don't believe in imposing my opinion upon another person."

"I just want to know what you think."

". . . I think the answer is already within you."

"Oh, for God's sake! If you're going to get mystical, or whatever you call this, I'm going to hang up."

"Good. Hang up and call me back when you've assembled your thoughts."

Assemble my thoughts, my ass! He pulled that crap on me when we first met, but it isn't going to work this time.

Who is this man to me, anyway? Somebody who donated his sperm to my birth mother, that's all. End of his connection to both Saskia and me. Later, when she was in worse trouble than the pregnancy, he didn't return her phone call because he was preoccupied with the woman he eventually married.

Why should I care what he thinks?

Assemble my thoughts. Hah!

"I'm sorry I hung up on you."

"I know you are."

"I've assembled my thoughts."

"Yes."

"And I know what you mean by the answer already being within me. I can't refuse this case, because I'm a truth-seeker. If working on this Nagasawa investigation can help me to understand why Joey killed himself . . . Well, it's something I have to do."

"Not so difficult to figure out, was it?"

Tuesday

•

APRIL 17

Roger Nagasawa's apartment was in a narrow building on Brannan Street not far from South Park: five stories of gray cinder block over an original wood facade, each with a single casement window facing the street. Its concrete front steps ended in a porch large enough for a pair of wrought-iron chairs and a small glass-topped table; all three were secured by chains to rings that had been attached to the building's wall. To the right stood a former warehouse that now housed a health club; the building to the left was a live-work loft conversion, now stalled by the city's six-month moratorium on such projects while a study on growth and development was conducted.

I took out the keys Glenn Solomon had given me, got the front door open. The lobby was small, perhaps ten feet square, and carpeted in threadbare brown that bunched up in the center, as if stretched out of shape by too many vigorous cleanings. An elevator with an accordion grille that screened a door with a porthole window was opposite the entrance, its cage waiting. I stepped inside, punched the button for the top floor, and it began a groaning ascent.

When I'd appeared at Glenn's office in Four Embarcadero that morning, he'd betrayed no surprise that I'd decided to take the Nagasawa case. We agreed on business matters, signed a contract, and he promised to let the family know I'd be contacting them. Then he turned over the keys to Roger's apartment, which he had owned and his parents had left untouched since his suicide. I'd come directly here to commune with the dead.

The elevator jerked to a stop. I waited till it stopped bouncing, then stepped out into a tiny space where the sun glared down through a skylight. A fly buzzed fitfully against its glass, and dust motes danced on the warm air. A door was set into the wall to my left, an impressive collection of locks and numerous coats of paint—the latest being white—spoiling what must once have been a handsome piece of woodwork. I started keying locks from the top down.

The room beyond was white walled, with bleached pine floors and a long sofa of unnaturally dyed turquoise leather perched on a clear acrylic base. Cubes of the same acrylic were positioned to either side, their tops empty of anything but dust. I shut the door and walked to the center of the room, my footfalls loud on the bare boards. A state-of-the-art entertainment center stood opposite the sofa, housed in more cubes.

Through wide archways I could see two other rooms: a bedroom at the front, with a door to a bathroom opening off it, and a dining-and-kitchen area. More skylights and windows at either end admitted light made harsh by the unadorned walls. I moved toward the dining area, where an oval glass table rested on a crimson lacquered base shaped like a piece of driftwood. The straight-backed chairs positioned around it were a matching crimson and looked uncomfortable. A galley kitchen with brushed chrome appliances ran along the wall to my left, separated from the main room by a white marble-topped bar.

I skirted the table and looked out the rear window. Five stories below in a small backyard someone had planted a garden with neatly spaced rows. An optimist, I thought. How could anything grow with the grimy walls of buildings towering over it on four sides and blocking out the sun?

There was a seat under the window. I perched on it, taking in the entire elongated space. Stark white walls. Minimal furnishings. Nothing on the table, nothing on the bar but a single crimson pottery bowl. Similarly bare counters behind it. Platform bed in the far room, covered in a violently yellow comforter. Three splashes of bright color, like paint splattered on a blank canvas. And where were the personal touches? Where were the objects that would tell me what kind of man Roger Nagasawa had been?

I went looking for them.

An hour later the picture I'd formed of Roger was still hazy, but fascinating. There were two sides of his personality represented in the flat—sides that most certainly had been at war with each other.

On the surface he'd been compulsively neat: Nothing was without its place, to the extent that he'd labeled where various plates and glasses went on his open-fronted shelves. The DVD and audio discs in the entertainment center were alphabetized, as were the books on the shelves in his bedroom. The computer workstation contained no discs whatsoever, and there was only a jumble of pens and pencils and a phone book in its drawer.

The machine was a Mac, like mine. I turned it on,

clicked to his Internet server, found he'd stored his password. When the connection was made, I found he had no new E-mail—which was to be expected—and no old or sent mail either. I signed off and clicked on the icon for the hard drive; there were no files stored there. Most likely he'd deleted them before killing himself.

On the shelves in the small bathroom, personal-care items were neatly lined up by type. The cord to his blow-dryer was wound tightly around its handle, the way a maid in a hotel will leave it. The towels—yellow, to match the comforter—showed signs of use, but were folded and aligned on their bars so the edges met perfectly.

But then there was the other side of Roger: Anything that wasn't in plain view was in a state of total disorder. A knee-high heap of dirty clothing in the bedroom closet, most other garments crooked on their hangers. Coats and hats and umbrellas dumped on top of a pile of papers and books in a closet off the living room. Utensils jumbled in the kitchen drawers. For a moment I wondered if someone hadn't trashed the apartment while looking for something, but there was no feel of such violation here. Roger, I decided, had simply been a clandestine slob.

A pantry off the kitchen was the absolute worst. Its small floorspace was covered with bundles of recyclables, gallon cans of dried and cracking white paint, dirty rags, flowerpots containing dead plants, and an oily pool of a substance that I didn't care to get close enough to identify. Bags of pasta and rice were spilled on the shelves, a bottle of pancake syrup had tipped over and bonded to a can of tomato juice, a cereal box had been gnawed by mice, whose droppings lay everywhere. The top shelf was given over to paper products, which Roger apparently had bought in bulk. Sandwiched incongruously between the toilet tissue and paper towels was a leather binder.

I pulled the binder from the shelf and took it to the dining area, where I sat down in a chair that was as fully uncomfortable as it looked. The binder was tan, with the initials RJN stamped on it in gold—the sort of gift most men receive at some time or another but seldom use. I opened it randomly to a vellum page covered with a backhanded script.

May 28
I'm not as depressed since I moved into the apartment. Sunny here South of Market, and there's so much light in the space. Am painting the walls white and will use bright accent colors to keep the good moods coming. And when the bad moods set in there's always a walk along the waterfront or bench-sitting in South Park. My fears about returning to the city were groundless.

I flipped ahead a number of pages, looking for evidence of a deteriorating emotional condition.

August 13
Dinner with the folks. Harry mercifully absent. But, God, that's a depressing house! Full of all that clutter. Japanese crap, as if they're trying to prove they haven't lost touch with their roots. Why didn't I notice it before? How did I breathe while I was living there?

When I came home tonight I boxed up the few knicknacks I'd set out. None of that clutter for me.

September 15
I met a woman tonight. Lady in distress. She's hip and beautiful. As we shared a glass of wine and conversation, I felt my reserve crumbling, that old magic returning. I'd better watch myself—it's bound to turn out as badly as it always has.

October 17
I can't believe the shit that's going on at work. You have to be there awhile before you fully tap into it, but I'm tapped now. For a while I was stunned, then I got angry. There's got to be a way to make those people act like human beings, but—

A knock at the door. I set the binder down and went to see who was there.

The woman who stood in the hallway was probably in her midtwenties: small, with closely cropped brown hair, large, thickly lashed hazel eyes, and multiple earrings in each lobe. Her stance was aggressive, one booted foot thrust forward, hands in the pockets of her black leather pants, but it didn't mask her nervousness. She blinked when she saw me.

"Who're you?" she asked in a voice not much louder than a whisper.

"A representative of the Nagasawa family's attorney. And you are . . . ?"

Some of the tension left her features; she unpocketed her hands and crossed her arms over her loosely woven sweater. "Jody Houston. I live downstairs. What're you doing here? Is the family getting ready to sell the apartment?"

"Eventually." I moved back and motioned her inside. She hesitated, looking around furtively, before stepping over the threshold. "Were you a friend of Roger's?" I asked.

"Yeah, I was. Look, if they're not planning to sell yet, what're you doing here?"

I told her my name and occupation. "I'm trying to establish a profile of Roger, find out about his last days. The family would feel better if they knew why he killed himself."

"He's been dead for two months. Why the sudden interest now?"

Glenn had cautioned me against mentioning a potential suit against *InSite* to anyone. "I don't know what prompted it. I haven't talked with them yet."

Jody Houston considered that, her expression thoughtful. She moved farther into the apartment, and her gaze rested on the open journal on the table. "That's Roger's diary," she said. "He always kept it hidden. And it's supposed to be private."

"I was hoping it would help me profile him."

She moved swiftly toward the table, picked up the journal, and cradled it protectively. "He wouldn't want a stranger reading it. If his parents are so interested in his reason for killing himself, why don't they try to find out themselves, rather than hiring you?"

"Maybe it would be too painful for them."

"Then they should leave well enough alone."

"That's not up to either you or me." I went over to her

and pried the journal out of her hands. "Rightfully, this belongs to Roger's estate."

"His estate." She looked around the apartment, sighed.

"Please," I said, "won't you help me? Tell me about Roger?"

Her eyes moved back to the journal, and for a moment I thought she might try to snatch it from me. Then she sighed again and leaned against the bar.

"Well, if you think I can help . . . Rog was a quiet guy. Sensitive. Not easy to get to know. We'd see each other coming and going, smile and nod, but that was it. Then one night I dropped my keys down the elevator shaft, through the gap between the cage and the floor. It'd been a really horrible day, and I went a little ballistic. Came up here and pounded on the door. He helped me fish the keys out of the shaft, I invited him in for a drink, and from then on we were friends."

"Romantically involved?"

"No. He would've liked it that way. After a few days he came on to me. I told him no. I was getting over a bad relationship and . . . Well, that's not important. So we agreed that we'd just hang together. But I knew that he thought he was in love with me, and he let the people at work think we were an item."

So Jody was the hip, beautiful woman with whom things were bound to turn out badly. "So you hung out . . ."

"Yeah. We had keys to each other's apartments, came and went. I'm a graphic designer, work at home, so I was always here to turn off the coffeepot if he forgot to, stuff like that. And we'd go to the movies, have dinner. We even drove down to Big Sur for the weekend once."

"You say you're a graphic designer. You ever do any jobs for *InSite*?"

"Well, sure. At least for a while. But never again."

"Why not?"

Her lips twisted and her eyes grew jumpy. "Because they're a bunch of assholes, that's why. They stiffed me on my last fee. I was lucky to be only a freelancer, though; that place is the office from hell."

"How so?"

She seemed to be listening to her words, and when I repeated the question she shook her head. "I've said all I'm ever gonna say on that subject." Quickly she pushed away from the bar and started toward the door. "There's someplace I've got to be."

"Can we talk another time?"

"No, I don't think so. I'm sorry for Rog's folks, but there's really nothing I can say that will make them feel any better."

I followed, hoping to persuade her, but she slammed the door behind her. It stuck, and by the time I got it open the elevator cage had begun its descent.

I was climbing the stairway to the second-story catwalk at Pier 24½ when I heard the voice of my office manager, Ted Smalley, yell *"Fuuuuck!"*

Now that was cause for concern; Ted is not a man given to obscenities. I took the steps two at a time and hurried to the door of his office. No one was in the outer room, but from the back, where we kept the supplies, fax and copy machines, a black cloud drifted.

At first I thought something was on fire, but as the cloud

wafted toward me I saw it was a gritty powder. I stepped out of its path and called, "Ted? What happened?"

He emerged from the back room, his face and clothing resembling an old-fashioned chimney sweep's. His black hair and goatee, normally frosted with gray, looked like the recipients of a bad dye job.

He said, "I'm gonna *kill* him!"

"Who, for God's sake?"

"Neal, that's who!"

I'd been afraid of this.

The previous fall, Altman & Zahn, the legal firm with whom I'd shared the suite of offices, had moved to more spacious quarters across the Embarcadero, and I'd taken over their portion of the lease in order to expand my own operation. The first order of business was to hire an assistant for Ted, and as his partner, Neal Osborn, had recently been forced by rising rents to close his secondhand bookshop, Ted suggested they work together. I had reservations: Neal possessed no office skills, and I knew from experience with my nephew Mick and Charlotte Keim how lovers' quarrels can disrupt a professional environment. But Ted had been at his most persuasive, and late in February I'd finally given in.

"What did he do this time?" I asked.

"The toner." Ted ran his hand over his forehead, smearing the powder that adhered to it.

"The toner for the copy machine?"

"Right. It ran out this morning, and I asked him to replace it. He'd never done that before, but I figured anybody could follow the directions. He was back there hovering over the machine for quite a while, till it was time for his lunch break. After he left I saw the toner light was still flashing, so I decided to fix the damn thing myself." He paused, out of breath.

"And?"

"And he'd left the box that holds one of those extra-large containers of toner on the coffee cart next to the machine. But he must've set it down where somebody'd spilled something. When I picked it up, its bottom gave, the container fell out, hit the floor, and—*boom!*"

"The toner exploded?"

Ted waved his arms, exasperated now by my lack of office know-how. "No, it didn't explode! That stuff can't explode! What happened was the idiot had taken the top off the container and didn't replace it. The impact . . . Well, we've got powder all over the place and the cleaning service doesn't come in till Thursday night and guess who'll get stuck sweeping up the mess? *Moi!*"

He was working himself into a frenzy. I motioned to him, said, "Come with me."

"I can't. The phones."

"It's the noon hour. Let the machine pick up."

He nodded and followed me along the catwalk to my office at the end of the pier, where I sat him down in the old armchair by the arched window overlooking the bay and Treasure Island. Then I fetched a box of premoistened towelettes that I keep for just such emergencies. While he scrubbed I dragged my desk chair over and sat next to him, feet propped on the low windowsill.

I said, "It's not working out, is it?"

". . . I guess not. Neal was a great bookseller, but he's hopeless in an office. Last Friday I caught him trying to send a fax through the slot where the paper comes out."

Even *I* could send faxes. "You're cutting him an awful lot of slack."

"Well, he's . . . Neal."

"If he's having so much trouble, why does he want the job?"

"He's got to have something to do. Even if we could afford it, he's not the kind of man who can stay home and tend to his knitting."

The image of Neal—a shaggy bear of a man—knitting made me smile. "Couldn't he continue to sell books online?"

"You've got to be computer literate to do that. Neal's even worse than you used to be." Ted turned concerned eyes on me. "Are you building up to telling me to fire him?"

I wished I could. But what Ted had said before held true for me as well: Neal was Neal, and I cared about him.

"No, I'm not. But you've got to find a way to use him that won't throw the entire operation into chaos. And you've got to promise me one thing."

"Sure. What?"

"That you won't kill him. It'd be very bad for business."

After Ted went back to his office, I booted up my Mac and accessed *InSite* magazine. This week's Top Hit was Bay Area oxygen bars—an article that didn't particularly interest me because I preferred to get my daily intake by breathing deeply, rather than snorting oxygen at ten bucks a pop. Personality of the Week was one of our urban activists whose not-so-inadvertent clumsiness at the groundbreaking for yet another development that the city didn't need had caused the mayor's fedora to be carried off on the breeze and eventually spiral into a sinkhole. The Poetry in Motion department reported on hip Bay Area limo companies. They Say Volumes interviewed the author of *Instant Connection in the Elevator and Other Places,* who advocated dressing up in outlandish costumes and cavorting in public places as a means of meeting women. Incredible Edibles was singing the praises of tofu for those who hadn't heard of it, presumably because they'd been living in underground caverns for the past two decades. Here, There, and Everywhere featured a club that was about to go belly-up and a restaurant I'd been eating at for at least a year.

Maybe there wasn't enough cool stuff to go around this week.

I clicked off the site, shut the machine down, and stared at the blank screen, gradually noting my own features. I was frowning. That frown had confronted me from a lot of reflective surfaces lately. Was it becoming permanent? God, I hoped not! I looked like my mother—

Which mother? McCone? Biological? Adoptive?

Adoptive. Definitely. Learned behavior. Ma had frowned a lot before she fell in love, divorced Pa, and had a face-lift.

Learned behavior could also be unlearned. I leaned close to the screen and rubbed furiously with my fingertips at the creases between my brows.

"So what's happening, Shar?" J.D. Smith asked.

J.D. was a good friend, a former *Chronicle* reporter who, as he put it, had recently gone over to the other side and was now freelancing for various electronic publications.

"Well, I've got an interesting case—"

"Don't tell me about it. Your last interesting case, you blackmailed me into putting you in touch with a confidential source."

"Whom I prevented from being framed for a felony."

"Well . . . So what's this one?"

"An undercover investigation of *InSite* magazine."

"That *is* interesting. I'd like to hear more about it."

"And I'd like to hear more about *InSite*."

"I know enough to fill a long dinner hour."

"Name the time and place."

In the hours before my eight o'clock appointment with J.D. I caught up on paperwork; spent some time discussing what constituted legal and illegal investigative tactics with my new hire, Julia Rafael; and made a list of the things I needed to do on the Nagasawa case. The first item was to talk with the members of Roger's family, so I put in a call to their home number, but received no answer. When I reached Daniel Nagasawa at his Bush Street eye clinic he said it would be best if he and I met there tomorrow morning. Margaret asked me to come to her publishing house's offices on Tillman Place near Union Square in the afternoon.

Their setting up separate interviews made me wonder if there might be trouble in the Nagasawa marriage. The aftermath of a child's death, particularly if by suicide or violence, could often exert pressure on previously undetected fault lines. I made a note to ask Glenn Solomon if that were the case.

Neither of the surviving Nagasawa sons was available at the numbers I had for them, so I left messages. The same was true of most of Roger's friends who had been named on a list in Glenn's files. With any luck they'd return my calls tonight or in the morning, and tomorrow would be my day to work intensively on my profile of Roger's state of mind—

"Shar?"

The voice was that of Rae Kelleher—my onetime right-hand who had resigned from the agency last fall after her marriage to my former brother-in-law, Ricky Savage. I looked up, saw her standing in the doorway, her freckled face glowing. She wore blue, her best color, and she held a champagne bottle in either hand.

I said, "You sold it!"

She nodded, a slight motion that told me how hard she was trying to contain her excitement.

I got up, rushed over, and hugged her. Then we were jumping up and down and making undignified squeaking noises. Rae bumped the bottles against my back, gasped, and we got ourselves under control before the wine became so agitated it would be dangerous to open.

"Don't say another word yet," I told her, and went to call Ted so he could round up the staff for a celebration. While Rae unearthed a third bottle from her tote bag and popped corks, I hunted up glasses. Soon everybody was filing in.

Ted and Neal, both looking broody at first, but snapping out of it as soon as they saw Rae and realized what her news must be. Mick and Charlotte, a handsome couple: he big and blond, she petite and brunette. When his father's marriage to my sister Charlene broke up, Mick had blamed Rae and vowed he would never forgive her; now I saw nothing but affection in his eyes as they met hers. Craig Morland, my FBI agent-turned-operative, was stroking his thick mustache and looking puzzled; Craig was part of our social circle, as he lived with a close friend of mine who was an inspector on the SFPD homicide detail, but he paid so little attention to what went on that I sometimes suspected he spent most of his time in an alternate universe.

And then there was Julia Rafael, two months on the job and looking ill at ease. A tall, strongly built Latina with a haughty profile and spiky hair, Julia had dragged herself up from one of the worst personal histories I'd ever encountered in a job applicant. I'd taken a chance on her because I figured that anyone with so much guts and determination to improve her lot in life couldn't help but succeed as an investigator.

I motioned to her and introduced her to Rae, whose smile she met with a brusque nod. Julia had few social graces—hadn't been given the opportunity to develop any in her twenty-five years—but I was confident that in time she'd possess a full complement of people skills. Beneath her rough exterior I sensed real value, both as an employee and an individual.

Charlotte and Mick were passing out glasses of champagne. When everybody had been served, I held up mine and said, "Here's to Rae! She's sold her novel!"

"Way to go, Kelleher!"

"All *right!*"

"Who's the publisher?"

"When can I buy my copy and get you to autograph it?"

"Did you get big bucks for it?"

At the last inquiry Rae laughed so hard she dribbled champagne over her fingers. "Listen," she said, "I'd've paid *them* big bucks to publish it. They're a little literary house in New York, and they tell me it should be out in about a year. And if I get to do any signings, you've all got to promise to come, so I won't be lonely."

A voice from the doorway said, "Anybody need more champagne?" Hank Zahn and his wife and law partner, Anne-Marie Altman, stood there, bottles in hand.

"How'd you know we were partying?" Rae asked.

"Ted called over to us. And Ricky phoned us from L.A. after you called him. Gave us the news and said to tell you he was able to charter a flight and will be home to celebrate this evening."

Suddenly my eyes stung and I had to turn aside. When Rae had resigned I'd been afraid our friendship would slip away as she became involved in her writing and life as a celebrity's wife. When Anne-Marie and Hank had moved their offices to Hills Brothers Plaza, I'd feared it was an end for us, rather than a simple relocation. Not so, apparently. Things had changed, but only for the better.

J.D. Smith and I sat at a sidewalk table at the South Park Cafe, sipping wine and waiting for our steamed mussels to be served. It was an unusually warm evening for April in San Francisco, and people wandered across the oval park or sat on its benches until tables opened up at the crowded restaurants. The branches of newly leafed sycamores moved in a gentle breeze; near the playground equipment a whippet caught a Frisbee with long-limbed grace.

Years ago, before the park became a trendy hangout, I'd worked a case there that ended in disaster for several people—both innocent and not-so-innocent. In its aftermath I took to walking the grassy ellipsoid in the darkness of the winter evenings, trying to make sense of the tragedy and my inability to prevent it. Eventually I recovered and so did South Park, which became home to galleries, cafés, shops, and architectural and multimedia firms. The cream of the dot-com establishment conducted their deals and spent money lavishly at the tables of the chic bistros.

Now I noted that the park was beginning to look a bit shabby again. FOR RENT signs appeared in many of the windows, and the talk in the café was more likely to be about which firm had closed its doors than which was floating an initial public offering. If the downward spiral of the high-tech market continued as predicted, South Park might very well return to being an urban secret known only to those who were brave enough to venture among its shady and often desperate habitués.

"So," J.D. said in his faint southern accent, "*InSite* magazine, nuts and bolts first. They've been in business over five years—which, as you know, isn't all that usual for online 'zines. Their funding comes from VC, who—"

"Wait a minute—Vietcong?"

He laughed, throwing his head back. He was a thin-faced, pale-skinned man with a mane of untamable red hair. Dressed in the expensively casual garb of the foundering new economy, he lounged in his chair, keen blue eyes following and assessing each good-looking woman who walked by. Now he turned them, sparkling with wicked amusement, on me.

"You're under the same illusion as I was. When I first started freelancing for *InSite* I'd hang out at the offices because that's how they do business, and I'd hear the honchos talking about the VC. And I'd think, 'Why're they talking about the Vietcong? They're not a political rag and, besides, that war's long over.' Imagine my chagrin when I realized that these particular VC are venture capitalists."

"It must be a generational thing. Go on."

He waited till the waiter had set steaming bowls of mussels in garlic broth before us, then tore a chunk of fresh sourdough off the loaf in the basket. "Okay, VC are people who make their profit by financing likely business ventures and taking them to IPO—initial public offering. A couple of years ago when *InSite* really began to take off they hooked up with Tessa Remington, of the Remington Group, and she rounded up investors and began to supply capital. Remington was seldom in the offices—not at all now, but that's another story—but she was a presence, much as Jesus Christ is a presence in your average parish church."

"And these honchos—who are they?"

"Jorge Amaya, the CEO. His family owns half of Costa Rica, or one of those Central American countries. He's the Remington Group's boy, was brought in to run the company because of his credentials—degree from the Wharton School, strong history of guiding firms to IPO. I don't know him very well, but he's superficially charming and appeals to women. Then there's Max Engstrom, publisher and editor in chief. He founded the 'zine, but agreed to turn over the reins to Amaya because he knew that was the price of getting funding. He's not very happy about it, and it shows in his behavior. But I'll get to that in a minute. Finally there are the department heads, those high on the organizational chart; they also wield a fair amount of power."

"What's the structure of that chart?"

"Similar to print magazines." J.D. signaled to the waiter for more wine. "Basically you've got Content, Art, Marketing, and Tech. Content breaks down into entertainment, food, travel, and so forth. Each is headed by an editor, with associates and copy editors working under him or her. Most of the people in Content are well educated, but with the kinds of degrees that translate into zip dollars, so they work their asses off trying to replace the person above them. It's a brutal atmosphere."

Roger Nagasawa had worked in Content, in the entertainment department. "This brutal atmosphere—what characterizes it?"

"Infighting. Excessive competition. In some cases, sabotage of a coworker's projects."

The office from hell, as Jody Houston had called it. "What about Art?" I asked.

"Less competitive, mainly because the staffers' skills are more clearly defined. They use a lot of freelance material, coordinate with Content and Tech. Now, Marketing, it's really a mess, mainly because they've never been able to keep anybody in the director's position long enough to develop a real selling product."

"Meaning?"

"Well, you take an e-tailing site like L.L. Bean. They've got an identifiable product—jeans, moccasins, sweaters. *In-Site,* on the other hand, is selling ad space, and they've had a hard time convincing prospective advertisers that an online 'zine is an effective venue. In a print 'zine, the ad's there in your face every time you turn to that particular page. But online, it's all too easy for a reader to click off on the connection to the individual advertiser's site and thus not receive the information being aimed at them."

"Like I do when a window offering me a product comes up before I access my E-mail. I just click on 'no thanks.' "

"Exactly."

"So is *InSite* losing money?"

"Struggling to keep its head above water, with infusions of cash from the Remington Group. Back when the dot-com bubble burst, Remington and Amaya considered going to IPO early, but decided against it. Instead, the Remington Group scaled back on its investment, slowed the growth."

"All right," I said, "what does Tech do?"

"It's a lot like Layout and Production at a print magazine. They're responsible for keeping the software and hardware functioning, as well as the links to the advertisers' sites. It's headed by a Webmaster who calls herself the WebPotentate—they all adopt offbeat job titles at *InSite*. She's a very big honcho, second only to Engstrom and Amaya. Dinah Vardon, her name is, and let me tell you, she's one scary woman."

"How is she scary?"

J.D. tipped back in his chair and closed his eyes. "How can I describe her? Do I own the words? She's single-minded, very focused, but that in itself isn't it. She wants what she wants, and she makes damn sure she gets it. An example might help. One day last year I was in Max's office, and Dinah came in. She wanted him to hire a guy for the Tech staff that he didn't particularly like. Made a good case for it, but Max said no, so she retreated. Fifteen minutes later she was back again with a new argument, new approach. And again at every fifteen-minute interval, until Max finally caved in."

"Tenacious."

"Relentless. It was as if there was an army of Dinahs; each time one was defeated, another somewhat different version took her place. Each wore away at Max's defenses till he waved the white flag."

"Okay, you said she wants what she wants. What is that?"

J.D. shrugged. "Power, I suppose. After that, whatever it is that will enable her to remain in power."

"Money?"

"Well, sure."

"Okay, earlier you said that Max Engstrom's displeasure at Amaya being put in charge is reflected in his behavior. I've heard he's a sadist."

"Max would say he enjoys an occasional practical joke."

"And you would say . . . ?"

"He's giving the Marquis a run for his money. But really, Shar, to understand the people and dynamics at *InSite,* you have to meet them and see for yourself."

"How would you recommend I do that, without them realizing I'm conducting an investigation?"

He regarded me through narrowed eyes; in the light from the candle on our table, his face looked reptilian. "If your investigation pans out, will it be newsworthy?"

"Eventually."

"And if I help you, will I get first crack at the story?"

"Absolutely."

He continued to stare thoughtfully at me. After a bit he nodded. "I have the germ of an idea. When it sprouts, I'll get back to you."

February 14

I've destroyed everything I don't want people to see and deleted all my files. I've mailed my note to my parents and E-mailed my brothers and said good-bye to Jody—even though she couldn't have known it was good-bye. Eddie will look out for her, and if she's intimidated in any way, he'll see that she finds the insurance policy I've left at her fingertips. Now it's time to go. I've always envisioned that I'd take this step off the Golden Gate. It's beckoned to me since I was a child. But given the circumstances and my many failures, the Bay Bridge seems more appropriate. The circumstances. The failures. I wish I could undo them.

I set down Roger's journal and went to turn off my office lights. Through the arched window I could look up at the underside of the span from which he'd jumped shortly before midnight on St. Valentine's Day. It hung high above the pier, the noise of the few vehicles passing over it at this late hour muted. Still, in my irritable state, the rumble and clatter above, as well as the steady hum of traffic on the Embarcadero, grated.

I looked toward Treasure Island, followed the curve of the bridge's lights toward Oakland. Tried to make sense of the journal entries, but couldn't.

At least he attempted to explain himself. Unlike Joey.

There had been nothing in the squalid rental house where my brother killed himself except the empty booze and pill bottles and his abbreviated note of apology. His few possessions, according to the sheriff's deputy, were suitable only for the trash. I'd asked him to have them disposed of before John flew up there to identify the body and arrange for its cremation. I'd told myself I wanted to spare him the heartbreaking details of Joey's last months.

Maybe I should have gone with him, looked over Joey's things. Why hadn't I?

Well, for one thing, I'd needed to make myself available to testify in a civil suit that week. But that was just an excuse. In reality I'd wanted to wash my hands of Joey's wasted life. On some level I'd needed to believe that his life was as senseless as his death.

Too late now. I'd failed him. And my family.

Wednesday

•

APRIL 18

The waiting room at Golden Gate Vision Center was large and crowded. I sat sandwiched between a man who was going over a legal brief and a woman who in ten minutes had had five calls on her cell phone.

Across from me was a glass display case full of red-and-blue Imari plates; a small sign on the middle shelf read HOW WELL CAN YOU SEE US? Subtle prodding of the clinic's prospective clientele to avail themselves of the corrective procedure, and more aesthetic than a vision-test chart. I closed my right eye and stared at the case with my left. I'd always had great eyesight, but three weeks ago during my monthly practice session at the firing range I'd thought I noticed some fuzziness, and while flying over the Pacific near Touchstone, Hy's and my seaside retreat in Mendocino County, I'd momentarily mistaken a large seagull for a distant plane.

Were my eyes starting to go? I closed the left, checked the right. The patterns of the Imari ware were sharp and clear. Good genes in that department: Elwood Farmer, an artist, was in his sixties and still didn't need glasses; my birth mother, Saskia Blackhawk, wore them only for reading the fine print in her law books.

The door to the inner office opened and a woman came out, followed by a tall man in a white doctor's coat. Not Daniel Nagasawa; this man was Caucasian. Almost everyone in the waiting room looked up when the woman said to him, "It's so wonderful to wake in the morning and actually be able to see the clock! Of course, seeing my face in the mirror is an entirely different proposition." A few people laughed and most looked relieved. This woman had come through the procedure and post-operative checks unscathed and satisfied. Help was just a flick of the laser beam away.

The woman left, the doctor went back inside, and I checked my watch. Ten minutes after nine; Daniel Nagasawa was late for our appointment. Much more delay, and it would have a domino effect on my tightly packed schedule. I had to be in Palo Alto at eleven to meet with his son Eddie, who had only the one hour free—

"Ms. McCone?" the receptionist said. "Dr. Nagasawa is ready for you. If you'll come on through I'll show you to his office."

The inner hallway was thickly carpeted, the walls hung with Japanese woodblock etchings. Daniel Nagasawa met me at its end, a stocky man in a blue sport coat and chinos, with narrow eyes that assessed me shrewdly. No glasses, of course—a perfect advertisement for his services. He ushered me into a room where objects covered every flat surface: files and books on the desk; more files on the floor; more books spilling off built-in shelves; two stylized sculptures of women in kimonos on pedestals; bonsai plants on the windowsill. I thought of what Roger had written in his journal about the clutter in his parents' home: "Japanese crap, as if they're trying to prove they haven't lost touch with their roots."

Dr. Nagasawa asked me to be seated and thanked me for agreeing to investigate, then went around the desk and sat in a leather chair, hands folded on a stack of papers, eyes attentive. I asked if he would mind my taping our conversation, and when he agreed, set up my recorder.

"I've been over Glenn's files," I told him, "so I'm familiar with the background material, but I'd like to hear it in your own words. I understand Roger lived with you when he returned to the city."

"Yes. He wanted to buy his own place, but he didn't have quite enough saved for a down payment. His mother and I offered to loan him the money, but he said he'd rather accept room and board. Roger could be prickly when it came to owing anyone." His gaze shifted to the far wall, and mine followed. A family portrait hung there, three boys standing behind their seated parents; their ages ranged from around ten to the late teens.

"Which one is Roger?" I asked.

"The boy in the middle."

The middle child even in the family portrait. A difficult place in the birth order. I'd been the middle child in my adoptive family, and it had made me feel set apart from my older brothers and younger sisters, turned me into something of a loner. Of course, as I'd learned last fall, there were other reasons for those feelings. . . .

I refocused my attention on Daniel Nagasawa. "How did that arrangement—Roger living at home—work out?"

"Very well. He came and went as he pleased, and did his best not to make extra work for our housekeeper. Roger is . . . was the most independent and considerate of our boys. We've yet to persuade Harry, the oldest, to move out, and Eddie brings his laundry home from Palo Alto every other weekend."

"A pleasant home environment, then."

Dr. Nagasawa's gaze muddied and he looked down at his clasped hands. "It was."

I waited, and when he didn't elaborate, asked, "What did Roger tell you about his experience at *InSite*?"

"Very little. He wasn't secretive, but he didn't share unpleasant things. We knew the job wasn't going well, though. He was tense and irritable. Worked long hours and didn't get enough sleep. Sometimes he'd be at the office all night, come home to shower and change clothes, and go straight back again. When I suggested they were working him too hard, he told me that was the way of the dot-com world. But he looked exhausted and was losing weight. After he moved out of the house we invited him for dinner frequently, hoping to make him eat a decent meal, but he rarely came."

"Did he seem depressed?"

"No. As I said, mainly on edge."

"But didn't he have a history of depression?"

"Certainly not. He was a happy-go-lucky child."

Perhaps as a child, but not as a man. At least that was what my reading of his journal indicated. Like many parents, Daniel Nagasawa hadn't really known his adult son.

"Dr. Nagasawa, what made you decide the people at *InSite* were responsible for Roger's suicide?"

He flinched. It was a reaction I could empathize with; to a person whose loved one has killed himself, the word has the force of a violent physical blow, no matter how often you hear it.

"The *karoshi* case in Tokyo was what turned my thinking in that direction. I read a very detailed account of it in a magazine, then searched out other articles in legal journals and the Japanese press. The conditions the victim was trying to cope with were so similar to those that some of Roger's friends—you have their names on the list I gave Glenn—to what they described to me after the memorial service. I talked to more of his friends, heard the same thing. Then yesterday . . ." He looked down again, straightened the edges of the stack of papers.

"Yes?"

"This is something I haven't even told Glenn yet. Yesterday evening a young woman called me. One who had been at the service. Jody Houston. She said she had heard we'd hired an investigator to look into the cause of Roger's death."

"She heard that from me. We met yesterday morning at Roger's building."

"That explains her call. She was very melodramatic, said one of the top people at the magazine had effectively murdered my son and was now threatening her. She wanted to see me immediately. Frankly, I didn't believe her. So I suggested she contact you and be prepared to present proof of her allegations. She became agitated and hung up on me."

"Did you try to call her back?"

"Not last night. But on reflection, I sensed she was genuinely afraid, so I looked up her number and phoned this morning. I reached a machine. I take it she didn't get in touch with you?"

"No, she didn't."

"Will you contact her, please? Ask if she's all right and find out what she knows?"

"I'll see to it right away."

There was just enough of a window of time in my schedule to stop by Houston's apartment. I drove over to Brannan Street and repeatedly rang the bell, but received no answer. When I dialed her number, I heard only her recorded voice. I left a message asking her to call me and saying that Daniel Nagasawa was concerned about her, then headed south to Palo Alto, reviewing my conversation with him and preparing for one with his youngest son.

"I don't have a clue about what was going on with Rog," Eddie Nagasawa said.

Not a clue, and he seemed strangely indifferent. Eddie was a handsome young man, stocky like his father, with a small gold loop in his right earlobe and a tiny tattoo of a spider above his left wrist bone. While the day was cool and overcast, he wore shorts and a sleeveless tee. He slouched in his chair at the Fine Eats restaurant on University Avenue, picking at something called a Feel Good Salad. I took a bite of my cheeseburger and for the second time that day mentally thanked Saskia and Elwood for their good genes; my metabolic system processes fat like most people's do water.

I asked, "What did Roger tell you about working at *InSite*?"

"Not much. He and I didn't talk often. He was six years older than me and had been away at school since I was twelve. I didn't really know him."

Hadn't I said the same of Joey? That we'd never had a real conversation? But I'd been lashing out in anger, while Eddie seemed all too calm.

"Your father said Roger was tense and irritable. Did you notice that too?"

"Couldn't help but. One time I tried to talk with him about the 'zine—it's cool, and my friends were curious about what it was like to work there—and he practically reamed me out. After that we kind of avoided each other."

"You saw him at the house?"

"On weekends." His mouth quirked up. "I bet when you talked with Dad he told you what a leech I am. Always coming home with the dirty laundry."

"Well, yes."

"I can hear him: 'My boys won't get outta the house. All our friends're empty nesters, but not us. We can't get them to leave.' Secretly he loves it. He knows we keep coming back because he and Mom are terrific." He frowned and pushed his salad away. "I hate what Rog did to them. They didn't deserve that."

So he *was* angry. "Suicide's a pretty hateful act."

"It ruins everything." He pushed back from the table, threw his balled-up napkin on the remains of the salad. "Why'd he have to come home, anyway? Why didn't he just stay back east? I mean, we were all doing great, and then there's Rog dragging around the house like a zombie. Next thing he's bought this apartment and can't even bother to come over to dinner. I mean, what's dinner once or twice a month? But no, he neglects and hurts Mom and Dad, then he throws himself off the bridge. And now everything's ruined."

"In what way?"

The anger was out now, sparking in his eyes, making him clench his thighs with his hands. A couple at the next table glanced over at the sound of his raised voice, quickly looked away.

"You wanta know how? Dad's obsessed with this lawsuit. He says he's gonna get the people who forced Rog to kill himself. Well, bullshit! Nobody forces you to do that. And Mom—she finally couldn't take it anymore. She moved out of the house and is living in her office, for Christ's sake. Me, I don't go home anymore. And Harry—Jesus!"

"What about Harry?"

"I guess you haven't talked with him yet."

"No."

"Well, when you do, you'll see what Rog did to him."

I'd planned to ask Eddie about Roger's final E-mail to him, as well as about the insurance policy his brother had wanted him to help Jody Houston locate, but that would have to wait till another time. After his angry outburst he'd abruptly ended our interview, saying he had to get to class. After walking back to the parking garage where I'd left my car, I took out my phone and began to make calls; its battery was low, and the unit emitted little chirps while I spoke. Not that the conversations were long. The friends of Roger I had yet to contact were either out of the office or on another line, and would have to get back to me about scheduling an appointment. When I checked with my own office for messages, Ted sounded out of sorts. Hy had called from Bangkok, he said. Otherwise there was nothing of importance.

Bangkok. Hy had flown there on Monday to train operatives of Renshaw and Kessell International, the corporate security firm in which he held a one-third interest, in hostage-negotiation techniques. I wrestled with time zones, the International Date Line, and quickly gave up.

"What time is it there?" I asked Ted.

"How the hell should I know?"

"Well, when did he call?"

"About two hours ago. Hold on."

I heard his swivel chair squeak, and then there was a thump and a curse. "Are you okay?" I asked.

"I am if you discount the fact that the stack of phone books just fell on my foot because *someone* piled them too high."

"Not me."

"For a change." In the pause that followed, pages riffled. "Yeah, here it is. International calling section. Bangkok's plus fifteen hours."

"That can't be right. It's to the west. Plus is to the east."

"Bangkok's halfway around the world, more or less. It's also east of here."

"But if I were flying, I'd go west."

"But you *could* fly east."

"Oh. I guess it works that way with everyplace."

"Unless it's north and south. Or northeast and southwest, or—"

The conversation was making my head ache. "Enough! Fifteen plus, huh?" It was twelve-twenty; that made it three-twenty in the morning in Thailand. Too late to return the call, unless it was urgent. "What did he say?"

"Who?"

"Hy!"

"Oh, him. He wanted to know if you got the rose."

"Of course I did." A single rose—dark red, almost black,

was delivered to my office every Tuesday morning; Hy had been sending them since a few days after we met, although the color had changed as the relationship deepened. "Why would he ask?"

"Maybe it's some kind of secret code." Ted liked Hy, but he tended to become sarcastic about his line of work. He disapproved of it and of him having enticed me into becoming a pilot—both too dangerous, in his opinion.

"Well, if you crack it, let me know," I said, and ended the call.

I looked longingly at my phone. Very late or not, I would have liked to talk with Hy. But my next appointment, with Margaret Nagasawa, was scheduled for one-thirty, allowing me little time to drive back to the city, park at the Sutter-Stockton garage, and walk over to the offices of Carefree Days Publishing on Tillman Place.

Tillman Place is one of the old-fashioned little lanes that abound in the city, a few blocks from the northeast corner of Union Square. Walking along on its cobblestones, I felt as if I had been transported back to the days of the Barbary Coast, when San Francisco was a wide-open town filled with miners down from the Mother Lode, seamen off ships out of faraway ports, and gamblers and con men and ladies of the night eager to fleece them of their hard-earned cash.

In college I'd made forays from Berkeley to the city and discovered a restaurant at the lane's end—the Temple Bar, a small, dark place where regulars rolled dice for drinks and society ladies stopped in for trysts after a hard day's shopping at I. Magnin. Magnin's is long gone now, its space absorbed into Macy's, and so is the Temple Bar. Gone also is the small bookshop that used to draw many a reader down the lane, but Margaret Nagasawa's publishing firm was housed in the building a couple of doors down from the shop's former quarters—proving that progress had not yet robbed Tillman Place of things literary.

Carefree Days' top-floor suite of offices was spacious and filled with light, even on this gloomy day. Brightly colored posters of book jackets hung on the walls in the reception area, and dozens of orchid plants bloomed in ceramic pots. When the receptionist led me to Mrs. Nagasawa's office, Roger's mother rose from behind her desk and came forward to greet me. She was small, almost frail in appearance, with gray hair sleeked back and tied in a ponytail. The tail gave her a girlish air, but the deep circles under her eyes and lines around her mouth said that her concerns were far from those of girlhood. She shook my hand with a surprisingly strong grip and motioned for me to be seated in one of a pair of wingback chairs. Then she took the other, smoothing the skirt of her stylish black suit as she sat.

I thanked her for taking the time to talk with me and glanced around the office. It was as fully cluttered as her husband's: manuscripts on the floor; books stacked helter-skelter on the shelves; sketches of jackets propped against the walls. Once beyond the desk she would have to tread carefully to avoid stepping on what could be the next *Wizard of Oz, Grinch Who Stole Christmas,* or *Harry Potter.* Eddie had said his mother was currently living in her office, but where? There was a sofa, but it too was piled high with books, boxes, and files.

Mrs. Nagasawa said, "I'm glad you agreed to gather evidence for our suit. It's a complicated job, calling for considerable expertise. And, of course, there are time pressures."

"Glenn said you were eager to serve papers on *InSite*."

"My husband is eager. And I am eager to have the matter over with."

"I spoke with Eddie earlier. He told me Dr. Nagasawa is . . . very committed to the suit."

She smiled faintly. "You're a tactful woman, Ms. McCone. Eddie said his father is obsessed with the lawsuit. I hear that every time I talk with him. I suppose he also told you I've moved from the house to an apartment in this building."

"Yes, he did."

She shook her head. "Eddie is so young. He thinks it's the end of our marriage. The end of his world as he's known it. He doesn't understand that in a good marriage you often have to give the other person space to do what he must, but that you don't necessarily have to allow him to poison your space."

"So the arrangement is temporary."

"Yes, and Daniel agrees to it. I wish our boys could understand."

"Harry doesn't understand either?"

A wary look, similar to Eddie's when he'd mentioned his older brother, crossed her face. "You haven't spoken with him yet?"

"No."

"Then I think it's best to allow you to draw your own conclusions."

My meeting with Harry was set for three o'clock at the family home in the exclusive Cow Hollow district. It was bound to be interesting.

"Let's talk about Roger," I said, taking out my recorder.

Roger, Margaret Nagasawa told me, had always been a sensitive child, easily hurt and full of empathy for others. When he was eight he bought three goldfish from the pet shop on Maiden Lane, and as they died one day after the other, he grieved as if they were human. If his brothers were punished for some infraction of the family rules, he suffered as if he were the miscreant. And if he accidentally hurt someone's feelings, he wallowed in guilt for days.

"He was aware his reactions were out of proportion," his mother said, "and not without a sense of humor. He was fond of saying that if he'd been born two decades earlier he would have felt personally responsible for the Vietnam War."

During his adolescence Roger became moody and withdrawn. He had only one close friend, a classmate named Gene Edwards. Gene was more sociable than Roger, and from eighth grade on always had a steady girlfriend; he and the various girls would fix Roger up with their friends, but the dates were unsuccessful at best, fiascos at worst. Finally Gene stopped trying. Then, in his senior year of high school, Roger fell in love.

"The girl," Mrs. Nagasawa told me, "was lovely, but wild and unpredictable. We didn't really approve of her, but she brought Roger out of his shell, so we decided to keep him on a loose leash. They were together twenty-four seven, as the kids say today. They made joint plans to attend U.C. Berkeley in the fall, but that summer she ran off to Hawaii with an older boy who was visiting her brother."

Roger had been devastated. He disappeared from home and, when he returned shortly after his frantic parents filed a missing-person report, he refused to say where he had been or what he'd been doing. From his appearance, they suspected heavy drug and alcohol use. After that he withdrew to his room, neither eating anything from the trays they placed outside his locked door nor answering them when they tried to talk through it.

"He proved he had backbone, though," his mother said, "because in three days he came out of there with a plan."

He had decided not to enroll at Berkeley—too painful in light of the plans he and his girlfriend had made. Instead he would work for Margaret's publishing firm for a year and study journalism at City College. He would also reactivate his application to the University of Michigan, one of several schools where he'd been accepted, and enroll there the following fall. He carried out the plan to the letter, left the next August, and except for brief visits at the holidays didn't return to San Francisco for close to seven years.

"Effectively we lost him," Margaret said. "It was as if he blamed us for what the girl did to him."

"I doubt that. He probably didn't want to be reminded of the relationship. What happened to her, do you know?"

"She married the boy she ran off with, then returned here, divorced, a few years later. At least that's what Harry says. He was a friend of her older brother, the one the boy from Hawaii was visiting."

"And her name is?"

"Dinah Vardon."

Dinah Vardon, the Webmaster at *InSite*. "Are you aware that she and Roger worked together at the magazine?"

Margaret's eyes flickered with surprise. "Roger never mentioned her. Perhaps she didn't matter to him anymore. Or perhaps they were able to put the past behind them and become friends."

"It's possible. This friend of Roger's—Gene Edwards. He's not on my list of people to interview. Were they still in touch?"

She looked away from me. "Gene's dead. He . . . killed himself two years ago, after his wife left him. On Christmas Day."

Another suicide, on another special day. Christmas, for Gene. Valentine's, for Roger. What day had Joey died? April sixth. He'd been dead for seventy-two hours before anyone found him. Nothing special about April sixth, though—

Nothing? Jesus! April sixth was Joey's birthday.

"Ms. McCone?" Margaret Nagasawa's voice sounded far away. "What is it?"

"Sorry. I was just thinking."

No, I thought, I wasn't thinking at all. Not when it came to my brother.

It was very late in Bangkok—or very early, depending on your point of view—but I badly needed to hear Hy's voice reassure me that I wasn't the monstrously uncaring person I felt like. Trouble was, I also needed a phone that didn't chirp at me every fifteen seconds.

As I merged with the sidewalk crowd on Grant Avenue, I looked around. Chichi shops, restaurants, and not a phone booth in sight. The prevalence of cellular units was forcing the phone company to phase out many booths, and it had been my experience that when you found a working one it was bound to be in an inconvenient and noisy spot. Besides, if I stopped to make a call, I'd be cutting it close for my appointment with Harry Nagasawa. I scuttled the notion for now and headed for the parking garage.

The family's home was on Vallejo Street in Cow Hollow, a district named for the dairy farms that once were prevalent there. Nowadays the only bovines associated with the place are cash cows—the buildings from which owners frequently milk huge profits. The Nagasawas' block was quiet and tree-lined, the house a large tan stucco with a blue tiled roof, a small front garden surrounded by a wrought-iron fence, and a pair of yew trees in gigantic blue urns to either side of the door. Impressive, even in this area of very impressive homes.

When I pushed the bell it rang softly. I waited, but no one answered. I rang again, and yet again. Had Harry forgotten our appointment?

Tires squealed a block away. I turned, saw a red Porsche careening around the corner. Rae called Porsches "asshole-creating machines," and she should know; Ricky owned one, and whenever either of them got behind the wheel they turned into maniacs. Obviously this car had exerted a similar affect on its driver.

The Porsche screeched to a stop at the curb in front of the Nagasawa house and stalled. A man leaped out, his black hair tousled and his chinos and Henley shirt looking as if he'd slept in them. A pair of sunglasses with one missing earpiece perched crooked on his nose.

"Sharon McCone?" he called as he came up the walk, tripping on an untied shoelace. "I'm Harry, Harry Nagasawa. Sorry I'm late, but I got tied up at the hospital—and now I'm untied." He let loose with a shrill laugh and bent down to fiddle with the lace.

"Housekeeper's day off," he said, speaking to the ground. "Otherwise she'd've been here. Well, that's obvious, isn't it? What I mean is that you wouldn't've had to wait outside." He straightened, launched himself at me, and shook my hand, pumping it up and down. Then he aimed a key at the lock and missed, nicking the door's varnish with its tip.

This man was a resident in cardiac surgery?

Harry finally got the door unlocked and rushed inside. I followed him into a large tiled hallway. It was filled with plants in more urns—silk, but good imitations—and several of a hand-painted type of chest that I'd heard referred to as *tansu.* Harry heaved his keys and sunglasses at one of them, and both slid to the floor behind it. He didn't appear to notice.

"Come this way," he said, and led me to a parlor to the right. The room was so crowded with objects that I stopped on the threshold to study them. Scroll paintings and statues and temple lamps vied for space with massive leather furniture. Tables were covered with embroidered silks and ivory and jade *netsuke.* Harry lurched across to a wet bar on the far wall, narrowly missing a porcelain cat that sat haughtily beside an armchair.

"Drink?" he asked. "You'll like this Viognier my father stocks for my mother. She doesn't live here anymore, but he still keeps it on ice, hoping."

It was too early for wine, but I sensed Harry was intent on drinking and would take offense at being forced to do so alone. As he plied the corkscrew without waiting for my assent, he babbled on about the vintage, and I realized I had yet to utter a word during our brief acquaintance.

He carried the drinks—something dark and strong-looking for himself—over to a coffee table and motioned for me to sit on the sofa. After I asked if I could record our conversation and positioned the machine, he gulped most of the liquor, closing his eyes as if he were taking medicine. And of course he was—the classic signs of a person who had been self-medicating in various ways were all present, and why wasn't anyone in his family or at the hospital doing something about it?

"You're here to ask me what I thought about Rog, right?" he said. "Well, I thought he was a total asshole."

No subtle probing necessary with Harry. "Have you always thought that way, or only since he killed himself?"

"Always. Rog was born a jerk. Whiney, sulky, self-righteous, self-involved. Sensitive, Mom said. Easily wounded, Dad said. A pain in the ass, I said. Of course, nobody listened to me."

"You expressed your opinion?"

"We kids were taught to always say what we think."

"How did Roger react?"

"How d'you suppose? He whined and sulked."

"Then it would be an understatement to say you weren't close."

"Rog was a loner, not close to anybody. During the time he lived here before he bought his apartment, he barely spoke. It was a relief to see him go."

"And I don't suppose he told you anything about what went on at *InSite*."

"He didn't talk about his job to any of us." Harry rattled the ice in his glass, went to the bar for a refill.

"What about his final E-mail to you? Did he say anything in it?"

"His what?"

"In his journal entry the day he died, he said he'd E-mailed both you and Eddie."

"Oh, that. I don't know what he said; I deleted it without opening it." He paused. "I sense you don't approve of our relationship."

"I'm not here to judge you."

"That's good, because you don't understand the situation. Nobody does. Rog gave my parents a lot of grief his whole life." He returned to his chair, flopped into it heavily. "He ran away from home because he was disappointed in love—at eighteen, for God's sake. By eighteen I'd been disappointed in any number of things, but I didn't turn my back on my family. For the next seven years, every time he paid a visit he put a downer on all of us. And then the son of a bitch knocked himself off. My folks're never going to recover from that."

"This disappointment in love—did you know the girl?"

"Hard not to, the way she used to hang around here. Dinah Vardon was a miserable little twat. Came from Pinole, or some such place. Was living with an aunt and going to school here because the circumstances at home weren't any too savory. She met Rog at a party, took one look at this house, and decided she'd love him forever in order to get her hands on our money. Dragged him around by his dick for a year, then ran off with somebody who had even bigger bucks."

"Are you aware she worked with him at *InSite*?"

"She *what*?"

"She's their Webmaster. Or WebPotentate, as she calls herself."

"Goddamn." His face went still, eyes thoughtful. "Maybe that's how he got the job. And it might explain—"

"Explain what?"

He shook his head. "Nothing you'd be interested in."

"I'm interested in anything having to do with Roger."

"This has no relationship to the lawsuit."

"Let me be the judge of that."

"Uh-uh. You go ahead and gather your evidence, but leave me out of it."

"Why, Harry?"

"Because I don't care about the suit. Tell you the truth, I don't care about anything anymore."

Dinah Vardon and her former relationship with Roger intrigued me, so I drove to my office and called J.D. Smith to ask how his plan to allow me an inside look at *InSite* and its staff members was shaping up. But J.D. wasn't available at any of his numbers; I ended up leaving messages and, for good measure, E-mailed him. Next I called a couple of Roger's friends and made appointments and tried Jody Houston again, but got no answer.

It was now nearly five; I added fifteen hours to the local time and came up with approximately eight in the morning. The message slip with Hy's number in Bangkok was on my desk. I dialed his hotel, asked for his room, and he answered on the first ring.

"About time, McCone," he said.

"How'd you know it was me?"

"I always know."

And I always knew too. We had an odd emotional connection that seldom failed us. "Why'd you ask if I got the rose?"

"The florist I was using went out of business, and I'm trying a new one."

"Well, it's here and it's beautiful." I stroked one of its velvety petals.

"Great. So how're you?"

"Oh . . . okay."

"You don't sound okay. It's Joey, isn't it?"

"Yes. We'll talk about that when it won't cost us a fortune. But I need to ask you something: do you think I'm insensitive and uncaring?"

"Where's that coming from? You're one of the most sensitive and caring people I know."

"I'm not so sure about that. It's occurred to me that I give people short shrift when it's not convenient to take the time or effort."

"Oh, I see. You couldn't find Joey, and now that he's dead you feel guilty."

"I didn't look hard enough for him. I gave up when it got difficult. And this afternoon I realized I didn't even notice that the day he died was his birthday."

In the silence that followed, I sensed Hy was carefully framing a reply. "Let me ask you this: when was the last time Joey sent you a birthday card?"

"He never did."

"So he didn't keep track of your birthday either."

"That's no excuse for me—"

"No, but it proves you're normal. People forget other people's birthdays all the time. It doesn't make them monsters, or even mean they don't care. Your problem is that

Joey's suicide had nothing to do with you, but because he was your brother you think it should've, so you're looking for ways to take the blame."

I thought about that, again touching the rose. The human mind and emotions worked in such convoluted ways. "Ripinsky," I said, "how'd you get to be so wise?"

"I'm not, particularly. But I have had some experience with suicides."

"Oh? I didn't know that."

"There's a lot about me you don't know. And I like it that way—keeps you off balance and interested. When I get back, I'll tell you about those experiences; maybe it'll help you put this thing into perspective. Meantime, we'd better hang up, or we'll never be able to afford to build that new deck at Touchstone."

The evening had turned damp and chill, and a strong wind blew off the bay and whistled through the streets and alleys of SoMa. It rattled newspapers in the gutters and swayed even the hardiest of outdoor plantings. As I walked along Brannan toward Jody Houston's building a siren wailed nearby and a dog howled in perfect imitation.

The windows of Houston's apartment were lighted, but when I pressed the bell there was no answer. I hesitated, fingering the front-door key that Glenn Solomon had given me. A small white cat crouched shivering against the jamb, and that decided it; I let myself—and the cat—inside and watched as it scampered away to scratch at the door of the first-floor apartment.

It was close to ten o'clock. I'd spent some time with Julia Rafael going over the file on her first real assignment—a skip trace so simple that I'd had to bite my tongue to keep from revealing where I suspected she'd find the defaulter—then read through my other operatives' daily reports, and grabbed a quick dinner at Gordon Biersch with Anne-Marie Altman, who'd been working late in her office in Hills Brothers Plaza. In between I'd lined up several appointments with friends of Roger and made repeated unanswered calls to Houston's apartment. Now I took the creaky elevator to her floor and paused outside her door. Music came from within—rock, turned loud. Maybe Houston hadn't been able to hear the bell. I pounded on the door and after a few seconds the volume was lowered and footsteps approached.

"Who is it?" a muffled voice asked.

"Sharon McCone. We met yesterday at Roger's apartment."

"I'm sorry? Oh, you must want Jody." The chain rattled, the deadbolt turned, and I was looking at a pretty woman in dirty sweats with a smudge on one cheek and light brown hair held atop her head by a scrunchie. She clutched a cleaning rag in one hand. "I'm her friend, Paige Tallman," she said. "She leased the apartment to me."

"Since when?"

"This morning. She knew I was looking for a place, and she called to ask if I wanted hers. I jumped at the chance, but God, it's a pit. I don't think she ever cleaned."

"Where did Jody go—and for how long?"

"Indefinitely, and she wouldn't tell me where. Said I'd be better off if I didn't know. I'm to hold her mail and packages till she sends instructions."

"What about the rent payments?"

"I gave her cash for first and last, and she has postdated checks for the rest of the year. After that, I don't know."

"Awfully sudden, wasn't it?"

Now the woman's eyes grew wary. "Who are you, and why're you looking for her?"

I repeated my name, told her my occupation. "Jody's connected with a case I'm working on, and she may be in danger. I need to find her."

Paige Tallman nodded, concerned but unsurprised. "I was afraid of something like that. There were some messages on the answering machine today—including a couple from you—that sounded like she was in trouble. And she acted really freaky this morning, rushing around and tossing stuff in suitcases. She wouldn't answer the phone or the doorbell, either."

"When did she leave?"

"Around noon. She couldn't wait to get out of here. She left a lot of her stuff; I'm supposed to box it up and hold on to it."

"She drive? Fly?"

"She doesn't have a car. I heard her call a cab—probably to go to the airport."

That meant I might be able to trace her. My travel agent had taught me a number of ways to get information from the airlines.

I asked, "Are you sure she didn't give any indication of where she was going?"

"No. She said that way nobody could force me to tell them."

But that didn't mean that they wouldn't try. Paige Tallman could be in for a very bad time. "Look, Ms. Tallman, this is not a good situation. Maybe you shouldn't move in just yet."

"I'm already in; I got my stuff out of storage this afternoon. After living on my sister's hide-a-bed for five months after I broke up with my boyfriend, this place is like heaven, dirt and all. Besides, I can take care of myself."

Tallman thrust her chin out defiantly, daring me to contradict her, and I realized how young she was—no more than twenty-one or -two. Young and full of bravado, as I'd been two decades before, and likely to get herself into fully as much trouble as I sometimes had.

"At least change the locks," I suggested.

"Can't afford to."

She didn't know who or what she might be up against, but then, neither did I. Maybe the threat wasn't serious; maybe Jody Houston was simply paranoid. Still, I couldn't leave Paige Tallman alone and at risk.

I handed her my card. "I'll make you a deal. When you hear from Jody, try to find out where she is and let me know. In exchange, I'll send a friend over who specializes in residential security. She'll install an alarm, free of charge."

Tallman looked at the card. "Thanks, Ms. McCone! What a day. This is the second time the right person's come along at the right time."

"And my friend will make sure the wrong person won't be able to come along tomorrow."

After I left Paige Tallman I climbed the interior stairway to the floor above and let myself into Roger's apartment. It was very cold there, as if each chilly night since his death had added its weight until the warmth of day could no longer penetrate it. The apartment smelled of fresh paint and furniture polish, but beneath those clean odors was filth and decay. Fanciful thinking on my part, I supposed, because I knew what the closet and cupboard doors concealed.

The other morning I'd noticed the phone up here was still connected; my cell had discharged by now, and I wanted to call Sue Hollister, my friend in residential security, right away. Sue was home and agreeable to coming over first thing tomorrow; I asked her to bill my office and gave her the Nagasawa case-file number for reference.

Then I turned on a small lamp in the living room and sat down on the sofa to listen to the silence.

When I was looking for my birth parents the previous autumn, Hy had taught me a useful technique: listening to the spaces between people's words, the pauses between statements. Listening, in effect, to what they censored. I hadn't tried it with a physical environment before, but I'd long contended that a place can tell you a great deal about the events that have transpired within it if you're patient and allow it to do so. Now I waited for the apartment to give me some hint of the past.

From outside came the normal city sounds: more sirens, more barking dogs, someone yelling in the street, a car burning rubber, an alarm gone haywire. But the apartment must be well insulated, because all of those seemed very far away.

In the kitchen the refrigerator made ticking noises. Then there was a swirling and gurgling. Something wrong with the coil, meaning costly repairs or even a whole new unit. Mine did that periodically, and every time I heard it I got depressed.

The wind was stronger now. It made small, shrill whistles as it seeped through the ill-fitting frame of the rear window. A skylight groaned ominously, and a piece of plaster beside it broke loose and crumbled as it hit the floor.

I thought of Roger coming back to the city, landing a dream job, expecting stock options, buying an apartment full of light. But then the dream job turned into a nightmare, the options didn't materialize, the apartment turned into a maintenance problem—

No. You can quit a job and find another. You can defer maintenance or take out a home-improvement loan. Those problems are not personal "failures." Those problems are not the "circumstances" that drive you over a bridge railing.

I listened some more. Tick. Gurgle. Whistle. Groan. Crack. There was something in between, a subtlety that I couldn't quite grasp—

The phone shrilled.

My heartbeat accelerated and I jumped off the sofa, scooped up the receiver, and answered in a voice made hoarse by surprise.

"Communing with the dead again?" The caller could have been either male or female, sounded like he or she had covered the mouthpiece with something. "It's not going to do any good. Better you should reschedule our appointment."

"Who is this?"

A silence. Caution? Surprise?

The receiver was replaced violently.

Roger, thank God, had favored state-of-the-art phone equipment. I pressed the key to view the number of the last caller, saw that the prefix was the same. Close by, then.

* * *

"McCone," Adah Joslyn's sleep-clogged voice said, "I can't do it till morning. Shouldn't be doing it at all."

"I don't ask for a lot of favors." I pictured the SFPD homicide inspector snuggled up in bed with my operative Craig Morland and her enormously fat cat, Charley. Warmth and comfort were the reasons she didn't want to run the check.

"Don't go all humble pie on me, girl! It ain't you."

I waited her out while she fulminated about late-night calls when I wanted something. Adah, who often denigrated her talents by claiming her straight-to-the-top career path was due to her being the department's "three-way poster child"—meaning half black, half Jewish, and a woman—was a terrific cop and a better friend, if inclined to be testy.

"Okay," she finally said, "fifteen minutes. But this is the last time, McCone. You hear? The last!"

"Phone booth," Adah said some ten minutes later. "Lobby of the Redwood Health Club on—"

"Brannan."

"You knew that, why'd you wake me up?"

"I know where the club is, not their phone booth number." The club was next door. Whoever called had seen there was a light here in the apartment.

Adah snorted. "*You* know where a health club is? When was the last time we swam together?"

"We'll go to the pool next week, I promise."

"Yeah, sure. You know, McCone, you and that crew of yours at the pier are really something."

I tapped my fingers on the receiver, impatient to hang up. "What does that mean?"

"Well, you wake me up on a night when I had trouble getting to sleep because my man's out boozing with your office manager—"

"Craig's with Ted?"

"Right. Seems Neal up and quit his job this afternoon. Harsh words were exchanged. So Ted's afraid to go home, and he and Craig're on a pub crawl."

Great. Now I had to worry about Neal, alone and miserable, while Ted, who couldn't hold his liquor, was out drinking with Craig, who could, and would probably tempt him to spectacular excess. Well, that was their problem—for now, anyway.

The health club was a twenty-four-hour operation, and the large windows that fronted on the sidewalk were awash with light. Inside, a dozen or so spandex-suited individuals used various instruments of torture, bearing grim expressions born of a determination to achieve bodily perfection. I've never understood why you would want your sweaty efforts displayed to every passerby—isn't it something better done in private?—but most fitness centers seem to favor this form of free advertising.

The lobby was empty, with no one at the horseshoe-shaped reception desk. The pay phone was in an alcove tucked between the entrances to the men's and women's locker rooms. I went back there and looked around, but there was no trace of the person who'd recently used it. Then I went to the entrance to the exercise room and studied the people. They were all concentrating on their machines and didn't notice me.

Well, what did I expect? The caller wasn't likely to have remained on the premises to work on his or her abs.

A black woman with curly auburn hair came through a door behind the desk marked Office. "Help you?" she asked.

"Maybe. A friend called me about half an hour ago from the pay phone. I was supposed to meet her here, but I don't see her. Is there someplace she might be besides the exercise room?"

"She a member?"

"I guess."

"What's her name?"

"Uh, Jody Houston." Since she'd lived next door, she might have been a member; if she was, maybe the woman would let me look around.

She went to her computer and tapped in the name. "Sorry, we're not showing her."

"Maybe you saw her make the call?"

"I haven't seen anybody on the phone tonight, but I've been in and out of the office, so I could've missed her."

I glanced toward the signs for the pool, racquetball courts, and juice bar. "Could I—?"

"Sorry. Members only."

"I understand. Thanks anyway."

"Hope you find your friend."

As I went out I reflected on the phone call. Implied threat there, and I suspected it was directed at Jody Houston, who had told me she had a key to Roger's apartment. Someone was watching the building, had seen the light. But why use a booth that was so close by, whose number Houston could have traced as easily as I had?

Of course—that was part of the threat: *I'm right here. I can find you any time I want.*

There were three messages on my home machine, two of them predictable and one intriguing.

My brother John: "Just calling to see how you are. After you left last week, I realized you were talking like you did because you're pissed at Joey. Well, guess what? So am I. We need to discuss this."

Not tonight, John.

Neal: "I guess you've heard that I quit. I'm not cut out for the job, and I should've known I couldn't work with Ted. Sorry for all my screwups. If you know where he is, will you call me?"

In a minute, Neal.

J.D. Smith: "Okay, Shar, I've got a sweet deal for you. So pick up . . . Are you screening your calls? No, you wouldn't screen this one. Why aren't you home, goddamn it? All right, I guess it can wait till morning. I'll see you at Miranda's at nine for breakfast. You're gonna love my plan."

Thursday

•

APRIL 19

To the casual passerby Miranda's would seem to be an ordinary waterfront dive. Gray weathered clapboard with salt-caked windows, it teetered on pilings over the bay's brackish shallows, clinging tenuously to mainstream San Francisco. It, as well as the nearby Boondocks and Red's Java House, were already on the city's endangered-species list.

Proposals for redevelopment up and down the waterfront had already threatened many venerable establishments. The plans ranged from desirable to the preposterous: among the latter were a Disneyesque faux-city theme park replete with earthquake simulations, and a full-scale floating replica of the *Titanic*. Such madness could strike at any location at any time, hence my concern for several of my favorite eateries.

Fortunately, Miranda's had assets that increased its chances of survival: its much-loved owner, Carmen Lazzarini; excellent food, courtesy of Carmen's new wife; aficionados in city government and on the Port Commission. As I waited for J.D. in a window booth I looked around and noticed a powerful member of the board of supervisors, a well-known actor, and an appellate court judge downing eggs and hash browns. Standees clustered by the lunch counter, drinking coffee while waiting for tables. Just as I was beginning to feel guilty for hogging an entire booth, J.D. pushed through the door and strode toward me, clapping the supe on the shoulder as he passed.

"Traffic!" he exclaimed, collapsing on the bench opposite me and shrugging out of his raincoat. "Fender-benders all over the place. Why is it that Californians forget how to drive when it rains?"

"Don't know. We ought to be experts, given the monsoons we've had recently."

"Parking's impossible too." He studied the menu and set it aside. "Makes me long for the days of my youth, when parking was plentiful and drivers in the Old South were courteous."

"You left Savannah because you found it dull and stifling."

"True. I came west looking for excitement and got it—congestion, rolling blackouts, high PG and E bills, higher rents, and now rain when the rainy season's supposed to be over. What's that the Chinese say? 'May you live in interesting times.' "

Carmen himself, wrapped in a stained apron, appeared to take our orders. The big man—whose real first name, I had found out after considerable investigation, was Orlando—had undergone a renaissance of sorts since meeting his second wife, Cissy. Beneath the apron he wore a teal blue silk shirt and stylish cords; hair implants dotted his head like seedlings in a vegetable garden. I couldn't help eyeing them and wondering if they'd ever grow. Carmen noticed, and I looked away, embarrassed.

J.D., a reporter to the bone, had no similar qualms. He asked, "How're those things doing, Carmen?"

"A few more little hairs every day."

"You know, your experience would make an interesting story, give other bald men hope."

"You think so?"

"Sure. I could write it up, chart your progress. We could sell it as a series to one of the online 'zines, and you'd be all over the Internet. Great publicity for the diner."

"I don't know, J.D." Carmen glanced at the crowd still waiting for tables. "We've got more customers than we can handle already, and while the Port Commission isn't selling us out to the developers yet, they're not about to give us the go-ahead to expand."

"Well, think about it, anyway."

"Yeah, I will. Now, for breakfast I can definitely recommend the Denver omelet."

J.D. made a face. "Orange juice, English muffin, hold the jelly."

Carmen snorted. "Why you bother with breakfast I don't know."

As he turned to go, J.D. said, "Hey, what about Shar's order?"

Carmen looked over his shoulder and winked at me. "Two eggs over easy, double side of bacon, hash browns."

J.D. blinked, astonished. "You have that all the time?" he asked me.

"Except when they've got chicken fried steak and eggs on special."

"Don't you know stuff like that can kill you?"

"Well, I don't come here every day. Unless I have a

breakfast appointment, I usually just have coffee and some tomato juice."

"It's a wonder you've survived this long."

"I've survived worse things at the hands of people who wanted me permanently gone. Breakfast doesn't scare me. Now, what's this plan you have for getting me inside—"

He held up a cautionary hand. "Don't mention them by name. I'm on to something, and I don't want it blown because somebody overhears our conversation."

"Okay. Go ahead."

He leaned across the table, his smile revealing small, sharp teeth, and I was reminded of Glenn's "wolf look." J.D. resembled a less ferocious species—possibly a ferret—but his hunting instincts transformed him all the same. It made me wonder what sort of creature I resembled when on the prowl.

"You and . . . the gang are going to play a game, and I'm to be the observer," he said.

"What kind of game?"

"Here's what I proposed to them: They create a puzzle of their own choosing, centered in their offices. You go in and have a day to solve it. The result of this battle of wits will be chronicled by me for their local celebrity series."

"And they went for it?"

"Yes. Why wouldn't they?"

"I don't know. The idea sounds kind of—"

"Silly. I know. But they're kind of a silly publication. Anyway, it gets you into their offices and gives you free run of them without arousing any suspicion, plus plenty of time to become acquainted with the players."

Silly or not, his plan had its merits.

"The publicity wouldn't hurt either," J.D. added.

"No," I said, "I don't want the article to actually appear."

"Why not?"

"This is an important investigation I'm conducting. I don't want to compromise it."

He considered that. "Well," he said after a minute, "I suppose I could have difficulty finishing the piece. Or simply write it so badly they'd refuse to publish it. They don't pay all that much anyway."

"I'll be glad to reimburse you—"

"Not necessary." He studied me, brows knitting. "The other night you said the results of this investigation would be newsworthy."

"Yes. They'll result in a civil suit revolving around a subject that's already attracted considerable attention."

"A civil suit?" For a moment he looked confused, then he smiled. "Now I understand—the Nagasawa kid."

I fixed him with a stony look.

"Okay." He held up his hands defensively. "I'll say no more. We'll play it your way. But remember—I get the story."

"Agreed. Now, when is this game supposed to take place?"

"Tomorrow. We're to meet with Max Engstrom at five-thirty today to go over the details."

I had no set plans for Friday, and today's last appointment was scheduled for three. I took down *InSite*'s address and told J.D. I'd meet him there.

By four o'clock I was back in my office reviewing the highlights of my taped interviews with Roger's friends and acquaintances.

Kelley Waterson, unemployed systems analyst: "A bunch of us used to hang together after work. We all had pretty intense careers, we were going to get as rich as Bill Gates. Right? Wrong! But back then the dot-com market was still sizzling, and we were all working our tails off for stock options, so we liked to blow off steam when we called it a day. We'd meet at Kodiak Rick's, that billiards parlor and brew pub on Third, shoot a few games to get the evening going. One night one of the women was late, and I asked Rog if I could use his cell phone to call and tell her we'd decided to amp up the evening by going on to one of the clubs. But he said he'd rather I didn't because it was a company phone, and Max Engstrom used the records of the employees' calls to keep tabs on what they did after work. Talk about a gross invasion of privacy!"

Matt Oppenheim, Web page designer: "Sometimes Rog and I lifted weights at the health club next to his building. Usually in the middle of the night, because we both had crazy schedules. You wouldn't believe how many people who're trying to stay fit are at the club at three in the morning. Anyway, one night I noticed he had bad bruises on his upper arm. When I asked about them, he shrugged it off, said he didn't know how he got them, he was clumsy and banged into things all the time. But he was not a clumsy man. The next time, I noticed scratches that looked like they'd been made by somebody's fingernails, and I insisted he tell me what had happened. He admitted there had been some serious arguing going on at the office, and he'd gotten into it with one of the VIPs. Now, I've worked in all kinds of offices, and seen all sorts of infighting, but this was unbelievable to me. I mean, physical fighting is just not acceptable behavior no matter what the circumstances. I advised him to consult his attorney, and he said he'd think about it. I guess, since you're here asking me about this, that he didn't."

David Kong, investment banker: "Invasion of privacy? Definitely. *InSite* is into that in a major way. They provide cell phones, credit cards, and Internet access to their employees, tell them to go ahead and use them for personal, as well as work-related, purposes. Then they use their leverage as the party who pays the bills to check phone and credit-card invoices and get the Internet server to divulge information about E-mail. I guess because of your line of work you know how much you can learn about a person from those sources. And it's not illegal, technically speaking, because the magazine is officially the client of record. . . . Why would they want to keep tabs on their people? I'd say it's a control thing. Engstrom and his buddies are total control freaks."

Fiona King, registered nurse, San Francisco General Hospital: "Roger Nagasawa sought me out after one of his coworkers was brought into our emergency room suffering from acute dehydration brought on by an overdose of laxatives. Roger thought the drug had been administered in her drinks at a company party. I told him the woman had suspected the same, and asked if she'd gone to the police or her attorney. He said she was afraid to confront their employer or file charges. Roger and I became friends after that. He was such a caring, sensitive man. We dated a couple of times, but . . . well, he was a glass-is-half-empty type, and my glass is always half full."

Suzy Bivens, bartender, Kodiak Rick's: "Sleep-deprived, that's what they all were, but manic too—especially when NASDAQ started tanking and they were watching their portfolios shrink and their job security turn shaky. Then there were the poor bastards like Rog, who didn't even have portfolios, because the 'zine had promised but not delivered stock options in lieu of real pay. After the bubble burst, the atmosphere in here really turned grim, and that hasn't changed. The regulars still come in, but it'll never be the same. But to get back to your original question, all of those people were wrecks, but the *InSite* staffers were the absolute worst."

Liz Lyman, consultant: "A consultant's a name for somebody who got laid off when everything fell apart and hasn't been able to land another position. But that's enough about me. Frankly, I don't want to talk about this last year, other than to say it's been horrible. About Roger Nagasawa and *InSite* magazine: it was a toxic combination. The top people there are not the type who like others to stand up to them. But Roger had been raised to fight things he considered wrong, and that did not go over well. There were screaming fights, physical fights. It was a hideous situation."

Emily Kurland, venture capitalist: "You know what the press has started calling us? *Vulture* capitalists. God, I hate that term! I'm a trust-fund baby, inherited a lot of money, and I've put it into socially responsible companies that I think may do our world some good. Sure I expect a return on my investment, and therefore I'm one hundred percent behind any firm I back. I don't want to pick their bones, see them fail. Sorry, I'm ranting, and you're here to talk about Rog. We used to see each other at Kodiak's. He was a very nice man. Depressed a lot of time because he'd lost his sense of a bright future with that magazine. But he was smart, he had a lot going for himself if only he'd use it. I kept after him to come up with a concept I could finance, so he could gain some control over his life. But something was going on at *InSite,* and he was determined to fight it. . . . No, I don't have any idea what. But I do know that Rog had a finely tuned sense of justice. He was a crusader, and if there was a way to make things right, he'd find it."

I shut off the recorder and went to the armchair by the window. It was a relic of my early days at All Souls Legal Cooperative, and I'd brought it along to the pier in a fit of sentimentality. I'd done some of my best thinking in that chair and, ugly and butt-sprung as it was, I didn't want to part with it. Besides, a good-quality handwoven throw had greatly improved its appearance.

So, I thought, after three days on this investigation what did I have?

Statements that the VIPs at *InSite* invaded their employees' privacy as well as psychologically and physically abused them. Statements that Roger had been determined to right the wrongs there. Hearsay, all of it, inadmissible in court. I needed actual witnesses to the abuse who would be willing to testify. And even then Glenn would have to establish that the abuse was severe enough to make Roger take his own life. Not an easy task, but Glenn relished that kind of challenge.

I'd interviewed all the potential witnesses on Glenn's list. Now it was time to tackle the people at *InSite*.

I hadn't visited the little neighborhood called Dogpatch in almost a decade, when friends who lived there were evicted from their ramshackle Victorian. It's an area little known to most San Franciscans, and even the residents are in disagreement as to how it got its name. Some say it comes from the hillbilly town in the *Li'l Abner* comic strip; others claim the five-block-square area was once home to packs of wild dogs. Whatever the explanation might be, it's an odd pocket of the city several blocks south of Pac Bell Park and the Mission Bay development, where new economy firms in renovated industrial space sit side by side with old cottages and working-class bars. And the only place, so far as I know, to boast of its own brand of ale, the oldest functioning shipyard in the country, and a Hell's Angels clubhouse. The denizens of Dogpatch take pride in its colorful past, when its sugar refineries, gunpowder factory, whaling station, and iron mills dominated the city's industrial economy.

As I drove to *InSite*'s offices in a former warehouse on Illinois Street, I noted that a good deal of redevelopment was slated for the area. A row of frame cottages was being torn down, and many other lots sat vacant; luxury cars and SUVs were slotted between battered sedans and trucks. When I passed the venerable Dogpatch Saloon I saw a briefcase-toting woman talking on her phone while she held the door for a man in shipyard worker's clothing—an amiable collision of the old and the new.

J.D. was leaning against the wall of *InSite*'s building when I pulled into a parking space by its loading dock. The morning's rain had let up around noon, and he'd traded his coat for a lemon-yellow sweater that clashed violently with his red hair. As he pushed away from the wall and walked toward me, I spotted a penny lying in a crack in the pavement, picked it up, and waved it triumphantly at him before pocketing it.

He grinned. "You're still doing that."

"For luck. I need all I can get." I'm always finding coins on the street and tucking them into the pocket of whatever garment I'm wearing—where they stay till they fall out in the washing machine.

"Well, maybe it'll bring us luck in there." He jerked his thumb at the building.

"We can hope." I started for the glass doors labeled with the magazine's logo—a hand holding a magnifying glass over its name—but J.D. stopped me. "From here on we don't say anything that'll give away our real purpose, even if there's nobody around."

"Don't tell me the offices're bugged?"

"Knowing Max Engstrom, it wouldn't surprise me."

"Someone told me he's a control freak. Does he gather information to coerce his employees?"

"Probably."

We walked through the doors into a linoleum-tiled anteroom with a second, solid set of doors at its far side. On the otherwise unadorned wall in between was an intercom with a surveillance camera mounted above it and a command panel for an alarm system. Not excessive security, considering the neighborhood. J.D. pressed a button and spoke, a buzzer sounded, and we pushed through into a scene of utter chaos.

Phones rang, fax machines and computers beeped, voices spoke loudly or, in some instances, shouted. About fifty casually dressed people filled the large space, and most of them were in motion—pacing, gesturing, popping up from and plopping down into their chairs. Their battleship-gray metal desks were lined up in rows three abreast; there were no cubicles, no dividers, no privacy. The floor was awash in crumpled paper, candy wrappers, and other litter; the desks were covered with files, notepads, coffee cups, and the remnants of meals. My senses reeled from the noise and the mixed odors of Chinese, Mexican, Italian, and good old American grease. Fluorescent light glared down from fixtures suspended on chains from the high ceiling.

I would have gone insane within an hour if forced to work in such a place.

A couple of people nodded to J.D. when we came in, but most didn't pay us any attention. He touched my arm and pointed to a staircase at the rear of the room that led up to a loft where glass-walled offices overlooked the main floor. A man—medium height, heavy, partially bald—stood in one, motioning to us.

"Max," J.D. said.

I followed him past the desks, up the stairs, and along a short hallway to a narrow corridor behind the offices. Max Engstrom waited for us outside his door. He was older than I'd expected—in his fifties—and massive in spite of his lack of stature. Around his large head grew a fringe of gray hair that merged with a neatly trimmed beard; lines furrowed his cheeks in an oddly corrugated pattern; his eyes, under thick brows, were shrewd.

"Mr. Smith," he said, nodding to J.D. "And this is the celebrated private investigator, Sharon McCone."

I offered my right hand, but he clasped both in his, scanning my face intently. Attempting to control me by refusing a simple handshake. Sizing me up, too, and whatever first impression he formed would govern whether he continued to take J.D.'s cover story at face value. I returned the pressure of his fingers and smiled girlishly—if such a thing is possible at forty-one—and said, "Celebrated, Mr. Engstrom? I doubt that. But I will be if you use J.D.'s story in your magazine."

It wasn't the response he'd expected. He dropped my hands, controlled a frown. "This, from a woman who's been written up in *People*?"

"If you saw the piece you must realize how much I regret it. Their photographer made me look like a thug, and their interviewer made me sound like an idiot."

"Well, I can promise you we won't do either. J.D.'s the best freelancer we've got, and the purpose of *InSite* is to present attractive people and things in the most favorable light."

Engstrom then ushered us into his office, a small space crammed with mission-style furnishings; a leather chair was swiveled toward the glass wall—an excellent vantage point for monitoring what went on below.

Engstrom saw me looking down and said, "This building used to be a sewing factory. When we remodeled it we kept this loft, which is where the supervisors sat. I've amused myself for countless hours by watching my staff's antics." His doting smile didn't reach his eyes.

"They seem a lively bunch," I said.

"They're like a roomful of kindergartners—bright, talented, and skilled kindergartners." He motioned for us to sit on the uncomfortable-looking sofa and turned his chair around to face us. "All of us at *InSite* believe that the workplace should be enjoyable—a home away from home. It fosters creativity. And what creativity doesn't get channeled into the work goes into the games. That's why J.D.'s idea for your game was so appealing to us."

"What kinds of games do they play?"

"Well, the water pistols are a good example. One of the tech staff came into possession of scores of them at a liquidation sale, which he distributed to all takers. They began working out their aggressions by firing on those who irritated them. Within days, the entire staff was armed and ready. Sneak attacks and retaliations are a common occurrence."

"Interesting," I said, trying not to show my distaste. There had been too many incidents of employees opening real fire on their coworkers. Maybe the water pistols were therapeutic, but to me they seemed only a short step away from the real thing.

Engstrom went on, "We're a family here. Long hours and working the occasional weekend are necessary in order to keep the magazine fresh—some of the content changes daily. We use a great deal of freelance material"—he nodded at J.D.—"but it still has to be edited, illustrated, and so forth. And the tech staff is on call twenty-four hours in case of problems. Most of us have newspaper backgrounds like J.D., so we run more like a paper than your traditional magazine."

A cheer went up from the floor below. As Engstrom swiveled toward the glass, J.D. and I got up to look. A pair of men were entering, one with a liquor case balanced on his shoulder, another laden with plastic sacks. The staffers crowded around them, herding them into the space under the loft.

"Cocktail hour," Engstrom said, swiveling back to the desk. "We work hard, but we also play hard. A daily happy hour is paid for by the company, and the currently fashionable cocktail and snacks are served. This week it's White Hot Zombies."

"What the hell're those?" J.D. asked.

"Damned if I know. I'm a martini man myself. But the point I'm trying to make is that we treat our staffers well. We provide a catered breakfast and pay for whatever they order in when they can't go home for meals. Expense accounts are generous. We provide cell phones, Internet access, and, in some cases, computers for home use. We allow pets and preschool children to be brought to work—although there's only one baby in the nursery right now, and no pets in the office, due to the travel editor's Great Dane having taken a violent dislike to the Edibles editor's Lhasa asshole."

"Lhasa *what*?" J.D. asked.

"Dog had a lousy personality."

In light of what I'd been hearing all day about *InSite*—which seemed to be common knowledge among Roger Nagasawa's social circle—Engstrom's speech sounded as if he were trying to convince us it was a pleasant working atmosphere—and perhaps also convince himself. My suspicion was confirmed when he rose suddenly and lowered the blinds on the glass wall. As he sat down again and fiddled with something under his desk—a control for the listening devices J.D. claimed were planted in the offices?—he said, "What I'm about to tell you is strictly on background, J.D."

"I understand."

"And you, Sharon—can I count on confidentiality?"

"Of course."

"I have a secondary motive for being intrigued by your game. Someone in our little family is disloyal. Someone in these offices is not working in the magazine's best interests. I've become aware of it in recent months, and whoever it is has to be identified and stopped. I want you, Sharon, to attempt to do so as you go about your game playing."

I glanced at J.D., who wore an interested expression. "What makes you think one of your employees is disloyal?" I asked.

"Important files have disappeared—files on unique stories our people are working on. In one case, a version of an especially good piece appeared in a rival publication. Invoices have vanished and gone unpaid till dunning notices arrived. Equipment that was running perfectly well the day before has malfunctioned. E-mail and voice mail messages have gone astray."

"And you're certain this is the work of an insider?"

"It has to be someone who has access to the premises and can find out other people's private passwords. Last week someone disabled the security system by disconnecting wires in an interior junction box."

"Any suspicions of who it is?"

"No. It shocks me to think any of my people could be responsible."

"Have you reported this to the police?"

"I prefer to handle it privately."

J.D. said, "So even if Sharon identifies the culprit, nothing about that would appear in my piece?"

"If it did, I wouldn't publish it, and I'd block publication anywhere else. Is that clear?"

J.D. held up his hands. "Just asking."

I said, "Are you proposing to hire me?"

"I would think the publicity you'll receive from the feature story would be sufficient compensation."

"Of course." And good that he felt that way, because I'd compromise Glenn's case if I accepted any payment from the magazine. "Let's get down to specifics now," I told him. "I think we're going to have a very interesting time here."

"Jesus Christ," J.D. grumbled as we settled onto stools at the bar of the Dogpatch Saloon, "couldn't Engstrom come up with a better game than that? Find out which staff member has a partial manuscript of a novel locked in his or her desk drawer! Doesn't the fool know that *every* journalist is secretly writing a novel?"

"You too?"

"Me too." He gave our order to the bartender and stared gloomily at the bottles arrayed across from us, avoiding my eyes.

"So what's it about?"

"About a hundred and eight pages."

"You know what I mean."

"All right—it's about my childhood in the Deep South. And it's a silly, self-indulgent piece of crap. I'll never finish, much less sell, it."

"Oh."

"But back to the game, it's so simplistic you'll have it figured out in a couple of hours."

"Not with everything else I'm supposed to do while I'm there. I wonder if these incidents he was talking about have any connection to Roger Nagasawa's suicide."

J.D. shrugged and reached for the drink the bartender set in front of him.

"Do you know many of the other people who freelance for *InSite*?" I asked.

"Sure. Like I said, the way you do business with them is to hang out, schmooze with the VIPs, wait for an assignment to drop into your lap."

"What about a graphic designer named Jody Houston?"

"I've talked with her a few times." He raised his eyebrows. "Wait a minute—weren't she and Nagasawa an item?"

"Just friends, or so she says. I talked with her briefly on Tuesday at his apartment." I explained about Houston's call to Daniel Nagasawa. "Now she's leased her apartment to a friend and vanished."

"Strange coincidence."

"How so?"

"You remember I mentioned a VC named Tessa Remington?"

"Uh-huh."

"Well, I meant to give you the skinny on her last night, but then I got sidetracked. A couple of months ago she disappeared. Left the Remington Group's offices for a late-afternoon meeting of the board of a nonprofit that she sits on, but never arrived there. Her husband notified the police the following morning, and because she's a mover and shaker, they got started on it right away, but they haven't turned up a trace of her."

"They think it was a voluntary disappearance, or foul play?"

"I don't know, but the investigation's more or less on hold. Her absence has created a real problem for *InSite,* according to what Max told me when I called him to propose the game. Remington was about to make a big deposit into their account, but she never got around to it, and no one else has the authority to follow through. Their reserves're dwindling fast."

"But they're still spending lavishly."

"Well, sure. Image is everything with these people. They learned no lessons from the dot-com bust."

"Do the police have any theories about what happened to Remington?"

"None they're sharing with the press."

Two people with connections to *InSite* had vanished—one voluntarily, the other maybe not. Had Tessa Remington, like Jody Houston, expressed fear for her life?

Back at the pier, I hurried upstairs, intent on accessing newspaper accounts of Remington's disappearance, but the sound of keys tapping in one of the offices the operatives shared stopped me, and I went in to see who was working late.

Julia Rafael hunched over her keyboard, a pencil thrust behind her ear, the tip of her tongue caught between her teeth. When I came up beside her she made an error and cursed as she hit the Delete key. "I'm a rotten typist," she said.

"I'm not too great myself. What's that?" I motioned at the screen.

"Report on the Doofus case."

"Doofus?"

"What I call Dreyfus. Guy's an idiot. Didn't bother to cover his tracks worth a damn. I'll have this on your desk in fifteen minutes." She was trying to act offhand about her success, but her dark eyes shone with pride.

"Congratulations! I didn't do that well my first time on my own."

"Well, like I told you, the guy's an idiot."

"How'd you like to take on somebody smarter?"

"Sure."

"I'll be in my office. We'll talk when you deliver that." I paused. "Unless you've got plans for tonight."

"Nope, no plans. I'll call my sister, tell her I'm gonna be late. She baby-sits my kid."

Julia was a single mother with an eight-year-old son. "I don't want to keep you from—"

"Hey, no *problema.* Tonio likes staying with Maria—she lets him get away with stuff."

"See you later, then."

As I waited for a connection to the *Chronicle*'s online files, I thought about the first time I'd met Julia Rafael. She'd come for an interview in response to an ad I'd placed in January for an investigative trainee, no previous experience necessary. Meaning not only would I be able to start him or her at the modest salary I could afford, but also instill my methods of investigation and—more important—my professional values in the individual.

It was raining the day of Julia's appointment, and she'd forgotten a hat and had her umbrella stolen on the bus. Her hair dripped water and rain had seeped through her cheap coat, staining her tan suit. Immediately I was impressed by the way she handled herself, making only brief explanations, allowing me to hang her coat near the heater, and accepting a towel for her hair.

The completed application she presented was brutally

honest: she'd been incarcerated by the California Youth Authority two times, each for drug-related offenses. During her second term she'd earned her GED. After she got out at twenty, she was dismissed from her first job as a motel maid for striking a customer who physically came on to her. A second job in a relative's convenience store ended because her boyfriend took to hanging out there and shoplifting. After that she landed a position with a federally funded neighborhood outreach program, working with at-risk teenagers, and things began to change for the better. But two months before she answered my ad, after she'd been on the job over four years, the program had lost its funding.

I wondered why she'd chosen to reveal her history with the CYA. Juvenile records are officially sealed, in order to give the individual a chance to start over. When I asked, she simply said, "If you hire me, it might come out later, and it would look like I was covering up. Besides, that's over now."

"Okay, tell me why you want this particular job."

"I figure in your business you help people. That was what I liked about my last job. And," she added with a small smile, "you said no experience necessary, and experience is one thing I don't have much of, unless it's bad."

And it had been very bad, that much I realized as I began to draw her out over a cup of coffee. She'd been born near Watsonville in Santa Cruz County, where her father worked in the artichoke fields, but he'd moved the family—his pregnant wife and four girls—to San Francisco's Mission district when Julia was five, in order to open a restaurant with a cousin. The restaurant failed, and the family's life spiraled downward into frequent unemployment, ever more cramped living quarters, alcoholism, and physical abuse.

Julia was on the streets dealing drugs and prostituting herself at twelve. Her first arrest was at thirteen. She'd had two abortions by sixteen, and at seventeen gave birth to a son whose father's identity was anybody's guess, and whom she'd sent to live with relatives in Salinas when she was sent back to the CYA.

"Why didn't you also abort that baby?" I asked.

"Because by then I'd grown up, had feelings. I wasn't innocent, but I knew the kid was. Didn't seem right to kill it. And the way it worked out, Tonio turned me around."

Pictures of her little boy saw her through the final incarceration by the youth authority. When she returned to the city, she was able to settle down, send for her son, and begin leading the normal life of a single parent.

"Don't get me wrong," she told me. "I'm not the model mom. I still like to party. If my older sister—who got out of the apartment before things really went to hell with the family—didn't live in my building, I don't think I could manage. But I'm working on it. I got to, for Tonio's sake. The way I see it, we saved each other's lives."

I'd concluded the interview thinking there was something too pat and calculated about Julia Rafael's presentation of herself, but next to her the other applicants I saw seemed lackluster. Honesty about one's past mistakes and determination in the face of the odds have always impressed me, and if she had a bit of the con woman in her, so much the better in this business. I gave her a hard day's thought, then called to tell her she had the job. So far she'd proven to be a bright student, and now, I felt, my investment in her was starting to pay off.

I finally located the Tessa Remington story in the Friday, February 16, *Chron*. It told me little more than what J.D.

had already recapped, except for the date of her disappearance—the fourteenth—her husband's name—Kelby Lincoln, CEO of something called Econium Measures—and that the police were asking the public to be on the lookout for her white BMW convertible, license number 2 KCV 743. A picture of Remington accompanied the article: a woman of about my age with short, sleekly styled blond hair and classically sculpted features. Her expression radiated poise and self-confidence.

The fourteenth. Valentine's Day. Roger had killed himself that night. Coincidence, or—?

"Sharon?" Julia stood in the doorway, her first report in hand.

"Come on in," I said. "Let's look that over and then get you started on your next assignment. It's a skip trace on a woman named Jody Houston."

Friday

•

APRIL 20

It was raining heavily when I arrived in Dogpatch at eight a.m. I sprinted from my MG to the doors of *InSite*'s building, pushed through them, and took off my sodden raincoat before using the intercom. It was too damn late in the season for this kind of weather!

When I went through the second set of doors I saw that the large room beyond was as chaotic as the previous afternoon. Several people stood in a row in a way that reminded me of a formal receiving line, with Max Engstrom at its head. J.D. wasn't in evidence. Engstrom stepped forward, took my wet coat, and hung it on a nearby chair. Then he clasped my hands, and said, "Welcome, Ms. McCone. The game's afoot."

I winced inwardly at his Holmesian imitation, but replied, "Yes, it is, Mr. Engstrom."

"Allow me to introduce some of the players—and my top people." He handed me over to a woman of my height and build who stood beside him. "Dinah Vardon, our Web-Potentate."

Vardon nodded, shaking my hand with a strong grip. Roger's former love was striking in a pale, severe way, her dark hair pulled back from her face and fastened at the nape of her neck. Her mouth was thin-lipped and humorless, and her gray eyes were shiny and cold; they reminded me of pebbles on the bottom of a stream, over which the currents wash but never move. Her face was devoid of makeup, and she wore all black—tunic sweater, jeans, boots. She didn't speak, but I sensed she was taking my measure and cataloging the impression for future reference. I could understand why J.D. found her scary.

Vardon passed me along to the man next to her. Engstrom said, "Jorge Amaya, our CEO."

Amaya—round-faced, black-haired, expensively attired in a dark suit—smiled at me, dark eyes dancing. "So we are to play games today, Ms. McCone. Delightful!" His Spanish accent imparted a melodiousness to his rather formal speech. When he clasped my hand, he gave it a little squeeze and winked at me. When I winked back, he looked pleasantly surprised.

As I went along the line, Engstrom continued his introductions, appending each person's self-created job title: Haven Maven (home section); Venue Vetter (entertainment); Gallivanting Gourmand (restaurant critic); Shaker and Baker (food editor); King of the Road (travel); Sherlock (research). When I expressed amusement at the offbeat titles, he preened and said, "Allowing the staff to name their own positions is another thing that makes their work enjoyable."

The introductions finished, Engstrom produced a whistle and blew three ear-piercing blasts. Apparently this was his customary method for getting his employees' attention, because the room instantly became quiet.

"Listen up, folks," he called. "The famous gambit's about to begin. This is Sharon McCone, ace detective. She's got until midnight to unmask which one of you has the partial manuscript of a novel in your desk drawer. Thwart her any way you can, but remember this rule: You're not allowed to lie to her. You can evade a question, refuse to answer, or mislead her, but you must tell the truth. So let the game, and your work, proceed!"

After a lingering scrutiny of me, the staffers returned to what they had been doing.

Behind us the door burst open and J.D. blustered through. "Sorry I'm late, Max. I—"

"I hardly expected you to be on time, so we got started without you. As of now we're on the clock."

J.D. shrugged out of his raincoat, draped it over the chair where Engstrom had earlier hung mine. Again he was wearing the lemon-yellow sweater; the fluorescent lighting rendered the clash with his hair even more hideous. He pulled a cassette recorder and notepad from his briefcase, fumbled with a tape. While he organized himself I said to Engstrom, "J.D. claims every journalist is working on a novel. Is it possible all the people here have partial manuscripts?"

He smiled. "Ah, your first question, and I mustn't lie. No. But I also must agree with J.D.; even I, at one time, harbored such an abomination—until I burned it. There was considerable competition among the staffers to be the target of your search. Eventually they drew straws."

"Then I'd better get started."

"Our offices will be your happy hunting grounds till midnight." He made an expansive gesture and turned away.

Bruce Dunn, the Gallivanting Gourmand, was a dedicated game player. He stonewalled me on every question, laid a trail of red herrings—which he said he preferred in cream sauce—and told me I should talk to Max Engstrom, who hadn't burned the manuscript of his novel as he claimed. When I said that would mean Engstrom had violated the cardinal rule of the game, Dunn told me Max was a law unto himself and a natural-born liar. "It's his nature." Although he spoke pleasantly enough, I detected an undercurrent of dislike for the publisher.

The Haven Maven, Lia Chen, was seriously annoyed at my intrusion on her work. "We're running a business here, not a theme park—and Max should know that!" Then she began talking about her just-published book on *feng shui,* and asked J.D. if he would plug it in his article. He replied noncommittally, and she scowled and turned back to her desk, muttering about Max and his asinine ideas. A seriously disaffected employee, and a good potential source for inside information about the situation here.

Courtney DeAngelo, the Money Mongrel, didn't like her title, which Engstrom had given her when she refused to come up with one of her own. "What does that mean, anyway? I'm an accountant, for Christ's sake. I try to balance the books and fend off creditors. With the current cash-flow problem, they ought to be spending less on fancy food and Mad Russians, or whatever it is they're drinking this week. Then I might be able to pay the janitorial service." I put her on my list of people to seek out for information.

One of the tech department staff members took time out from trying to correct a faulty link between the magazine's and an advertiser's sites to tell me about the annual mystery-game cruise he took in the Caribbean. "I wait all year for it, and then I come home and start waiting all over again." Was he happy working here at *InSite*? "As long as I've got problems to solve, I'm happy. Besides, the food's great. I like to eat." He patted his ample stomach for emphasis. A possible culprit for the game, but not a good source of information.

Kat Donovan, aka Sherlock, was a nervous individual. As soon as I came up to her desk, the head researcher blocked my view of her computer screen and put the machine in sleep mode. She really didn't have time for game-playing, she told me. She was behind in her work as it was. I bowed out gracefully, wondering if she was trying to clear her desk in time for a vacation; before she noticed me I'd seen she was scrolling down a list of cheap airfares.

I worked the first floor systematically and by ten had come up with a lengthy list of disaffected staffers who might be induced to talk candidly about Roger's tenure there. A breakfast buffet was set up in the area under the loft, and people had been making forays to it, carrying their plates and cups back to their desks. I decided to sit down there and observe office dynamics for a while.

The spread was impressive; sweet rolls, bread, bagels, lox, fresh fruit, juice, coffee, tea. And yet the Money Mongrel couldn't pay the janitorial service. I built a lox sandwich and took some fruit and coffee while J.D., who had been trailing me and ostentatiously taking notes, made a face and poured himself a small glass of juice. When we were seated at one of the round tables flanking the buffet he said, "I never tire of watching you stuff yourself."

I swallowed a bite of lox. "In my business it's a good idea to eat when you can, because you never know when you'll get your next chance."

"What about when you're not working?"

"Then I have to make up for the meals I've lost."

"I see."

"Ms. McCone?" Jorge Amaya, coffee cup in hand, stood beside me. "May I join you?"

"Certainly." I moved my chair, and J.D. fetched another.

Amaya sat down, smiling at me. "How are you enjoying our little game?"

"Pretty well so far."

"Max has told me what you are really looking for—our saboteur." When I didn't respond immediately, he added, "Ah, you have no comment on that. But surely you must feel free to share your findings with me, the CEO."

"I have no findings yet."

"And no opinions?"

"None."

"Max and I have discussed these disturbing incidents, and I have formed an opinion. He is putting too much emphasis on them. In the normal course of events equipment malfunctions and files stray. Do you not agree?"

"Perhaps. I understand you were brought in by the Remington Group after they began investing in *InSite*."

He seemed startled at the change of subject. ". . . That is true."

"You've guided other firms to IPO, are an expert in the process?"

"Correct."

"Exactly how do you accomplish that?"

"It is not an exact science. Like individuals, companies vary. *InSite,* for example. When the Rowland Group began looking at it, it was small but had a solid business plan and a money-making idea. My function was to create a bigger package deal, one that will attract shareholders. Remington made the initial infusion of cash, then I tried to take it to the next level. But the paid-subscriber program I instituted didn't become popular, and so far we have failed to interest the large advertisers. The burn rate of capital was extremely high when we received our mezzanine financing—"

"Mezzanine?"

He smiled as if I were a pleasant but not very bright child. "Intermediate financing. A second round. After that Tessa Remington and I agreed to slow the magazine's growth and wait out the economic downturn. Which is the stage where we are now."

I glanced at J.D. He was surreptitiously taping the conversation. "Is the magazine in trouble because of Tessa Remington's disappearance?"

Amaya hesitated, compressing his lips. "You know of this disappearance from where?"

"The *Chronicle.*"

J.D.'s tape clicked off. Amaya glared at the recorder, made a chopping motion. "Leave that. We are speaking privately." To me he added, "In your profession, you must encounter many disappearances. Tell me this—" His eyes moved away from me to Dinah Vardon, who had just come up to our table. "Ah, Dinah," he said with a sly smile, "we were speaking of Ms. Remington."

She stared at him—a flat, unreadable look.

Amaya appeared unfazed by her expression. "Perhaps you would like to join our discussion."

"I would like to talk with Ms. McCone and Mr. Smith, yes, but Max has asked that you meet with him in his office."

The CEO stood, nodding to us. "We will continue with this later, but now, when our esteemed publisher requests my presence, I must comply."

Vardon's eyes followed Amaya to the stairway. I caught

a conflicted expression there—contempt and anger, but something else that I couldn't put a name to. She sat down in the chair he'd vacated and sighed deeply. "If Jorge hadn't declared himself exempt from Max's nonsense titles, he'd be *El Maestro de Toroshit.* So, are we having fun yet?"

I said, "You don't seem to approve of this exercise."

"It's not up to me to approve or disapprove. If J.D.'s story lures more paid subscribers or interests more advertisers, we'll start making money and finally get to this IPO everybody's been jerking us around about. Then I'll be happy."

"You have stock options?"

"Up the wazoo."

"Do all staff members have them?"

"Only Max's anointed few. Let's keep that off the record, huh, J.D.? The problem is, the staff grew too fast and neither Max nor Jorge was willing to slice the pie into a lot of little pieces. So they're banking on people being young and gullible and not realizing till IPO time that they've been screwed and worked their butts off for nothing."

"And you don't care about that?"

"Why should I? I'm not willing to give half my slice to somebody else, either."

Brimming with compassion, Dinah Vardon was, but why should she be different than any of the other survivors of the collapse of the hot tech market? Would I have felt differently under the same circumstances? I'd've liked to think so, but maybe not.

I said, "Mr. Amaya was talking about Tessa Remington's disappearance earlier. What do you know about that?"

Something flickered in Vardon's eyes, but again I

couldn't identify it. "Very little except that she's left this company in an untenable position. I'd just like to know what kind of game she's playing."

"So you feel this disappearance is voluntary?"

"Of course it is. I know Tessa; she's sly and manipulative and will do anything to make a buck. I wouldn't be surprised if she was in hiding on some offshore island where she's got money stashed, waiting to make her next move."

"And what kind of move would that be?"

"I couldn't tell you that. I'm no financial wizard like her. But I will tell you this: if she doesn't surface soon, we'll all be polishing up our résumés."

"It's that bad?"

"It's that bad, and I've said too much already." She got to her feet and added to J.D., "If a word of this leaks out, Smith, you're dead meat."

"She's something, all right," I said to J.D. when Vardon was out of earshot.

"I'd love to know how she got that way."

"Roger's brother Harry said something about a bad background and a fierce desire to better herself, but that doesn't fully explain it. I've got a new hire in my office who could top any horror story Vardon might offer up, but compared to her, Julia's a sweetheart."

He looked at his watch. "Well, we can't sit here all morning psychoanalyzing the WebPotentate. What now?"

"I want to check in with Engstrom, get some information on the employees I've isolated as possible troublemakers. I don't know why, but I feel these incidents, plus Tessa Remington's sudden disappearance, may have a connection to Roger's suicide."

Halfway up the stairs I realized I'd violated J.D.'s dictum against saying anything in the building that might reveal my true purpose for being there. What if the buffet area was bugged and Engstrom had overheard our every word? But to my relief, the publisher was engaged in an argument; I could hear it as we turned into the hallway.

"Goddamn it, Jorge, this is *my* magazine! I founded it, I guided it through the lean years. We'll do things my way, or not at all."

I touched J.D.'s arm, pulled him back. Pointed to the far end of the hall, where the petite figure of Lia Chen, Haven Maven, stood listening.

Amaya spoke in reasoned tones. "We are buried in unpaid invoices. The equipment is on the verge of obsolescence. The Web-site links are barely functional. The only tangible asset we have is this building—and it's next to worthless—"

"We have talent. We have direction. That should count for something."

Chen looked up, saw us, and stepped back into one of the offices.

"Unfortunately, Max, talent and direction are of very little importance in the financial world. We have no choice—"

"Bullshit! We have a choice, and it'll be my choice—*Jesus Christ!*"

A blaring noise had interrupted Engstrom's last pronouncement. Now another sounded. *Honk-honk-honk*, like the alarm in a prison-break movie.

J.D. shouted, "Fire!"

Between the strident bleats I heard a hissing, and then the automatic sprinkler system switched on.

"Shit!" J.D. grabbed my hand and pulled me toward the stairway. He pushed through the door and dragged me with him. Down below staffers either stood stock still looking up at the spraying water or grabbed their possessions and thronged toward lighted exit signs at either end of the building. I pulled away from J.D. as he started down the stairs.

No smoke. No flames. Not even the hint of a smoldering electrical short.

Footsteps thundered behind me. Max Engstrom and Jorge Amaya rushed down, grabbed my arms, and pulled me after them.

"Wait!" I shouted. "There's no fire. Your alarm's malfunctioned."

Engstrom stopped, letting go of me and nodding in agreement, but Amaya kept dragging me toward the rear exit. The floor was slick, and we slid the last couple of yards, then burst into an alleyway where it was raining harder than inside.

People milled about, talking excitedly, oblivious of the downpour. Engstrom came out, leaned against the building's wall, panting. Amaya had let go of me, and when I looked for him he was gone.

The fire department arrived quickly, cordoned off the entire block of Illinois Street, and evacuated everyone from the alley. J.D. and I stood in the crowd beyond the tape, watching as firemen entered the building. The rain continued unabated, but most people were so soaked they no longer cared.

"My favorite sweater," J.D. said mournfully, peeling the sodden wool away from his chest. "Good thing I bought a second, just in case."

"You have two of that?"

Fortunately my astonishment didn't register with him. "When I find something I really like, I always buy two."

Clearly the man was color blind.

After a while most of the firemen departed and the captain of the squad took Max Engstrom inside. Jorge Amaya, who had been hanging around by the loading dock, followed them.

J.D. said, "Max'll probably want to hire you for real now."

"And that would put me in an extremely awkward position. It's one thing to gain entrée to their offices by a ruse, but another to accept them as a client."

"Well, start thinking of an excuse for not taking him on."

"Time pressures. That's always a good one." But would Engstrom believe me, when I'd agreed to dedicate an entire day to a game for the sake of some free publicity? I worried on that for a while, then worried that I might already have compromised Glenn's case against *InSite*. By the time Engstrom emerged from the building I'd moved on to the fact that I'd really gathered very little information this morning.

The publisher approached us, his gaze troubled and remote. When he spoke, it was to J.D. "You realize the game's off. Of course, we'll pay a kill fee for the story."

"We could start over next—"

"I'm afraid not. There's a great deal of damage here; we

may have to suspend publication." To me he added, "Thank you for your time, Sharon. I'm sorry it didn't work out. And I'm afraid I'll no longer be needing your investigative services." Before either of us could ask what the source of the malfunction was, Engstrom turned and walked away.

When he was out of earshot I said, "I understand how the damage must be discouraging to him, but he seems totally defeated."

"Something the firemen showed him, maybe. I've got a friend on the Commission whom I can ask about that."

"Why don't you? Also, talk with any of your sources who might be able to shed some light on Tessa Remington's or Jody Houston's disappearances."

"You putting me on your payroll?"

"No, but if the two of us work together, we might come up with one hell of a story for you."

J.D.'s eyes narrowed thoughtfully.

"How many times have you been nominated for the Pulitzer?" I asked.

"Twice."

"Three's a charm."

It was nearing noon, and the day that had begun so promisingly now loomed empty. Because I'd expected to be at *InSite* till midnight, I'd scheduled no appointments, and nothing pressing was going on at the office. I supposed I could take some personal time and sort through my ideas about the case while doing chores. At home I had a ton of dirty laundry and two cats who would surely be cranky and in need of attention because of the rain. There were messages on the answering machine that I'd been avoiding. Unwanted E-mail to be dealt with. Dust mice in the corners. Real mice in the crawl space . . .

I went by the house for some dry clothing, then headed for the pier.

Not much activity there. Ted's Neon was parked in its space, and for a moment I contemplated stopping by his office to ask how he and Neal were getting along, but decided I wasn't up to it. He hadn't wanted to discuss his partner's abrupt departure when I'd spoken with him yesterday, and I'd learned from long experience that he'd confide in me when he was ready, and not before.

I went upstairs and along the catwalk, waving to Craig Morland, who was taking a break and doing pushups on his office floor. Craig was into fitness, trained for the annual Bay to Breakers race, and had interested Adah in working out alongside him. Now, if they could only put Charley on a diet . . . Two weeks ago Craig had told me the cat's vet had pronounced him "officially obese."

There was a single message slip on my desk. Paige Tallman, the friend who had leased Jody Houston's apartment, had called. I dialed her number, and she answered on the first ring.

"I heard from Jody last night," she said. "She wouldn't tell me where she was, just that she'd gotten to her new place okay, except the airline lost one of her suitcases and still hadn't found it."

"She say anything else?"

"Asked if anybody had been looking for her. I didn't mention you."

"Thanks. How's the security system working out?"

"Great. I want to thank you again for sending your friend over. She gave me some safety tips, and I feel loads better."

"Good."

"I told Jody I didn't appreciate her leaving me in a risky situation, and that I'd had the system put in. Made it sound like I paid for it myself."

"What was her reaction?"

"Kind of defensive, and then she said she had to hang up."

"Well, you know where to find me if she calls again." I said good-bye, then buzzed Ted. "Is Julia in the office?"

"Out to lunch."

"When she comes back, tell her I want to see her, please."

The Nagasawa case file lay on my desk, Ted's transcriptions of yesterday's interviews attached to the back cover. I began going over them, highlighting words and phrases, looking for new lines of investigation. This evening I'd run by Kodiak Rick's, the bar where Roger's crowd hung out, see if there were others who'd known him who might be willing to talk with me. Right now I'd try to track down the *InSite* staffers who might be weak on loyalty, feel them out about Roger's treatment at the magazine. I was especially interested in talking with Lia Chen, who earlier had been eavesdropping on Engstrom's confrontation with Amaya.

I took out a list of the employees' addresses and phone numbers that Engstrom had provided me with yesterday and marked the ones I wanted to see, then began calling. None answered their phones. Possibly they were still at the office, trying to salvage their soaked workstations. Finally I gave up and retreated to my armchair for some miscellaneous brooding.

"Sharon?" Julia Rafael's voice, trying to contain excitement. "I've got something on Jody Houston."

"Grab a chair and tell me about it."

She wheeled my desk chair over and flopped down, fingers nervously playing with the edges of her case file.

"Okay," she said, "like you suggested, I started by calling the airlines' frequent-flyer programs, going down the listings in the Yellow Pages for the major carriers. But when I got to Air France, I figured out that I oughta concentrate on the companies that run relatively short flights out of SFO, Oakland, and San Jose. I mean, Houston didn't take much luggage, so she probably wasn't going far, right?"

Not necessarily, but apparently her logic had proved correct. "Go on."

"Well, it wasn't much of a shortcut. I kept striking out till I got to United. They had a frequent-flyer number on file for her."

"And from that you got her flight information. Where'd she go?"

She frowned. "Don't you want to know how I did it?"

Allowing her to live out her triumph for a few minutes wouldn't hurt and, besides, critiquing her techniques was part of her on-the-job training. "Of course. How?"

"I said I'd lost my frequent-flyer card and couldn't remember the number. I didn't have any statements because I make it a rule to recycle stuff like that as soon as it comes in, so I couldn't refer to them. But now I needed to know if I had enough miles to travel to Texas for my aunt's funeral, and— Well, you get it. I acted kinda lame, and the clerk felt sorry for me, so she looked up the miles. Twenty-nine thousand, two hundred and three."

"And from there . . . ?"

"I go, 'That doesn't sound right. Did last week's trip to

L.A. get posted?' And she goes, 'There's no L.A. trip, but we're showing Wednesday's flight from San Francisco to Portland.' That's where Houston is—Portland area."

"Julia, that's great!" I was already at my desk, leafing through the Yellow Pages to the airlines section.

Julia followed me. "I didn't get too dramatic or anything?"

"No. I think you have good instincts about how far to take it with whoever you're talking to. Let's try you on this." I thrust the phone book at her. "Call United's lost luggage department. A source told me Houston's bag didn't make it to Portland and, as of last night, it hadn't been found. What do you ask them?"

"Um . . . I tell them I'm her and . . . I say I want to verify the address in the Portland area that the bag's to be delivered to, since it hasn't arrived yet. What if it already has?"

"Doesn't matter. Say there must be a mistake—"

"And I want to verify it anyway. If they ask for a claim number, I'll do the I-lost-it routine."

She was good—and, as I'd suspected, she was also a bit of a con woman. I handed her the phone receiver.

She dialed and performed as if she'd been doing this for years. When she hung up she handed me the paper on which she'd scribbled the address.

Thirty-two Beach Street, Eagle Rock, Oregon.

Julia said, "They told me Houston's bag was located in Omaha and should be there by morning."

Strange. I'd once had a bag sent to Omaha by mistake. Maybe Nebraska was the purgatory of lost luggage.

Eagle Rock, Oregon. I buzzed Ted, asked him to check

his atlas. After half a minute he said, "It's on the coast, about two hours southwest of Portland."

I considered the distance, compared the flying time in Two-five-two-seven-Tango with the speed of a commercial airliner. "Book me on any flight for Portland," I told him.

It was Friday night, so I hadn't been able to get a flight north till eight. The sky was dark but clear by the time I left the Portland area, the two-lane highway well marked and smooth beneath the wheels of my rental car. About halfway to the coast, where Route 18 and 99W divided, I saw the turnoff for McMinnville and felt a twinge. For a few years Joey had worked in a restaurant there—possibly his longest tenure of employment—and I'd always promised to visit and sample what he claimed was world-class cuisine. But I never had and now, like so many other things I'd promised, it was too late.

High cirrus clouds appeared as I approached the coastal ridgeline, whipping across the moon like horsetails. The road bisected a meadow, meandered through woods, began climbing, then descended. At its intersection with Oregon 101, I came up against a wall of thick, stationary fog. I checked the odometer and turned north, driving slowly past the small settlements scattered along the shore: Neskowin, Oretown, Pacific City. Then I began looking for the old-fashioned wooden water tower that the rental-car clerk, a native of the area, had told me was the landmark for Eagle Rock. It loomed up suddenly, dark and bulky through the fog.

As I came closer I spotted a long line of mailboxes fastened to a rough board stand. Beyond them high wooden fences, most of them overgrown by vegetation, shielded the roadside houses from view. Tall trees—some type of pine—formed a canopy over an unpaved lane leading into the settlement. I turned left, pulled my rental up to the mailboxes, and got out.

The boxes were of different sizes and shapes: standard Postal Department issue; birdhouses; tin drums; lighthouse replicas. Some were painted with flowers or abstract patterns; others were corroded and battered by the elements. Gaps between them indicated vacation homes where no deliveries were made, and the space for 32 Beach was empty. I took out my flashlight and checked names; what few were painted on the boxes were not familiar. Then I got back in the car and went in search of Beach Street.

The cottages I passed were small, built mostly of clapboard or weathered shingle. Lights shone dimly in a few windows. Some of the dwellings had fenced yards, but most were fronted by gardens where plants grew lushly, encouraged by the moisture of the climate. The intersecting lanes were marked, but poorly, their signs bleached and pitted. I crept along, shining my flash on them, and finally located Beach—a short block ending at a stone seawall. The house numbers proved impossible to read from the car, so I parked under the low-hanging branches of a cypress tree at the lane's far end and proceeded on foot. The fog was thick there, muting the sound of the surf. A dog barked in one of the yards as I passed, and another answered from a couple of blocks away.

Number 32 was pale clapboard, with an overgrown front garden and a carport to one side. A vehicle was parked in the driveway: Ford Taurus, this year's model, an Enterprise

Car Rental sticker on its bumper. I tried the doors, which were locked, then took down the license plate number.

The plants in the yard were rhododendrons, set close together and several feet taller than I. I worked my way through them till I could see the front of the house. Lighted first-story window with blinds shut; lighted dormer window upstairs, curtained. In the dim yellow glow of a bare bulb on the porch I saw an envelope wedged into the frame of the screen door. I stepped up there, snagged it, and retreated into the bushes. It contained a five-dollar bill and a scribbled note signed by Houston. "United Airlines—Please leave bag here."

I considered my options, then went through the bushes and walked back down the street to the car. At Houston's cottage again, I carried my own travel bag up the front path, keeping my head down; if Houston were looking outside, she wouldn't recognize me, would naturally assume I was an airlines courier. I knocked loudly. There was no immediate response, but after a minute I heard motion and an erratic intake of breath on the other side of the door.

"United Baggage, Ms. Houston," I called. "Thanks for the tip, but I've got to get your signature."

Silence, then Houston's voice spoke up close. "I signed the note. Won't that do?"

"Sorry. You know how it is with the Department of Transportation—forms, and more forms. It'll be my butt if I don't get it on the dotted line."

A sigh of resignation. "All right."

A chain rattled. I dropped my bag and braced myself. The deadbolt turned, the door opened, and I shoved through, knocking her off balance. She staggered back against the newel post of a steep staircase, face pale, eyes wide. Then she put her hands over her mouth and sank onto the bottom step. A whimper sounded in her throat.

I felt for a light switch, got the overhead on. Kept my distance as I said, "It's okay. I'm not here to hurt you."

A wisp of relief crept into her eyes, and after a few seconds she took her hands from her mouth. There was a spot of blood where she'd bitten her lower lip. "I . . . know you. You're . . . ?"

"Sharon McCone. We met the other day at Roger's apartment."

". . . Oh, right."

"I spoke with Daniel Nagasawa. He told me about your call. I've been trying to contact you."

The blood from her lip was dribbling onto her chin. She wiped it with her fingers, wiped the fingers on her jeans. "How'd you find me? Nobody knows, not even the friend I leased my apartment to."

"I'm a private investigator. Tracing missing persons is one of the things I do." I handed her my card.

She put it in her pocket without looking at it. "What d'you want with me?"

"To talk. I'd like to help."

"Help? Yeah, sure, like you give a shit about me."

"I 'give a shit' about any innocent person who's so frightened she abandons her whole life and runs."

Her eyes moved jumpily—left, right, left. "I can take care of myself."

"I don't think so. Look at you: you're so scared you practically peed in your pants when I came through the door. You've been here since, when? Wednesday night? I'll bet you haven't changed your clothes, washed your hair, or bathed. Have you been out of the house? Do you even have enough food on hand?"

"I've been out, damn you! I've got food!" She ran her hand through her cropped hair, added in a weak voice, "I'm fine."

"Jody, I meant it when I said I'd like to help."

"Why should I believe you?"

"Because for the moment I'm all you've got."

Houston led me to the kitchen at the back of the house—a tiny room with an adjoining breakfast nook containing a table and built-in benches next to a window that overlooked the backyard. Before we sat she moved two full grocery bags to the counter by the refrigerator, giving me a pointed look that said, "See—I have been out, I do have food."

More rhododendrons crowded in close to the window, tapping on the glass in the rising wind. Houston shivered and lowered the canvas shade. "Those bushes really creep me," she said. "They're like hands trying to reach inside."

"Whose place is this?"

"My great-aunt's. At least it was. She's eighty-nine, in a rest home in Portland. Last year she signed the deed over to me."

And that meant her ownership of the cottage could be traced. I'd have to get her out of there.

"Okay," I said, "let's talk about Roger, and what has you on the run."

She fidgeted. Clasped and unclasped her hands. Finally she began to speak—haltingly, breaking off whenever a real or imagined sound startled her. The wind baffled around the small cottage; the branches clawed at the glass; beams creaked and groaned. She sat on the edge of the bench, ready to leap off at the slightest provocation. I'd seldom questioned anyone more frightened.

It had started, she said, on a cold, blustery day the previous November when she and Roger holed up in her apartment, ordered pizza, shared a joint and some Chianti. Roger was depressed, and not only by the weather. The smoke and wine loosened his customary reserve, and he broke his silence about his job.

"He said he and Dinah Vardon had gotten into a physical fight, and Max Engstrom had threatened to fire him. Not Dinah, just Rog, even though she was the one who attacked him."

"Did he tell you what the fight was about?"

"He was standing up for a tech department staffer Dinah had humiliated to the point of tears. He called her—Dinah—a monster, and she came after him, scratched him up pretty bad. Rog was furious with her and the other VIPs at the 'zine, said he wanted to expose their abusive behavior to the press. I told him he'd better collect some solid evidence, because the press doesn't like to turn on one of its own."

Three days before Christmas Roger appeared at Houston's door with champagne and caviar and lobster tails. He wanted to celebrate his finally having found a way to get the evidence he needed to expose the abuses at *InSite*. Jody was concerned about his manic behavior, but she went along with the celebration.

"He wouldn't tell me exactly what he planned to do—except that he was going to take all of them down. A lot of what he said that night didn't make much sense at the time. You see, with Rog, it was like he was speaking in code, and sometimes I really had to work to get at the meaning behind it. His perceptions didn't come from the same place as mine—which was one reason why I could never love him. I mean, don't you at least have to understand what the person you love is saying?"

Early in the new year, Jody continued, she invited Roger to dinner. Once again he was out of sorts, edgy and preoccupied. When she first asked what was wrong, he dismissed his mood as a figment of her imagination. But as the wine flowed, he admitted that his plan to expose the abuses at the magazine had gotten sidetracked.

"He'd found out some things, but when he tried to fit them together, they didn't compute. And he'd gotten off in a wrong direction, forced somebody to do something unethical for him, and now the person's career was in jeopardy."

"He didn't go into the specifics?"

"No. Rog could be secretive. I told him maybe he should just give it up and look for a new job. But he said he couldn't do that. Once he got started on something he couldn't quit."

"Okay, what happened then?"

"I screwed everything up."

Late in January Roger had grown more optimistic. He told Jody he'd uncovered something wrong at the magazine—something more serious than management's poor treatment of the employees—and it was only a matter of time till he had the evidence he needed to go public with it. Again he wouldn't go into specifics, except to say it was major. He discussed his options, said he favored taking the details to the print media, as it would be a difficult sell to an online publication or even television. The *Chronicle,* he thought, would be the ideal venue.

"Did he contact anyone on the paper?"

"Not that I know of. To tell you the truth, he made me uncomfortable. He was completely obsessed with getting back at those people, and at the time I wondered how much of this stuff wasn't coming from his imagination."

On the last Friday of the month Jody received a call from Max Engstrom asking her to come to his office to discuss her most recent freelance assignment; there, in the presence of Jorge Amaya and Lia Chen, he rejected her graphics for a story on California housing markets as not being up to the magazine's standards.

"I was pissed. There was nothing wrong with my work. I'd had to struggle to come up with something that was visually interesting, and it had taken longer than it should have. And I was counting on their check to pay some overdue bills. I tried to be reasonable at first, but Max wouldn't listen."

For most of the meeting Engstrom stood with his back to Jody, staring out his office window at the beehive of staffers below. Jorge Amaya examined his manicure and smirked. Lia Chen squirmed and refused to make eye contact. When Engstrom made an imperious gesture of dismissal, saying his mind was made up, Houston lost it.

"Totally lost it. I reamed into him. Said the trouble with his magazine was that the people in charge didn't give a fuck about the staffers or freelancers—in fact, took pleasure in hurting and humiliating them. Max told me I had no proof of that, and I said the scratches on Rog from when Dinah went after him were proof enough. And then I made my big mistake."

"Which was . . . ?"

"I said they'd better tell Dinah not to put her claws on Rog again, and the rest of them better watch their behavior too, because he and I had proof of everything that was going on there, and could nail them bad. And then I stormed out."

That night Jody told Roger what she'd said. He seemed shaken, but quickly covered up, trying to make light of it. She suggested that if anyone asked him, he should tell them she was simply making idle threats, and he said he'd do that. And he'd also be more careful in collecting his final pieces of evidence.

"But after that night everything was different between us. He started to avoid me. If we ran into each other he'd be polite, but he turned down my offers of drinks and dinner. Then on Valentine's Day he showed up at my door around ten in the evening. I thought he wanted to apologize for ignoring me, but instead he asked if he could use my computer to send a couple of E-mails; his server was down. He was in my office for five or ten minutes, then thanked me and left. I thought about going up after him, taking him a bottle of Valentine's Day wine. I mean, I valued the friendship. In a way, I loved him, even if I wasn't *in* love with him. But then I thought, the hell with it. He'd been using me, was all. So I didn't go up, and around eleven-thirty I heard the elevator going down from his floor. And the next morning there it was on the TV news: Roger Nagasawa, son of prominent . . ."

"Hey, don't cry."

"I can't help it."

"Those E-mails, did he leave them on your computer or delete them?"

"He deleted . . . Oh, God, I don't know what to do!"

"About what?"

"I don't know who to trust."

"Try me."

"But how do I know . . . ? I'm in worse trouble than you can imagine."

"Then you need me to help you get out of it."

". . . Okay. All right. But before I tell you anything else, there's something I better show you. I'll get it. It's upstairs."

She got up and went along the hallway. I waited, listening to the gusting of the wind and the rattling of the windowpanes. A roofbeam gave a tremendous crack, and I looked up apprehensively. When several minutes passed and Houston hadn't come back, I went upstairs after her.

The second story was one room, with a dormer window at the front. The window was open, and Houston was gone.

Saturday

•

APRIL 21

The white curtains billowed out from the window, and fog-damp touched my face. Somewhere on the floor below a clock chimed—one, two, finally a dozen times.

Dead midnight.

I hurried to the window and looked out. No sign of Houston. A drainpipe was within easy reach of the sloping front porch roof; from there the drop to the ground was short. I ran downstairs and outside. The Taurus was still in the driveway.

So what had happened here?

Houston hadn't wanted to trust me, but I thought I'd won her over. Terrified as she was, what could have prompted her to run away into the night on foot—especially when she was so close to confiding her fears in me and getting the help she needed?

I stared into the shadows, looked down at the ground. Something wrong here. The travel bag that I'd carried from the car in order to impersonate an airlines courier wasn't where I'd dropped it when I pushed inside the cottage. I peered into the shrubbery, went along the walk checking to either side. Nothing. Had Houston taken it?

The small microfiber bag that I kept packed in the trunk

of my MG—in case, like today, an investigation took me out of town on short notice—contained nothing important. Some toiletries, a change of jeans and tee and underwear, a knit dress and shoes suitable for pretty much any occasion. My business card was in the identification slot on the bag, and in a side pocket were some rough notes on the investigation that I'd made on the plane. That was it.

I went back inside the cottage, locked the door, returned to the second story. Checked out the view from the window. Houston would have been able to see most of her front garden and the street. Had she spotted someone out there? Fled either to or from that person? A suitcase and a tote bag sat on the floor, partially unpacked. What Houston had taken out was draped over a wicker chair. The bedclothes were rumpled and twisted; Jody had been wrestling with her demons. I went through the luggage but found nothing of significance.

Downstairs was a small bathroom; a jumble of toiletries lay on its counter. A prescription bottle was lined up next to an electric toothbrush in its charger: Ambien, a mild sleep aid. In an unpacked travel pouch I found a compact of birth control pills. The presence of the prescriptions might mean Houston would return for them; possibly she was watching the cottage, waiting for me to leave.

In the kitchen, I unlocked and cracked open the window in the breakfast nook. Then I shut off all the lights, left by the front door, got into my rental car, and drove away. An alley intersected Beach Street three doors east of Houston's cottage; the houses in between were shuttered and dark. I drove for two blocks, parked by the seawall, cut back to the alley, and followed it to Beach. No lights came on in any of the houses I passed; no dogs barked; I saw no one on the street. At Beach I crossed Houston's neighbors' backyards and slipped through the shrubbery to the window I'd left open. Raised the sash and climbed inside.

The cottage was so quiet I could hear the tick of the clock in the front room. Cold from the open window upstairs had penetrated the first story; the smell of old ashes, dry rot, and mildew was borne on the air currents. I shut the kitchen window and moved toward the front of the house, feeling my way with outstretched hands. The clock chimed the half hour.

By the time I reached the entryway my eyes had adjusted to the darkness. The staircase rose to my left, and beyond it was an archway leading to a front room. I went in there, saw the back of a sofa and a potbellied woodstove. The clock—ornate and ugly—sat on a round table by the window. I went over and peeked through the closed blinds. Nothing but the swaying branches of the rhododendrons and the Taurus in the driveway.

I decided to fetch a quilt I'd seen on the bed upstairs and camp out on the sofa in case Jody returned. But as I was crossing between it and the woodstove, my foot slipped and I nearly fell. Something slick coated the floorboards. I leaned down, and it smelled—

Like blood.

I fumbled in my bag for my flashlight, shone it down. The substance was blood, all right, a fair amount of it. Sticky, congealing. I moved the light in a wide arc and saw marks on the dusty planks, as if something had been dragged across them. . . .

I followed the marks to where they stopped in the hallway. The wall under the staircase was board-and-batten; black iron hinges and a latch showed where a door was set into it. Before I touched the latch I pulled the sleeve of my sweater over my hand to avoid leaving fingerprints.

The closet was small, with a steeply slanting ceiling and coats and hats and umbrellas hanging from wall pegs. A row of cardboard cartons was stacked below them and in front of it lay a man. The stillness enveloping him was total, the stillness of death. The rag rug on which he'd been moved was flung over his head and he wore—

I knew that sweater. At least I knew its mate, the one that had gotten soaked in the sprinklers' downpour at *InSite,* and then in the rain outside.

For a moment I was unable to move. Then, feeling sick, I knelt and pulled the rug away from his head. His unruly cowlick wafted around. I touched his neck, found no pulse. His flesh was cooling, but not yet cold. I turned him over, stared into empty eyes that were already glazed and flattened. Congealed blood stained the front of the sweater.

I closed my eyes, but found no comfort in darkness. After a moment I put him back the way he'd been, replaced the rug, and stood. A wave of dizziness overcame me; I staggered over to the stairs and collapsed there.

Why, J.D.? Why? *What were you doing here?*

The answer, of course, was obvious. I'd asked him to look into the Remington and Houston disappearances. He contacted his sources, came up with a lead—probably from someone who knew Jody owned this cottage—and flew north before I did, on the trail of a story. What had happened between him and Houston and why she'd killed him I couldn't guess. Only Jody knew that, and she was on the run again.

I'd believed her story of being afraid for her life. Been taken in by her nervous sidelong glances and startled reactions. Assumed she was terrified when in reality she'd fooled me until she figured out a way to make her escape. The only thing Houston had been afraid of was me finding out she had a body stashed in her closet.

The body of a man who had been my friend for nearly a decade.

We'd met at a party at a mutual friend's apartment, and when I complimented him on a recent feature article, J.D. flushed with pleasure and exclaimed, "Nobody reads the bylines on stories. Nobody!" And I said, "I do."

Once he'd taken me along as an undercover companion for a piece on panhandlers, and we netted five dollars and sixty-two cents, which we spent on pizza slices and Cokes.

Each year he enlisted my aid in soliciting funds for his favorite charity, a literacy project. We joked that I made a better panhandler than fund-raiser.

Two years ago, when his date bailed on him, he'd taken me to the city's big charity extravaganza, the Black and White Ball. We stepped all over each other's feet the whole evening.

Last fall he'd visited Hy and me at Touchstone, and we went on a whale-watching cruise. J.D. threw up fifteen minutes out of Point Arena. Next fall he planned to try it again, fortified by Dramamine—

I closed my eyes and hot tears leaked out. A sob choked me, the sound small and pathetic in the empty house. It took several minutes before I had myself under enough control that I could take out my phone and dial 911.

* * *

"This complicates matters considerably," Glenn Solomon said. "Don't misunderstand me. I'm not indifferent to your pain over your friend's death, particularly as it comes so close on the heels of your brother's suicide. But I have to think about the situation from my clients' perspective."

It was close to eleven in the evening, and we were seated at a big stainless-steel table in the kitchen of Glenn's Russian Hill condominium. Unlike his offices, which were full of mahogany antiques and oriental carpets intended to soothe the most nervous of clients, the condo was up-to-the-minute chic, incorporating the bold, bright colors and clean-lined furnishings that were the hallmarks of the work of Glenn's wife, interior designer Bette Silver.

Glenn reached for the remote control and turned on a TV—one of three in the spacious room—mounted under the cabinet opposite us. A local newscaster with laminated hair was speaking, his face solemn but his eyes betraying the glee that a juicy story brings out in his kind. Then a photograph of J.D. appeared, and I looked down at the files spread in front of me.

"They picked up the story from their Portland affiliate," Glenn said. "Tomorrow his picture'll be on the front page of the *Chron,* along with commentary from his former editor, colleagues, first-grade teacher, and the family dog. They tend to overdo when one of their own buys it." He glanced at my face, saw my distress. "Sorry. I was speaking in generalities."

The newscaster's voice droned on, but I heard only phrases: ". . . isolated seaside community on the Oregon coast . . . veteran reporter . . . two-time Pulitzer Prize nominee . . . body found by a visitor to the cottage, where his rental car was parked in the driveway . . . all-points bulletin on Jody Houston, owner of the cottage, who is said to have been in the area . . . anyone having information is requested to contact . . ."

Glenn shut off the TV. "It's a good thing the sheriff's department up there was willing to keep your name out of it, but it won't be long before—"

"Look, can we go over these files, please?" My voice rasped with pent-up emotion.

Glenn heard it. "Sure. Give me a recap from the beginning."

I paged through the documents and transcripts, touching on the high points and ending with last night's conversation with Houston. When I finished Glenn got up, fetched a bottle of brandy, and set it and two snifters between us. "Conclusions?" he asked.

"A few. Tentative. First, I think Houston was telling me the truth, but not all of it, so far as Roger went."

He raised a skeptical eyebrow as he poured our drinks.

"She was panicked because she had J.D.'s body in the closet—much too panicked to be able to weave a story like that out of whole cloth. So she gave me some of what she knew, hoping I'd be satisfied and leave."

"There's a grain of truth in it, I'll give you that."

"More than a grain. There's a consistency with things that other people told me about Roger. Let me read you some." I paged to the first of several paperclips I'd attached to pages.

"These are exact quotes from his friends and acquaintances. 'Rog was basically a decent guy. Very decent. He once told me he'd always wanted to be a person who could make things right. And he acted on that principle. He even gave blood once a month. How many of us do that?' " I flipped to the next paperclip. "'He always struck me as naive, but in a nice way. Easily shocked when it came to stuff most people take for granted, like marginal business practices. And after he got over being shocked, he got angry.' Another friend says, 'When I first met him he seemed depressed, but last fall he changed, acted like he was high most of the time. Maybe he was taking Prozac?'"

"Was he?" Glenn asked.

"According to his physician and the coroner's report, no. I think he was experiencing a natural euphoria, because of his resolve to bring down the VIPs at the magazine. Here's a telling statement: 'Was Rog depressed for a long time before he killed himself? I guess so. I mean, aren't all suicides depressed? But he wasn't depressed enough to give any of us cause for concern. He seemed . . . well, the word purposeful comes to mind. Like maybe he was putting his affairs in order?' And this is even more telling: 'Yeah, Rog was real quiet and single-minded toward the end. Like he had a plan and was following it to the letter. But the last time I saw him, on the street outside his building the night he went off the bridge, he seemed . . . well, sad. Deeply and profoundly sad, the way people get when they feel all their dreams've been taken away from them. I don't mean the ten-million-dollar house or the new Benz or the yacht—the kind of stuff yesterday's Silicon Valley tycoons're moaning about. Whatever Rog had lost, it meant a hell of a lot more than money. Maybe he felt he'd lost himself.'"

I shut the file, waited for Glenn's comments.

"Okay," he said, "it tends to back up what Houston told you. And it reveals a different Roger than I knew. For instance, until I read his journal, I had no idea he'd been drawn to the idea of suicide his whole life."

"Neither did his parents."

Glenn closed his eyes, spoke from memory. " 'The circumstances. The failures. I wish I could undo them.' " When he looked at me again, his eyes were moist.

I covered his hand and after a moment his fingers curled around mine. How many times had he read those lines? He must have loved his godson very much.

After a bit he said, "I understand what you're trying to tell me, my friend. Roger's life hadn't worked out anywhere near as he'd planned. The woman he loved didn't love him. He was disillusioned and disgusted by any number of people. Given his predilection to suicide, it was a given."

I nodded.

"During this past week I did an extensive analysis of the literature on the Tokyo *karoshi* case. While the basis for suit fits Roger's situation as Daniel and Margaret understood it, it's not at all compatible with what you've found. I very much doubt that I can use it as a precedent in an action against the magazine—or pursue a wrongful-death suit of any kind. But there's a larger issue here, given the Houston woman's fear and J.D. Smith's murder."

"Yes."

"Then we'll proceed. Keep digging into this. Find out what Roger had found out that made him so sad. And why that woman killed your friend." He sighed deeply, looking very tired. "It's getting late. Tonight I think it's best you stay here."

"Why?"

"The press has a way of finding things out very quickly, and there are leaks in even the best of law-enforcement agencies. You may have reporters camped on your doorstep."

"I'll check on that." I went to the wall phone and dialed my next-door neighbors, the Curleys, whose daughter Michelle looked after my house and cats whenever I was away. Her mother, Trish, informed me that Channel 7 had been first on the scene, followed by Channel 4, whom she'd had to tell not to block her driveway.

"'Chelle's got the cats and house secured," she added. "And she's having fun being rude to the reporters. What do you need?"

"Nothing, tonight. But I'll be in touch tomorrow. Tell Michelle thank you."

I replaced the receiver, and when I turned saw Bette Silver coming across the room—a slim figure with a luxuriant fall of white-blond hair, wearing a brilliant purple kimono. A similar robe in shades of green hung over her arm.

She said, "Let me show you to our guest room, dear."

Sunday

•

APRIL 22

". . . As a further twist to the story, this channel's news team has learned that the individual who discovered Smith's body was San Francisco private investigator Sharon McCone. A high-profile detective whose cases have often been chronicled in both the local and national press, McCone has not been available for comment. There is some speculation that she may have been working with Smith on an investigation relating to the death cottage's owner, San Francisco graphic designer Jody Houston, but what separately led them to the isolated community of Eagle Rock—"

"Garbage!" Glenn shut off the TV. "'Death cottage!' 'Speculation!' Whatever became of who, what, when, where, and how?"

I didn't answer, staring glumly down at the French toast Bette had set in front of me. I'd been looking forward to it, but now I didn't feel I could eat a single bite.

Glenn dug into his food with a gusto fueled by indignation. "If they can't find news, they create it—that's the rule of thumb today. Look at the way they've blown the power crisis out of proportion. I've had people calling me from all over the globe asking if I'm reading by candlelight like Abe Lincoln. I tell them the only people in the dark here are those who believe this isn't a conspiracy by the utility companies and their suppliers to drive rates up and line their own pockets."

"Calm down, dear," Bette said. "The effects of deregulation—"

"Bah!"

I said, "Well, I've tried to conserve energy."

"That's because you, like Bette and I, have a sense of community. But for every one like us, there're a dozen who simply don't give a shit. And the lights're still on now, aren't they?"

"The rolling blackouts—" Bette began.

"Only happen when the utilities are under fire and afraid they won't get their way. A conspiracy, pure and simple."

Bette rolled her eyes at me. Glenn was still waiting for the truth to come out about the Kennedy assassinations, as well as any number of other events, and she was accustomed to his rants.

Instead of allowing him to continue along those lines, I said, "Given the media interest in me, how the hell am I supposed to carry on with this investigation? By now there'll be reporters staking out the pier, as well as my house."

"Set up a temporary headquarters elsewhere. You're welcome to stay here. Right, Bette? We've got plenty of room, a fax machine, computer—"

"No. I've been talking with a lot of people about Roger. It won't take the press long to ferret that out, as well as my affiliation with you."

"Then go to a friend. How about Ricky Savage and his wife? Big star like him, he must have good security."

"I don't involve people I care about in my investigations. Even people with top-notch security."

"Understandable. A hotel? No, too much chance of being spotted. What about your other house—Touchstone?"

"Glenn, Touchstone's over three hours away, in Mendocino County. I'd have to fly back and forth—"

"Right. Where, then?"

"I have an idea."

For a number of years Renshaw and Kessell International had kept a guest suite in their Green Street building, to be used by clients who for one reason or another felt their safety to be in jeopardy. Since Hy had joined the firm he'd worked mainly out of the San Francisco offices, rather than world headquarters in LaJolla, and he'd made security at the converted warehouse at the base of Telegraph Hill a top priority. After a drive-by shooting the previous fall, that claimed no lives but seriously shook up its target, the then-resident of the suite, as well as RKI's staff, he'd decided to move the accommodations for at-risk clients to a less obvious location.

As I left my MG in the garage at RKI's apartment building at Twenty-eighth Avenue and Balboa and went through the door to the lobby, I thought how clever Hy had been to choose this neighborhood. It was definitely not a place where one would expect to find residing in seclusion the CEO of a multinational corporation who had been targeted by kidnappers, or the deposed president of a third-world nation and his entourage.

The Richmond district, as the area is called, has long

been a place bypassed by mainstream San Francisco. Originally home to the city's Russian community—and boasting of a number of Orthodox churches—it has undergone influxes of various groups over time, the largest being Asian. But with the collapse of the USSR, the tide of Russian immigrants swelled anew, as families exiting eastern Europe were reunited with their California relatives.

Despite its diverse cultures, the neighborhood is generally thought of as a dull, fogbound place where old men and women go about bundled in coats, hats, and scarves in the middle of summer. Coffeehouses, clubs, and chic restaurants fail to take hold there. Shops cater only to basic needs. No sightseeing buses detour out that way. It—whatever "it" currently is—simply doesn't happen there, making Richmond a perfect place for a safe house.

I'd called Green Street from Glenn's condo to inquire if all three apartments were occupied. No, I was told, a client was using the first-floor unit, but the second story was vacant. I said Mr. Ripinsky had authorized me to stay there if space was available, and the switchboard operator didn't question me further. He was aware of Hy's and my relationship; I came and went frequently at their offices and often used the firm's operatives for jobs that they were better suited to than my own people.

The building was thirties vintage, and the lobby—cracked beige plaster walls, threadbare carpeting, scarred woodwork—hadn't been redecorated since the sixties. The aura of genteel neglect was deliberate, and most people wouldn't notice the well-concealed surveillance cameras and bullet-proof glass. Only the installers would be able to trace the web of wiring that supported the alarms, motion sensors, and listening devices. A glass-paned door in the wall opposite the garage entry was curtained on the inside in faded flowered chintz, but when I pushed through I was confronted by a bank of monitors worthy of a minimum-security prison.

Allen Lu, supervisor of the site, looked up and nodded to me. Here in the safe house, he was more casually attired than he would have been at Green Street, but his maroon-and-gray blazer—uniform of RKI's rank-and-file personnel—hung over a chair in readiness for high-level visitors.

"Hey, Ms. McCone," he said. "Downtown told me you'd be coming." Lu's eyes flicked back to one of the screens, where a portly, shaggy-haired man paced, drawing deeply on a cigarette. Normally Allen would have blacked out the picture when someone entered, but to RKI staff, I was almost family. I said, "Nervous guest, huh?"

"Mr. Jones has a severe case of the twitches. I wish he'd settle down; he's making *me* antsy."

It wouldn't do any good to ask who "Mr. Jones" was or why he was there. Allen would be aware only of the potential sources of threat to him; with RKI, information was dispensed on a strict need-to-know basis. I said, "Which apartment may I use?"

"Either on floor two. Don't smoke, do you?"

"No."

"Front's nonsmoking. You'll get some noise from the bus line, but it's better than breathing the old secondhand."

"Then I'll take it."

"You need full surveillance?"

"No." I didn't want him and his subordinates monitoring my every move. "I'm here to avoid newspaper and TV people."

"Oh, right. I saw the morning broadcast. Just the entrances and the hallways, then. If somebody comes around, how d'you want us to deal with them?"

"Find out who they are, warn them off. I'll take it from there."

"Will do." He turned back to his screen. "Mr. Jones" was now pouring himself a glass of whiskey. "Easy, guy," Allen muttered. "It's only one-twenty."

While the exterior and the common areas of the Twenty-eighth Avenue building were deliberately shabby, the apartments themselves had been remodeled luxuriously. Usually the temporary residents were high-powered and wealthy individuals; discomfort on top of restricted freedom of movement could make them difficult to deal with. RKI's theory was that the clients were better off satiated and comfortable than hungry and on the attack.

I hadn't visited the building since the interior designers had been given carte blanche, so I took a few minutes to explore the unit. Two large bedrooms with a bath off the hallway, the former in restful shades of blue and green, the latter sparkling white marble with a Jacuzzi tub and stall shower. Michelle Curley had packed a bag, and her mother had delivered it to me at a rendezvous point near the Portals of the Past in Golden Gate Park; I dropped it on the bed in the blue room and proceeded along the hallway toward the front of the apartment.

Beige walls in the living and dining rooms, with warm burnt umber trim and deep piled carpeting to match. Large entertainment center and comfortable leather furnishings to curl up on in front of the brick fireplace; refectory table that could easily seat ten. The kitchen was small but well equipped and stocked. I snooped through the fridge, noting with approval several bottles of sauvignon blanc from Annapolis Winery, on the coastal ridge some forty-five miles south of Touchstone. All the comforts of home. . . .

As I was passing through the dining room again, voices outside drew me to the window. A group of thirty to forty Asians in dark suits and pastel dresses milled about on the opposite sidewalk balancing plates of cake and cups of coffee. I peered at the sign on the building, made out the words CHINESE GRACE BAPTIST CHURCH. Although San Francisco—with its provincialism, poor public transit, dirty streets, and often childishly squabbling politicians—can drive me crazy at least once a day, I'm always entranced at the way it manages to defy the stereotypical. J.D. would love this scene—

J.D. He'd reveled in the city's nonconformity and diversity. He had friends and acquaintances and sources from the Golden Gate to the Daly City line and beyond: people of all age groups and ethnic backgrounds, of all professions and circumstances. Yesterday one of them had told him something that sent him to Eagle Rock, Oregon. Drawing on my memories of our conversations, I made a list of people to call. But before I began my search, I dialed Adah Joslyn.

"The Department's not assisting on the Smith case," Adah said. "Tillamook County Sheriff's Department contacted SFSD."

"I suspected they had, but I hoped you would know who—"

"'I don't ask for many favors.'" It was a surprisingly accurate imitation of what I'd said to her on Thursday night, but I wasn't in the mood for even good-natured jibes. When

I didn't respond, Adah said soberly, "I'll call over there, find out who's in charge, tell them they'll be hearing from you. After all, this is about J.D. I liked him. Everybody did."

"Thanks, Adah. By the way, how did Craig's evening with Ted go?"

"Neither of them told you?"

"I didn't think to ask Craig, and Ted's been kind of remote."

"Well, Ted got smashed and puked all over the side of Craig's new Explorer."

"Better outside than inside, I guess."

"Marginally better. But it gets worse. After he got him cleaned up some and in the Explorer, Craig decided he shouldn't take him home and risk grossing out Neal, so he brought him here. Grossing me out instead. We doctored him with aspirin, tucked him in on the couch, and he would've been all right, except Charley took a fondness to him and curled up on the pillow. As you know, Ted's developed an allergy to cats. So the next morning he felt even shittier than he deserved to, and I had to listen to him kvetch all through my breakfast. And now, it seems, Neal doesn't want him back, so we're stuck with him, and he's driving us both crazy."

No wonder Ted hadn't wanted to talk much recently. "This is my fault. I gave Ted the go-ahead to hire Neal."

"You didn't give him the go-ahead to puke on Craig's SUV or move in with us, though—which is the only reason I'm still talking to you."

I ended the call on that quasi–high note and began phoning J.D.'s friends and sources.

* * *

Thom Lynds, J.D.'s former editor at the *Chronicle,* sounded subdued. "He stopped in here to use my computer Friday afternoon. He did that sometimes when he didn't have time to go home and use his. God, I can't believe somebody killed him!"

"What time was that?"

"Probably between three and four. I don't remember the time. How could I know it would be important?"

"He was on the Internet?"

"Uh-huh."

"You see what kind of information he accessed?"

"Nope. I went for coffee and by the time I came back he was on his way out. Said he had to catch a plane. You know, when he went over to the electronic side, I bet him he'd be back within two years. I lost."

Deb Schiller, J.D.'s woman friend for the past year, had been crying. "It's bad, Shar. I can't imagine my life without him. And what makes it worse is that we fought Friday night. I had tickets for *The Vagina Monologues* and reservations at Aqua, and then he called me from an airplane to say he couldn't make it, he was on his way to Portland. So I yelled at him like I always do. He got defensive like he always does. And I hung up on him."

"Don't be too hard on yourself, Deb. You couldn't've known what was going to happen."

"That's what I keep telling myself, but it doesn't help."

"He say why he was going to Portland?"

"A lead on a hot story—what else?"

"But he didn't tell you what the story was about?"

"I didn't give him time to. Now I wish I had."

* * *

Dave Lesser, urban activist and J.D.'s frequent source of information on who was about to act up and why, was full of himself as usual and didn't seem all that broken up over his death. "Yeah, he called in the middle of the afternoon on Friday, asked how he could get hold of somebody on the Coalition for Wireless Privacy. I gave him the phone number of their director, Alana Andrews."

"What does this coalition do, exactly?"

"Lobbies for legislation against electronic eavesdropping, that kind of stuff. Me, I don't worry about it. I don't put anything in E-mails that I don't want the world to hear. I got one credit card, don't buy off the Internet, guard my Social Security number like it was Fort Knox."

"Did J.D. say why he was interested in the coalition?"

"Nope. He guarded his stories like I do my SSN. I'd pass on info to him, he'd give one of my causes a plug, and we were both satisfied. Say, did you see his piece on the Hapless League putting the dead rats in the mayor's office?"

The Hapless League was an organization Lesser and his cohorts had formed to play practical jokes on city officials. "No, but I think I saw something about it in the *Chron.*"

"Well, you should check out J.D.'s version in *Salon.* You can say stuff on the Internet that you can't in a so-called family newspaper. He reprinted the text of our note. Way cool. You wanta know what it said?"

Do I have a choice?

"'We saved your life today. Killed a bunch of shit-eating rats.'"

Such eloquence.

* * *

Alana Andrews's machine picked up. The message said she would be out of town for the next ten days. I didn't bother to leave a message.

Jane Harris, J.D.'s landlady, sounded depressed. "I didn't see him at all on Friday, but I heard him upstairs in the late afternoon, rumbling around like he was in a hurry. Then he rushed down the stairs, banged the door on the way out, and was gone."

"Has the sheriff's department been here?"

"First thing this morning. They searched the apartment and took a box of his things away with them."

"So the apartment's sealed now?"

"If you consider a little bit of plastic tape a seal."

"Do you?"

"Look, Sharon, you're talking to a seventy-three-year-old hippie. At my age I've learned to trust people over thirty, but I've still got my reservations about authority. You want to come over and have a look around, I'll let you in."

On my way to J.D.'s building on Waller Street in the Cole Valley district near U.C. Med Center, my cell phone rang. Although I'd had the phone for upwards of a year and a half, I still wasn't sold on—or proficient at—using it while driving, so I pulled into a bus zone to answer.

"Sharon?" Jody Houston's shaky voice.

I couldn't mask my anger as I demanded, "Jody, where are you?"

"I didn't do it. I didn't kill J.D."

"Where *are* you?"

"I came home from the grocery store and there was a strange car in the driveway. So I parked down the block and snuck back to the cottage and went around it looking in the windows. He was on the living room floor."

"Why didn't you call nine-eleven?"

"At first I was scared the person who killed him might still be in the house. Then when I realized they weren't, I was scared the police wouldn't believe me. I mean, it was my house, and I knew him."

"You could've told me. I'd've handled it." But would *I* have believed her?

"I know I should've, but when I went upstairs I looked out the window—"

Sudden silence.

"Jody? Jody?"

Only static on the line now. I looked at the digital display on the phone, saw the words "no service." There are dozens of places in the city where wireless reception is spotty to nonexistent—and I was idling right smack in the middle of one.

I didn't kill J.D.

I didn't know whether to believe her or not, but I took out the card of the Tillamook County detective in charge of the case and reported Houston's call.

Jane Harris was what I call an unreconstructed hippie: gray hair hanging down to her waist; dangly earrings and sandals and tie-dye. The odor of incense mingled with the smell of marijuana in her ground-floor apartment. Beanbag chairs, bead curtains, and Flower Power wallpaper were alive and thriving there.

I'd met Jane a few times at dinner parties at J.D.'s apartment, and over the course of our mostly one-sided conversations had learned her personal history. She'd been married to a minor Beat poet in the fifties, a minor rock musician in the sixties, a minor artist in the seventies, and in the eighties a major distributor of soft drinks who had died and left her well enough off to buy the building and become a benevolent landlord. Her rents, J.D. had told me, were proof that her favorite decade lived on in her heart.

And apparently it was a generous heart. As she waved me into her living room she continued a conversation on her cordless phone: "Now, don't worry about a thing, honey. I'll contact J.D.'s pastor"—she rolled her eyes at me—"and discuss the service. I'll arrange for the flowers and get some ideas for places to hold the reception afterward. He had so many friends, we'll need a good-sized space. . . . Right. By the time you and Mr. Smith arrive here, all you'll have to do is choose."

Half a minute later she ended the call and turned to me, sighing. "His poor mother. She's so upset she can hardly think. He was an only child, you know."

"What's this about a pastor? I've never known him to set foot inside a church."

"The parents are very religious. Doesn't matter to him anymore, and if it'll give the Smiths some comfort, I can handle a few white lies."

"You're a good friend, Jane."

"Not all that good. Something was wrong with J.D.'s hot-water heater; he complained of a sulfuric smell. But I kept putting off calling the plumber because I'm budgeting toward a new roof. Now I feel terrible. The poor boy had to smell rotten eggs during his morning shower on the day he died."

Regrets . . .

I was a neglectful landlady.

I hung up on him.

I thought about going up after Roger, taking him a bottle of Valentine's Day wine. . . . Then I thought, the hell with it. . . . And the next morning there it was on the TV news. . . .

We were close. But apparently not as close as I thought.

There must've been signs. We could've helped Joey.

No, I wasn't thinking at all. Not when it came to my brother.

The hell with regrets.

I said, "I'll take a look at J.D.'s apartment now."

Every time I'd visited J.D. I'd been impressed by how he managed to convey an aura of simple elegance with furnishings that for the most part he'd purchased at Cost Plus. Plain woven grass mats, canvas director's chairs, rattan tables and bookcases were accented by colorful framed museum posters of art exhibits, and a jungle of tropical plants grew in the window bay. Interspersed were what he referred to as his "finds"—interesting junk, basically, that he cleaned up and displayed in unusual ways. Various engine parts, pieces of pipe, old tools and bottles all became treasures after his careful reclamation. I stood in the living room fingering a model of an airplane made from a spark plug, some sheet metal and wire, with the business end of a leather punch as its propeller. He'd often tried to give it to me, but I'd refused, thinking it was better off with its creator. Now I slipped it into my purse—something to remember him by.

I went down the short hallway to where two bedrooms flanked the bath. The one where he slept showed signs of a hurried departure: bed unmade, clothing—including the soaked yellow sweater that was the twin of the one in which he died—tossed on a chair, drawers left partially open. The office across the hall was equally untidy, with books strewn on the floor and papers mounded beside the computer. I sat down at the workstation and turned the machine on. It was a type I wasn't familiar with, but I played around and finally accessed his recent files. None were of interest except for some notes he'd made Thursday night on our conference with Max Engstrom. It was titled "Bullshit 101." He'd apparently had no time on Friday to record whatever had sent him to Oregon on a flight that the newscasts said had departed SFO two and a half hours before mine.

I shut off the machine and left the room. The apartment had a westward exposure, and the afternoon sun had begun to warm it. It still felt lived in, as if at any moment J.D. might walk through the door and ask, "What the hell're you doing here, Shar?" But soon his parents would arrive, the memorial service would be held, and his home would be stripped bare, repainted, readied for new tenants. A few years from now few people would remember that a talented man who died before his time had once lived there.

I remained in the living room for a moment, trying to say my good-byes to his lingering presence, then turned toward the door. There was an old-fashioned wood-and-brass coat tree next to it, and J.D.'s raincoat, which he'd worn Friday morning, hung from it. I'd forgotten about mine up to now, had left it at *InSite,* but he must've gone back inside for his.

I took the coat down. It still felt damp in places. I stuck my hand into the left pocket, found nothing but lint. The right was full of pieces of paper. I removed them and stepped into the adjoining kitchen to examine them.

Receipt from Miranda's for our Thursday morning breakfast; he'd insisted on buying. Parking ticket, weeks old and mangled. Business card of a personal shopper at Nordstrom's. Folded sheet of yellow scratch paper.

I smoothed the sheet out on the counter and studied it: Circled names with arrows connecting them in multiple ways: Nagasawa, Houston, Remington, Engstrom, Vardon, Donovan, Chen. They formed an ellipsis, and the arrows crossed and crisscrossed in a confusing pattern. Below were words and abbreviations with question marks after them: Afton? Econ? CWP? ER? LR? TRG?

I stared at the diagram till the lines and circles blurred, finally shook my head. It had meant something to J.D.—but what?

As I was walking back to my car from J.D.'s building, I glanced up at Parnassus Heights where the U.C. Medical Center complex loomed, and thought of Harry Nagasawa. Roger's brother interested me because, while he professed intense dislike of him, he'd apparently fallen apart in the aftermath of his suicide. Harry had terminated our interview very abruptly, and I was certain there was more I could learn from him, if I approached him in the right way. I decided to walk up the hill and see if he was on duty at the hospital.

It was windy on the Heights, and even on a Sunday afternoon Parnassus Street was clogged with buses, taxis, and other vehicles. Visitors streamed into the buff-colored hospital bearing flowers, plants, gift packages, and stuffed animals. I checked the directory, took the elevator to the cardiac care unit. A nurse with curly black hair hunched over a computer terminal behind the reception desk; when she turned to me I saw her eyes were tired.

"I'm looking for Dr. Harry Nagasawa," I said. "Is he here today?"

Surprise animated her drawn features. "Dr. Nagasawa's no longer on staff."

So they'd caught on to his substance abuse. "When was he let go?"

"He was put on suspension in January, pending a disciplinary hearing, and offered his resignation a week later."

"But—" What had he said when he arrived at the family home for his appointment with me last week? *I got tied up at the hospital.* "D'you know if he's on staff someplace else now?"

"Sorry, no. Are you a patient?"

"An old friend. Can you tell me why he was suspended?"

She glanced around, obviously torn between hospital policy and the temptation to gossip. Leaned toward me and said in a low voice, "I don't know all the details, but I believe it had to do with him accessing confidential patient records."

"Patients other than his own, you mean."

"Right. I've heard a couple of rumors. One is that he was altering the records. The other is that he was passing them on to another party. Either way, that's a very sensitive area, and the board was happy to receive his resignation."

I thought of what Roger had told Jody—that he'd forced

someone to do something unethical, and the person's career had been put in jeopardy.

Harry?

"Any way you can find out whose records they were?"

"If you're his friend, why don't you ask him?"

"I didn't even know he wasn't on staff any longer. I doubt he'll want to talk about it."

"Well, I'm sorry, but I can't help you. As I said, it's a very sensitive area, and nobody's discussing it."

Except the people who are floating those rumors—and you.

I left the hospital and crossed Parnassus to the parking garage, where I took the elevator down to Frederick Street at the base of the Heights. A roundabout walk back to my car would give me time to ponder this latest turn of events.

The governing board of the medical center hadn't wanted to make public what Harry had been doing with confidential records, so they'd allowed him to resign quietly—so quietly that his own family members weren't aware he was no longer on staff there. Easy enough for him to conceal: his mother was no longer living at home, and his father was preoccupied with his busy practice and the impending wrongful-death suit. Chances were he hadn't been taken on by another hospital; the signs of substance abuse were so severe now that any health-care professional would have spotted them.

So what did Harry do with his days? Absent himself from the Cow Hollow house at the appropriate times, in case the housekeeper noticed his presence and called attention to it. But where did he go? The movies? A girlfriend's home? The bars? How could he fill the time a resident's busy schedule demanded? He was out of control, unsuited for any other vocation, or even avocation. Tomorrow I'd put an operative on the Nagasawa house—Julia could use some experience in surveillance—in order to find out where Harry went and get a handle on how to approach him.

I was halfway down the short block of Arguello Boulevard that runs between the medical center's garage and Kezar Stadium—a restored 1925-vintage football field that now hosts high school games—when one of the row of Edwardian houses caught my eye. It had once been the home of my client and old friend Willie Whelan. Willie, a professional fence who had, as he put it, gone legit by establishing a chain of cut-rate jewelry stores, had caught the eye of a talent agent while doing his own over-the-top TV commercials. Now he lived in New York City, where he starred as an immensely popular villain on a soap opera. Rae, who had survived a fling with him during his days as "the diamond king," taped the more amusing episodes and shared them with me.

I smiled wryly in remembrance of the old days. The investigation that had brought Willie and me together seemed simple next to the tangle of facts and questions I faced today. More and more I found myself relying on sophisticated equipment, technical assistance, and experts of all sorts. Fortunately, I knew an expert who would work on Sunday for the price of a meal.

Mick and Charlotte's condo, which he had purchased last fall with the help of his father, was small, starkly white, and would have been characterless at the hands of many people. But they'd each put their individual stamp on it. A specially constructed hall tree held Charlotte's collection of fancy evening bags and sequined baseball caps—my favorite was a black one with silver stars. Mick's motorcycle memorabilia—logos, scale models, framed advertisements—lined up on a plate rail that he'd installed at eye level. The furnishings were mainly Ikea, and carefully chosen.

When I arrived there around four-thirty, they were enjoying a glass of wine in the living room. The balcony door was open and the rumble of traffic on the Embarcadero was deafening, even in the last hour of a Sunday afternoon. Mick closed it, Charlotte brought me a glass of Chardonnay, and I got down to business.

"You hear about J.D.?"

Their faces turned somber. "Yeah," Mick said. "Must've been tough for you, finding him. A couple of reporters called here, wanting to know if we knew where you were. They got Dad and Rae's unlisted number, bothered them too. I said I hadn't heard from you; Dad wasn't as polite."

I nodded. My former brother-in-law could be prickly when anything penetrated his shield of privacy. "Well, I'm staying someplace where no reporter can get to me."

"RKI's building."

"I didn't say that."

"Nope, you didn't. Right, Sweet Charlotte?"

"I didn't hear a thing."

Mick asked, "So what's happening? This isn't a social call."

"No. I'd like to trade you a dinner in exchange for letting me run some things by you on your day off."

"Cool. There's a new place we've been wanting to try, but money's tight this month."

Actually the promise of a dinner on the agency wasn't necessary. As I outlined certain details of the case, both of their expressions became focused and fascinated. They were natural investigators and enjoyed a challenge. When I finished, I asked, "Anything come to mind?"

Charlotte said, "Roger wrote in his journal that he'd deleted all his files and destroyed everything he didn't want anyone to see?"

"Right."

"But he didn't destroy the journal full of very personal stuff."

"No."

"That makes me think that he wanted someone to see it, someone who knew he kept it."

"Maybe, but it was hidden in a very unlikely place."

"A place that maybe the person he wanted to read it knew about."

"Of course—Jody Houston. When she saw I'd been reading it she recognized it and said he'd kept it hidden. And she tried to get it away from me."

Mick said, "That last journal entry, where he said he'd left an insurance policy for Houston, it sounds like a message to me."

"Could be. But insurance against what?"

"Hard to say, but if I were you I'd want to take a good look at the files he deleted."

"How? They're gone."

"Not really. It's very difficult to completely delete anything. And if you have the proper skills, you can retrieve most files."

"I don't understand."

He glanced at Charlotte. "You explain it. You're better at putting stuff in layman's language."

"Okay," she said. "Take my personal computer." She motioned at a workstation in the corner. "A Windows PC. I receive or send an E-mail, hit the Delete key, and the mail's stored in the recycle bin. I empty the bin, and it's gone—right?"

"Right."

"Wrong. It may be gone from the bin, but somewhere in the machine's memory it still exists. It's just not easy to get at. There are a number of firms whose sole business is to go into the offices of clients and retrieve deleted files from their employees' computers, in order to investigate possible improprieties. The service is called computer forensics and, believe me, there's a growing demand for it."

Mick said, "I've been meaning to talk to you about offering it as an agency service. Most of the work has to be done after business hours when the employees have gone home, but you can charge substantial fees—"

"Get me something in writing," I said. "An actual description, including initial outlay, operating expenses, and a fee structure. Then we'll discuss it. Is it common knowledge that you can do this?"

"Not really. If more people knew, they wouldn't say the things they do in their E-mail."

"Do either of you have the skills to copy what might still be in Roger's machine's memory?"

They grinned at each other.

Mick said, "The head of our new computer forensics programs would have such skills. Yes, indeed."

* * *

The apartment on Brannan Street seemed even colder tonight. The refrigerator still made its ominous gurgling sounds, and more plaster had fallen from the ceiling around the skylight. Mick and Charlotte were oblivious of the chill; they carried a portable computer into the front room, set it up at the workstation, and began tinkering.

"This'll take about half an hour," he told me. "Go watch TV or something. You're hovering like a great big buzzard, and it's distracting me."

Dismissed, I wandered through the living room and, after a couple of turns around the dining area, sat down at the table.

A great big buzzard.

What did you have to do to command the respect of your employees? Not hire relatives, I supposed. Mick had been on to me since age seven, when he figured out that I really wouldn't kill him as I'd threatened to when he wouldn't pick up his toys.

Now they were laughing in there. I strained to hear.

He: ". . . bitchy lately."

She: "Yeah, Hy's definitely been gone too long."

He: "Better not come home jet-lagged, because she's gonna jump his bones—"

Me: "Not everything's about sex, you know!"

Silence. Then suppressed giggles.

Me: "Go ahead, laugh! You'll laugh even harder when you find out your free dinner is at an In-N-Out Burger."

But, God, they were right. I missed Hy in more ways than one.

I got up and went into the kitchen. Opened the door to the pantry and peered inside. The pancake-syrup bottle was still married to the tomato-juice can. The oily substance still lurked on the floor. I closed the door, went to the fridge, studied the jars of pickles in cloudy brine, the bottles of salad dressing. Opened the freezer and reinventoried its contents. Torn bag of lima beans, spilled and stuck to the shelf. Blue ice, container cracked and staining the frost beneath it. Regular ice, shrinking in its trays. Baggie full of mystery meat.

I slammed the freezer door shut, looked around the stark white room. The only spot of color was the red pottery bowl that matched the table base and chairs. Inside it was a jumble of keys: a set similar to the ones to this building that Glenn had given me; spares for the Toyota Roger had left with its flashers going on the bridge when he jumped; a standard dead-bolt type with a purple rubber band twined through the holes at its top; another larger key on a chain with a plastic tag, nothing written on the tag to identify it.

I picked up the two loose keys and examined them. Turned them over and over in my hands. Keys which, like the others, Roger had left behind because he knew he'd have no further use for them. No further use for anything anymore.

Back at RKI's apartment. A stack of hard copy of the more interesting files we'd found on Roger's machine on the refectory table. Half-eaten mediocre Chinese takeout beside it. Headache flaring up as I tried to separate the important from the unimportant. Most seemed to be in the latter category, but how could I be sure?

I reached into my jeans pocket, took out the two keys that I'd impulsively removed from Roger's apartment. Fingered them, set them down. Went to the kitchen, removed one of the bottles of wine from the fridge. Opened it, poured myself a generous glass that I carried back to the living room. I needed to relax for a while; maybe later my thoughts would flow more freely.

I dialed my home phone, listened to my messages. Nearly everyone I knew, it seemed, wished to be briefed on the recent events. I wrote down names and numbers and contemplated the list: two calls were mandatory, in order to allay maternal anxiety.

Which call to make first, though? Which mother? My adoptive mother sounded frantic: "Sharon, you're all over the news! Another one of your horrible murders!" *My* horrible murders, Ma? You make it sound like I commit them. My birth mother sounded her usual levelheaded self: "Sharon, it's Kia. I've seen the report on CNN. Do you need legal advice?"

I opted for Saskia Blackhawk, attorney-at-law.

"How are you?" she asked.

"Holding my own. And you?"

"Holding."

"Robin and Darcy?" My half sister and brother.

"Robin's working her tail off this first semester in law school, loving every minute of it. Darcy's . . . well, Darcy." My half brother had purple hair, multiple piercings, and a drug dependency. Not unlike Joey, except he had artistic talent and was gainfully employed by a Boise TV station.

As if she knew I was thinking of him, Saskia said, "I'm sorry about your brother."

"How did you hear?" She'd been traveling, and we hadn't spoken for weeks.

"Elwood told me."

"You're back in touch with him?"

"We talk, yes."

"Does this mean . . . ?"

"No. Elwood's too traditional for me." Meaning in the old Shoshone ways. "Too withdrawn from the real world. Tom Blackhawk was a man of passion and conviction; if I ever have another romantic relationship, it'll be with someone like him. About Joey . . . How are you dealing with the loss?"

"Well, at first I was really angry. I'd lie awake in the middle of the night and feel the rage building. I'd think of every nasty, shitty thing he ever did to me."

"Such as?"

"You really want to know?"

"If you care to tell me. I'm interested in what happened all those years we were separated."

"Okay, then. These are only a few examples. He hung my favorite stuffed animal—a kangaroo named Roo-Roo—from a tree in the canyon behind our house. I can still see him doing it, his rotten face pinched with meanness. The day I wore my first training bra, he announced at the dinner table, 'Shar's got her big chest on.' He went out with my best girlfriend in high school and told everybody she'd given him head. And you know what he said to me about not attending this big party we threw for Ma and Pa's wedding anniversary a few years back? 'Blood's not thicker than water, Shar. It's just a different color.'"

"And after you thought of all those things?"

"I felt better. But then to make up for dwelling on them, I started to feel guilty because I'd failed him for not finding him on time. That passed, too. Now other memories're filtering in."

"And they are?"

"You sound like I'm on the witness stand."

"Sorry, unfortunate habit. Robin and Darcy hate it too."

"I don't hate it, exactly. It's just that . . . Well, you sound like I do a lot of the time."

Saskia laughed—amusement tinged with relief. She and I were continually struggling to find common ground that would help us define our relationship.

"Okay," I said, "the other memories. The gentle way he picked me up and made me stop crying after I fell off the monkey bars in the park and skinned both knees. One Christmas—his eyes were so wide and anxious while he watched Ma unwrap this *hideous* cookie jar that he'd spent a month's paper-route money on. And I mean hideous. A donkey in a sombrero and chaps playing the guitar. She pretended to like it, and he was so happy. There was this fat, ugly kid in the neighborhood that the bullies were always picking on. One day they held him down and tried to make him eat a slug. Joey tore over there and took them all on, and after his wounds healed, he kind of looked out for the kid. He called me the night before I graduated from Berkeley, loaded and proud that I was the first in the family to get a college degree, and informing the whole bar about it. He must've put half the other drunks on the phone to congratulate me before I convinced him to stop running up a big bill. And his postcards to Ma never said much, but he always signed them 'I love you.' "

"In the balance, positive memories, then."

"Yes." I was surprised to realize that my eyes were moist. "I guess it means I'm coming to terms with him dying, but I still don't understand why he killed himself."

"Maybe you never will."

"I'm not a person who deals well with not knowing."

"Neither am I, but sometimes you have to accept that you won't. And speaking of not knowing, tell me exactly what happened in Oregon."

After spending ten minutes bringing Saskia up to date on my investigation, I checked my watch. After eleven. Late to be calling Ma, but I knew she wouldn't rest till she heard from me, so I dialed her number in the adult community of Rancho Bernardo, north of San Diego.

"Thank God!" she exclaimed. "I've been so worried! First your brother, and now you."

"Ma, I wasn't the victim. I only found him."

"I know that! But when I heard, I was afraid . . . This family, we're so snake-bit."

Snake-bit. An old western phrase that Ma had used her whole life till she remarried and decided to become a lady who lunched and joined book-discussion groups. Maybe she was beginning to reconcile the former Katie McCone with the present Kay Hunt.

"Why're we snake-bit?"

"Your father died—"

"Pa had a heart attack. He was in his seventies. It happens."

"Charlene and Ricky divorced—"

"And are both happy with their new spouses. As you are."

"Well, yes. But little Kimmie died, and then John and Karen divorced, and he's never remarried."

She was into ancient history now. "A lot of marriages don't survive the death of a child. And as far as I know,

John has a great life and an excellent relationship with Karen and the boys."

"Well, you found out you were adopted—"

"But I'm still your daughter."

My affirmation made her fall silent. Then she said weakly, "Joey . . ." A sob.

Oh, Ma, don't . . . "Joey's still your son, too. Wherever he is, he still loves you."

A long silence. Then she said tartly, "Don't lie to me."

"What?"

"You don't believe that. You must be aware that I know you've lost your faith."

"Well, I . . ."

"And do you know how I recognize it?"

"No."

"I recognize it because I've lost mine too."

Impossible. Ma had always described herself as "very devout."

"When did this happen?"

"That's not relevant. The reasons and circumstances are personal. But I will tell you this: If I hadn't lost it when I did, I would have lost it the moment I heard Joey was dead. A good God would not have planned for my son to sink into despair and kill himself. A good God would not have planned that for our Joey."

I asked, "So how do you go on, without the faith you've leaned on your whole life?"

"You simply go on. You suffer, and then you heal. You grieve, and then you let go. Maybe that's proof that there's something bigger than what the Church taught us, I don't know. But you do go on."

Wise women, both my mothers.

Subj: No Subject

Date: Tuesday, February 6, 2001, 10:16:21 AM

From: tothemax@insite.com

To: tremington@trg.com

Tessa:

Since Jorge seems strangely indifferent to the situation here, I am going over his head and communicating directly with you. I do not understand the delay on this latest round of financing. I happen to know you have signed commitments from the limited partners far in excess of what's been doled out to us, and it's in your best interests to keep us going until the market corrects and the climate is right for an IPO. Please respond asap.

Max

Subj: Your inquiry

Date: Tuesday, February 6, 2001, 4:29:45 PM

From: tremington@trg.com

To: tothemax@insite.com

Max—

Your inquiry received and duly noted. Timing is an issue here, and there are complicated factors which would mean nothing to you. We will put out the call for capital to the limited partners by the middle of

next week, latest. Please bear with me. If you feel the need to communicate directly in the future, make sure to copy Jorge.
Regards, Tessa

Subj: No subject
Date: Thursday, February 8, 2001, 9:31:07 PM
From: Kdonovan@aol.com
To: webpotentate@insite.com

I'm putting the research materials you requested on disc and dropping them at your place, rather than sending them as a file or leaving them in your in-box at the office. I don't trust the privacy of E-mail there, and this isn't something you'll want to look at in the presence of others. You'll be happy to know you were right about the situation.
K

Subj: No subject
Date: Friday, February 9, 2001, 11:07:43 AM
From: webpotentate@insite.com
To: Kdonovan@aol.com.

Thanks for your good work, and for dropping the disc off personally. It's useful stuff. Payment forthcoming. I assume all your searches were done on your personal machine, since you have privacy issues about the office?

Subj: No subject
Date: Friday, February 9, 2001, 6:22:07 PM
From: Kdonovan@aol.com

To: webpotentate@insite.com

Yes, all the work was done here at home, so privacy is insured.
K

Subj: Amaya
Date: Tuesday, February 13, 2001, 10:12:01 AM
From: tothemax@insite.com
To: tremington@trg.com

Tessa:

I'm not copying Jorge on this regardless of your prior instructions. We had another of our incidents last night—burglar alarm repeatedly going off, security company calling me at home at all hours—and he's acting very cavalier about it. Frankly, he's a piss-poor CEO. He may have the credentials, but he doesn't give a shit about the magazine. I urge you to replace him.

Max

Subj: Amaya
Date: Tuesday, February 13, 2001, 2:57:54 PM
From: tremington@trg.com
To: tothemax@insite.com

Max—
Please calm down! "Acting cavalier," as you put it, is simply Jorge's style. If you don't want the security company calling you, refer them to him. He is, after all, in charge there.
Regards, Tessa

Subj: No subject
Date: Wednesday, February 14, 2001, 9:32:18 PM
From: artfulroger@earthlink.com
To: happyhacker@sonic.com

This is important, guy, and by the time you get it you won't be able to reach me for clarification, so please print this out and follow it to the letter. Jody is going to be upset after tonight, and I want you to look out for her. Somebody may try to intimidate or even hurt her, and in that case it's important you show her the stuff I asked you to teach me. Then she'll know how to protect herself.

I've done something that I don't want anybody ever to know about unless it's the only way Jody can be safe. The folks, you, and even Harry don't deserve it being made public. If anybody comes around asking about me, distance yourself. Call me a bastard, say you hate my guts, whatever it takes. This is for your own safety.

Love you, guy—
Roger

Subj: DON'T DELETE THIS BEFORE READING!
Date: Wednesday, February 14, 2001, 9:40:02 PM
From: artfulroger@earthlink.com
To: rx@aol.com

I'm sorry. I was on a mission and not thinking about what my demands might do to you. I never should have used you that way. I know I can't make it up to you, but I've put a request in a letter to the folks that you have my apartment. Live in it or sell it, I don't care. Maybe it'll help you get a fresh start.

Regretfully—
Roger

I'd isolated the first seven messages from dozens in a file labeled "Project 'Zine" on Roger's computer's hard drive. They were the only additions to the file in the two weeks before his death. The remaining two were the only ones sent on the day of his suicide. There had been volumes remaining in the computer's memory—story outlines, idea lists, financial and tax information—but none of it seemed relevant compared to these. Now I tried to analyze what I'd read.

Max Engstrom's mail to Tessa Remington confirmed how deeply in trouble the publication was, as well as his growing frustration with the sabotage and Jorge Amaya's performance as CEO. Remington's reaction, while not unsympathetic, seemed curiously unconcerned.

From the list of staff members I identified "Kdonovan" as Kat Donovan, the magazine's head researcher, job title Sherlock. I recalled her as a short, overweight woman with beautiful red hair who had been rather nervous and impatient with my presence on the day of the game. I wondered what kind of extracurricular sleuthing Sherlock had done for the WebPotentate. Sensitive material, since she didn't feel free to do it at the office or send it internally, and apparently Dinah Vardon shared her concerns.

Nothing about these messages or the others in the Project 'Zine file gave any indication of why Roger killed himself or what he'd done that he didn't want made public unless necessary to protect Jody Houston. Nor did they hint at whom or what she needed protection from. His final messages to his brothers Eddie—happyhacker—and Harry—rx—were filled with guilt and remorse. And it appeared that when I'd talked with Eddie he'd distanced himself from Roger, as his older brother had instructed him. His anger was probably genuine—I could recognize that from my own recent emotional state—but his statement that they weren't close was a lie. As for Harry, I suspected that Roger was the one who had put him up to accessing confidential hospital records, but for what reason I hadn't a clue.

I checked my watch. Almost midnight, too late to call Eddie or Harry. Then I remembered I wanted to assign Julia to conduct a surveillance on Harry tomorrow. If I could get a handle on his activities, I might acquire the leverage to make him open up. For a moment I hesitated at phoning a single mother with a young son at this hour, but Julia knew she'd signed on for an irregular schedule, and would resent being given special treatment. I picked up the receiver and made a nuisance of myself for the last time that day.

Monday

•

APRIL 23

The phone rang as I was lying in bed contemplating my plan for the day. I regarded it warily. A reporter? No. By now, with no new developments, press interest in both J.D.'s murder and me would be on the wane. Besides, all calls to this number were prescreened by the command post downstairs, and I'd given them only a limited list of names to be put through. I picked up.

"So how do you like your home away from home?"

"Ripinsky! You must've talked with Green Street."

"Yeah, they told me I'd authorized your using the apartment. I'm curious as to why I had to do that."

I explained, heard the pain in his voice when he reacted to the news of J.D.'s death. Hy had seen entirely too many people die before their time, including his wife, environmentalist Julie Spaulding, whom he'd watched waste away from multiple sclerosis. Such experiences had molded him into a man who regularly needed reassurance that those he cared about were all right—the reason why, in spite of an uncanny emotional connection that allowed us to tap into each other's feelings over time and distance, we spoke frequently when apart.

"I suppose you're feeling guilty because J.D. went up there while he was helping you with your case," he said.

"Not really. He was a reporter to the bone. I couldn't've stopped him even if I'd known he was going. I just wish I'd gotten there sooner. Maybe I could have prevented the murder. And, of course, I'm going to miss him."

"Me too."

"So when are you coming home?"

"That's one of the reasons I called." Now his voice took on a familiar tone, a formality and remoteness that said he was about to tell me something I didn't want to hear. "I have to go to Manila. A situation's brewing with one of our clients."

"The Philippines? Didn't they just have a 'situation' there?"

"Well, it's a volatile political climate."

I'd get no more details from him. Need-to-know again, and even I was excluded.

"McCone? You're not angry? Or afraid for me?"

"No."

"You're in a bad place right now, and I'm not there for you again. Is that it?"

"I can handle this."

"You can. But should you always have to?"

"What're you saying?"

"The job is just something I do. I'm good at it, and it makes me feel valuable, but it doesn't define me. You say the word and I'll let Gage and Dan buy me out."

"You'd do that? For me?"

"In a heartbeat."

Knowing that he'd make such a sacrifice was all I really needed.

I said, "You're with me, no matter where you are. Go on, get yourself packed and on your flight to Manila. You're the best man to handle any 'situation.' "

Charlotte Keim, a restaurant snob if I'd ever met one, looked around the linoleum-and-vinyl interior of the Koffee Kup and wrinkled her nose. "Tell me one thing," she said. "Why're we meeting way out here in the Avenues?"

Despite its appearance, the coffee shop had redeeming qualities—among them its location near RKI's building, and the presence of corned-beef hash and eggs on its menu. I frowned at Keim, waited for the waitress to take our orders and depart before I replied.

"I'm here because I'm staying close by," I said. "And you're here because I need to ask you how venture capital works."

Keim, a former RKI operative whom I'd lured away with the promise of more interesting work and a less paranoid atmosphere, was an expert in the financial area. Now she forgot her displeasure at what she considered a substandard eatery. "How much detail do you want?"

"The basics will do for now."

"Okay, that's easy. You have a venture capital firm. X Company. They establish what's called a start-up fund and solicit signed commitments from investors—called limited partners—to come up with a certain amount of cash when it's needed. When the VC find a likely company to invest in, they put out a capital call, requesting the promised bucks from the partners. The fund remains in existence till the start-up company is sold or goes public—or folds, the scenario we're seeing more frequently these days. But if all goes well, when the fund closes, the limited partners realize their return on investment."

"And what's in it for the VC?"

"Most invest their own capital as well, so they realize the same kind of return as the limited partners. And they charge the fund management fees, usually in the neighborhood of two or three percent of total assets. That probably doesn't sound like much to you, but we're talking many millions per fund, and most VC oversee several."

"A high-risk way to get rich, then. I would think the volume of investing would be down nowadays."

Keim waited while the waitress put a plate of blueberry pancakes in front of her. From the look on her face as she sniffed them, I could tell that the Koffee Kup was about to triumph over its shabby appearance and unfortunate locale. My corned-beef hash looked to be classic—sliced right out of the can and slapped on the grill—nothing fancy, just the way I like it.

As she poured syrup, Charlotte went on, "VC investment was down about forty percent first quarter of this year, but rich people and pension funds're still reaching for their checkbooks. Historically, venture capital investing has produced a return of around twenty percent. Where else can you realize that much in this market?"

"I guess the VC are steering away from the dot-com firms, though."

"Definitely. They're waiting to see what the market trends will be before they choose which companies to finance. I read in the *Wall Street Journal* that overall there's thirty to forty billion dollars in unexercised capital commitments out there."

I considered that, sipping coffee. "All right, you have a

capital call when the initial investment is made. Then there's what I've heard called mezzanine financing."

"Right. It happens at various stages before they go to IPO."

"And the fund manager is the one who decides when they'll be made. What factors enter into that?"

"How the company's growing is one. If it's going too fast for the timetable they've set up, they may opt to slow growth. Or if it's in trouble, a big infusion of cash at the right point can help. Companies are like individuals in a lot of ways; you've got to treat each one differently in order to maximize performance."

Like my employees, I thought. "So if a company's in trouble an infusion of cash is considered the proper solution."

"Another round of financing would be in the VC's best interests, yes. But there's also the scenario of cutting their losses and running. The firm might have valuable assets that could be sold at a profit. Or they might come up with a buyer who would be willing to take it off their hands. I've even heard of cases where the VC wanted to cover up some irregularity, so they just let the companies fail. Almost anything could be a reason for not coming up with the needed capital."

Almost anything—including a sudden disappearance.

My phone rang as I was crossing Mission on Tenth Street, heading toward the pier. I picked it up from the passenger's seat and answered.

"Sharon?" Julia Rafael, calling during her surveillance on Harry Nagasawa. "The subject left his home at nine-thirty-two. I followed him across town to a bar on Sixteenth Street near Folsom, where he had a couple of pops and made a drug buy. Apparently he used some of the merchandise in the car before he left his parking space. Now we're heading northeast on Market and, man, is he driving crazy."

"Stay on him and keep me posted." I made a left turn and doubled back on Ninth.

"He drove along Franklin and turned left on Lombard. Could be headed for the bridge."

Or he'd spotted her and would turn toward home.

"I'm right behind you. Stay on the line."

"We're in Seacliff now. El Camino del Mar. He's turning . . . You know that short block that dead-ends before you get to the recreation area? He's pulling over by McKittridge Park."

I knew that block all too well.

"Maintain surveillance, but don't approach him. I'll be there in a few minutes."

In the 1950s, when the three-acre bluff-top land near the Golden Gate National Recreation Area was occupied by a conservative think tank, an infamous murder had been committed in a dovecote on the property. A few years ago my own investigation on behalf of the woman who was convicted of the crime revealed the true identity of the killer. The think tank, which by then had moved to other quarters, donated the land to the city, with the stipulation that it be named Cordelia McKittridge Park, in memory of the young debutante who had been brutally murdered. What was then an overgrown tract occupied by a decaying mansion is now beautifully landscaped, with benches and a gazebo; a series of three large decks connected by staircases lead down to the bluff's edge, commanding views from the Golden Gate to the open sea. Old San Franciscans know where to look for the foundations of the razed mansion and dovecote, but many visitors to the park have no idea of its bloody history or who Cordelia McKittridge was.

The evil of years past still lingers in the park, however: a rape and a stabbing have occurred there since its establishment, and two people—both suicides—have plunged to their deaths from the bluff top. It's as if the place is infected by an ineradicable virus that can be contracted by susceptible visitors.

I pulled my car up behind Julia's shabby orange van, noted Harry's Porsche three spaces ahead of it. Julia wasn't in her vehicle, but as I entered the park I spotted her sitting on a bench on the first deck. She saw me and pointed down at the far platform; Harry leaned on the railing at the bluff's edge, staring at the roiling surf and jagged rocks below.

Unease gripped me as I hurried past Julia to the steps. A woman with two large dogs was ascending, blocking my way. I squeezed around them, heard a growl and the words "Watch it, asshole."

An artist had set up his easel on the middle deck and was daubing his canvas with colors that reflected the brilliance of the morning, but nighttime memories of this place flashed through my mind: thick mist hanging in the trees, the groan of foghorns, the glitter of light on a handgun . . .

Harry had straightened, his palms braced flat against the railing. His stance bothered me—resolute, intense. Just as I started across the deck, he climbed over the rail onto the sloping ground behind.

"Oh my God!" I ran toward him.

He turned, threw me a glance that showed no recognition. Then he looked around as if surprised to find himself there. His foot slipped, and he fell heavily; the ground at the cliff's edge began to crumble.

I vaulted the railing and grasped him by the shoulders, frantically digging my heels into the ground. He lay limp, unresisting as he slid, pulling me behind him. The crash of the surf on the rocks below was deafening. I could smell brine and Harry's alcohol-laced sweat. I dug my heels in harder, straining my calf and thigh muscles, and finally managed to arrest our slide. Harry's head flopped back against my chest; his eyes were dull, blank—empty even of fear.

My heart was pounding erratically and I drew short, ragged breaths. Behind me I heard shouting and running, and then hands were reaching for us—Julia's and a male stranger's. I kept a firm grip on Harry, allowed them to pull both of us to safety.

Another suicide.

But this time it didn't happen.

This time I prevented it. . . .

". . . and on the local news this evening, we'll have more about that San Francisco private investigator who keeps turning up when tragic things happen—or almost happen—to people—"

"Dammit!" I shut the TV off. After a brief hiatus when I'd thought press interest in me had died down, I was once again a hot news item. Thank God Julia and I had retreated to RKI's well-guarded fortress as soon as the police finished with us at McKittridge Park.

I glanced at her. She'd been uncharacteristically silent as I surfed the channels for one of the stations' noon-hour trailers for its newscasts, and from her rounded shoulders and drooping head I could see she was depressed. She felt the pull of my gaze and looked up.

"He totally weirded out, didn't he?" she said.

"Yeah, he did." When the paramedics had loaded Harry onto an ambulance, he'd appeared catatonic. "Maybe now his parents will get him the help he needs."

"Does shit like this happen to you a lot? Almost getting killed saving some asshole?"

Or defending myself from same. "It's happened. But most of the time the upsetting events in my business aren't anything worse than a client stiffing me on a fee."

Julia didn't look convinced. "I guess today wasn't really so bad, was it? I mean, it turned out all right."

"Right."

"But sometimes it doesn't. You've seen people killed, haven't you?"

"Yes."

"When was the first time?"

"A while after I started at All Souls Legal Cooperative. One of Hank Zahn's clients was murdered."

"How long had you been an investigator when that happened?"

"I was around thirty, and I'd been in security off and on since I graduated high school."

"But how long had you actually been an investigator?"

"Three years. Why?"

"I'm trying to figure out the odds."

"Of what?"

"How many times shit like that will happen to me if I stay in this line of work."

Was she thinking of quitting? I couldn't believe that. Julia was a tough woman and, while she'd witnessed Harry's attempted suicide, she hadn't been the one he almost took with him. The images I'd be carrying for the rest of my life were not hers. Still, I had to reassure her, help her deal with the situation.

Carefully I said, "You may never see something like that again. Not all investigators work in the field. If you build your computer skills and opt for a desk job—"

"No way. Not me."

"Well, it's one possibility."

"Not for *this* woman. I get half crazy when I spend more than a couple of hours sitting in that office. I'm always having to get out, take a walk. Craig's the same way. That's why he's always lying around on the floor exercising. We're action people, like you."

"Then you'd better find a way to deal with the unpleasant things that'll come along. I can recommend one method: compartmentalize."

"Say what?"

"You picture a compartment in your mind. One that locks. Then you put the memory in there and close it."

She frowned. "You must have one hell of a huge compartment."

"The size of a bank vault, now. But you can start small. Maybe you'll be one of the lucky people."

"You've seen my résumé. Luck doesn't figure."

"That's already changing. For starters, I'd suggest a compartment the size of a safe-deposit box."

Julia smiled. Of course, she hadn't yet thought of the obvious: any self-created mental compartment comes with an easily pickable lock.

"Ms. McCone, this is Eddie Nagasawa. Glenn Solomon gave me your number." His voice was rough with emotion. "I want to thank you for saving my brother's life."

"You're welcome, Eddie. I'm glad I could get to him on time."

"D'you suppose . . . Could we get together, talk in person?"

I'd wanted to ask him some questions anyway. "Name the time and place."

A pause. "I'm on my way up from Palo Alto to be with my folks, but I'd rather not do this at the house. D'you know where Roger's apartment is?"

"Yes. As a matter of fact, I have a set of keys to it."

"So do I. I'll meet you there in an hour."

When I arrived Eddie was drinking wine—an inexpensive red that he'd brought with him. He offered me some, and I didn't refuse. We sat across from each other at the glass table in the dining area and, at his request, I described the circumstances of his brother's attempted suicide.

"Are you sure he intended to jump?" he asked.

"Well, he didn't leave a note in his car, if that's what you mean. He'd been drinking, and my operative thought he'd also done some drugs. He may have been thinking of suicide, climbed over the railing to test his limits, and fell because he became disoriented."

"But there's no way to know for sure."

"No."

"God, I wish I could believe he would've climbed back over. I keep thinking . . . I've got this life, you know, and up until Rog died it was a good one. Four-point GPA, great friends, great girlfriend, all that stuff. But now it's screwed because it looks like there's this suicide gene in my family. How do I know I won't go nuts and try to kill myself too?"

I hesitated, unwilling to talk about my own affairs, then decided Eddie could benefit from my experience. "My brother committed suicide. Recently. But I've got another brother and two sisters; they've all lived through some pretty horrible things, but none of them has ever considered that was a way out. So, you see, it doesn't have to be an inherited tendency. And you seem a lot more together than Harry or Roger."

"I hope so. I've gotta be there for my folks. Harry too."

"They're having him committed?"

"To a private hospital run by a friend of my dad's."

"Well, maybe his story will have a better outcome than Roger's."

He shrugged.

"There are a few questions I'd like to ask you," I added.

"Sure. Go ahead."

"You and Roger were closer than you indicated to me?"

"Yeah. When I was a kid and getting kicked around by Harry, he stood up for me. He was always there to listen when I had a problem. Even after he left home I could call him any time. I only said all that shit about him because I was pissed off at him for killing himself."

"And because Roger told you to distance yourself if anybody came around asking about him. For your own safety."

"How'd you know that?"

"His last message to you."

His gaze moved toward the bedroom where Roger's workstation was. "Jody show it to you?"

I nodded, rather than waste time going into how I'd accessed it. "He also wanted you to look out for Jody in case someone tried to intimidate or hurt her. Show her something you'd taught him. Did you?"

"Yeah."

"And that was how to access the files he'd deleted on his computer?"

"Right. Look, I don't know if I should be talking about this with you. I mean, Jody was really scared, and then she left town. And I can't believe she killed that reporter. Something happened up there, but it isn't what the press and the cops claim."

"That's what Jody says."

"You've seen her since?"

"She called me."

"What did she tell you?"

I recapped my conversation with Houston.

Eddie asked, "Do you believe her?"

"There's a ring of truth to what she says. I wish she'd turn herself in, let the authorities sort it out."

"Me too. Even if they put her in jail, at least she'd be safe."

"Safe from whom?"

"She wouldn't tell me. It's so complicated. I need to explain from the beginning. But no tape recorder, okay?"

"Okay."

"Last December Rog called me, said he'd read an article about how you could retrieve deleted files from computers' hard drives, and asked if I knew how to do it. I did, and I showed him."

"And he retrieved files and E-mails from the computers at *InSite*."

"Hundreds of them. Why, I don't know. Next he asked me about getting hold of the medical records of a couple of the 'zine's employees who he suspected were victims of poisoning by somebody at the office. I didn't want to get involved in anything like that, but both people had been patients at U.C. Med Center, so I suggested he ask Harry. Harry didn't want to do it either, so Rog blackmailed him—threatened to tell our folks about his drug habit."

"And Harry cooperated, but was caught and forced to resign."

Eddie nodded. "After that he really got into the drugs and the booze. I tried to warn my folks, but by then they were so caught up with grieving for Roger and getting this lawsuit you're working on going, that they ignored everything else. And, I suppose, they didn't want to hear what I was saying."

"Was Harry the one who told you about having to resign?"

"No, it was Rog. Harry and I don't talk, hardly ever. He's got a mean streak, and it's gotten worse since he started doing drugs and drinking heavily. I don't blame Rog for what happened to Harry. He's smart, and he had the makings of a good surgeon, but he couldn't handle the pressure. Even if Rog hadn't put him in a position where he lost his job, he'd've crashed and burned sooner or later anyway."

"So after Roger died, you kept in touch with Jody?"

He poured more wine, drank deeply. "Yeah, I called her, said if there was anything I could do for her to let me know. She told me she was okay, but she didn't sound good, so I started calling once a week, and we'd talk. A couple of weeks ago she admitted that she had a key to his apartment and had found and read his personal journal. Trying to make sense of what happened, I guess. In the final entry there was a message for her, she claimed, something about an insurance policy. Now, Rog wasn't the kind of guy to take out life insurance, so I suspected what he meant. He wanted me to show her how to retrieve his files."

"And you did, of course."

"Yeah. She was mostly interested in the one labeled 'Project 'Zine.' Of course, there was a ton of stuff in the computer's memory besides that. I didn't have the time—or the heart—to go through all of it with her, so she had me walk her through the retrieval process a few times, and I guess she accessed the rest later."

I'd scanned the rest of the files, and could think of none that might be construed as insurance for Jody.

I asked, "You talk with her after that?"

"I called once. She sounded pretty bad—scared—and she cut the conversation short. After that I left messages, but she never got back to me."

Interesting. Jody must have been able to read more meaning into Roger's files than I had—enough to make her flee the city.

After Eddie left to be with his parents, I stayed in Roger's apartment, going over my interrupted plans for the day. Then I took from my purse the yellow sheet of scratch paper I'd found in J.D.'s raincoat and studied it. The abbreviations and words with question marks after them interested me—two in particular. Econ and TRG. Tessa Remington's E-mail address was trg: The Remington Group. And the newspaper account of her disappearance gave the name of her husband, Kelby Lincoln, CEO of a firm called Econium Measures.

I went to Roger's workstation, took the city directory from its drawer, and looked up both the firm and Lincoln. No listings. Next I called information, asked for listings in the Greater Bay Area. Again, none for Econium Measures, but there was a Kelby Lincoln in Atherton, on the Peninsula. I dialed the number, and the man who answered warily confirmed he was Remington's husband. But when I explained I would like to talk with him about his wife's disappearance, his tone hardened.

"I'm not interested, Ms. McCone."

"Please hear me out. I'm working for Glenn Solomon, the criminal-defense attorney, on an investigation of *InSite* magazine, one of the firms your wife's company has invested in—"

"And I suppose they want their funds and are claiming I've misappropriated them. Well, the hell with them."

"I'm not representing the people at the magazine. Quite the opposite, in fact. I've discovered some irregularities there, and wonder if they might have a bearing on Ms. Remington's disappearance."

A pause. "You say you're working for Glenn Solomon?"

"Yes. His office will verify—"

"That's not necessary. I take it you'd like to meet with me in person."

"If possible."

"I tell you what: I have a dinner appointment in Marin this evening. I could meet you for drinks in the city—say, around five-thirty."

"Good. Where?"

"Do you know the Beach Chalet?"

"Yes."

"It's on my route to the bridge. I'll meet you in the bar."

The Beach Chalet at the western end of Golden Gate Park, facing the Great Highway and the Pacific, is a San Francisco institution that has seen both good times and bad. Designed by noted local architect Willis Polk, and completed in 1925, it was originally conceived of as an elegant watering hole for day-trippers to what was then still the countryside. During the Great Depression, a WPA artist was commissioned to augment the grandeur by decorating the terra-cotta tiled ground floor with murals depicting vivid city scenes. The Chalet, however, never quite became the favored destination the city fathers had hoped it would, and by the time I first began visiting San Francisco, it was not a place where any sane woman would have ventured without a weapon or a strong male escort.

Upstairs, the Veterans of Foreign Wars, who had managed the building since World War II, held infrequent meetings. Downstairs was a dark, smoky bar where men in bikers' garb swilled drinks, played pool, and often laid one another out with their cues. The murals were coated with grime, the tiles sticky with miscellaneous vile substances. On one occasion my friends from Berkeley and I were forced to flee the patrons' wrath because one of our party was black. Finally even the bar closed, and the building stood fenced off and vacant; occasionally a rumor would circulate that a restaurant was negotiating a lease with the city, but it wasn't until the late 1990s that the Chalet re-opened. Now it—and the murals—are restored to their former splendor, with a Parks and Recreation Department visitors' center on the ground floor and a restaurant with sweeping ocean views on the second. Today it's a favored spot for locals, tourists, beach walkers, and anyone else who enjoys a good meal on the edge of the Pacific.

Kelby Lincoln had described himself to me—tall, blond, tanned, with gold-rimmed glasses—and when I entered the bar area I spotted him on a stool at one of the high tables that take advantage of the view over the diners' heads. He stood as I approached, nodding gravely; his handshake was weak, as if he feared contamination from another person's touch.

I slipped onto the opposite stool. Lincoln asked me what I wanted to drink and went to the bar. He was slender and fit looking, and his deep tan appeared to be of the saltwater variety. When he returned he squinted in the glare of the sunpath on the water and replaced his clear lenses with dark glasses.

"Have you found out anything about my wife's disappearance?" he asked.

"So far, nothing conclusive. But it appears to be linked to the other events I'm investigating, and I was hoping you might be able to shed some light on them."

"I'll be glad to help, if you think you can turn up something that may lead to Tessa. But the police and the detectives I hired"—he named a highly respected local firm—"had no success. The police investigation is on hold, and I terminated the detectives' employment last month. Since then I've been more or less waiting for the other shoe to drop."

"Meaning?"

"Well, whatever word I finally have of Tessa won't be good."

"Let's talk about the day your wife disappeared. You last saw her . . ."

"At breakfast. She planned to spend the day at her office, then attend a five-thirty meeting of the Committee for Wireless Privacy and come straight home."

"This committee—it's a nonprofit?"

"One of Tessa's causes. She feels strongly about abuse of the new technology. That night we were to meet friends for dinner at our club at eight, so when she wasn't home by seven-thirty I contacted the committee chairman. She said Tessa never arrived for the meeting. I called around to a number of her friends and associates, but none had seen or heard from her. In the morning I notified the police."

"Were any of her possessions missing?"

"None that I could tell. The police made me look through them thoroughly."

"I'm sure you've been asked this before, but was there trouble in the marriage?"

". . . Well, it was . . . a marriage. It had its ups and downs, but what marriage hasn't?"

"And you had no reason to suspect she might be seeing someone else?"

". . . No."

Interesting hesitations there. "Did anyone report anything unusual happening to Ms. Remington before she disappeared? Annoying phone calls, or someone following her, perhaps?"

"Nothing like that."

"Has anyone contacted you concerning her?"

He sighed wearily. "Oh, yes, people have contacted me. That's why initially I was reluctant to talk with you. I'd categorize them either as sickos or clairvoyants. The sickos claim they've seen her in such locations as a drug den in Seattle, an S and M club in Los Angeles, a lesbian bar in New Orleans. One of them—a cocaine dealer—asked for a million dollars to lead me to her body; I brought in the police and they had me set up a meeting, but he didn't show. The clairvoyants throw out hints—she's near water, she's being held in a cold, dark place—and want to collect a retainer before they'll reveal more. This experience has taught me a great deal about human nature, Ms. McCone."

"I imagine so. What about activity on her credit cards or bank accounts? Anything there?"

"Nothing at all. Originally that led me to believe she was dead. My wife is not a woman who can do without her creature comforts."

"You say 'originally.' Has something happened to make you think otherwise?"

"Yes, just today. Something I don't want to tell the police about." He swiveled his head, scanning the room from behind the dark glasses. It was cocktail-time crowded, and no one was paying any attention to us. "I don't know if I should be telling you this," he went on. "If Tessa turns up unharmed, it could ruin her professionally."

"I can keep a confidence."

"Legally?"

"I don't have the same status as an attorney when it

comes to confidentiality, but if the occasion merits it, I can have an extremely bad memory."

He thought about that for a moment, and it seemed to satisfy him. "Nominally I'm head of a corporation called Econium Measures. It's really Tessa's company. She uses it to hold and disburse investors' funds. I'm only a figurehead, don't know much about its operations, and only sign documents when she tells me to."

"Why is your name on it, then?"

"Legal reasons, she tells me. I've always suspected it's because she's more comfortable being able to introduce her husband as the CEO of something, rather than as a man who does nothing."

"Nothing at all?"

His face grew melancholy. "Nothing, according to her. I'm a classical pianist, although I've long ago lost my passion for performing. But I still compose, and a number of my works have been performed by others, both here and on the East Coast. Unfortunately, I'm not financially successful, so Tessa refers to music as my 'little hobby.' You asked earlier if there was trouble in the marriage. There is, and it stems from my lack of appropriate ambition."

And his wife's lack of appreciation for a pursuit that didn't bring in large sums of money.

When I didn't respond immediately, Lincoln knocked back what was left of his drink and took our glasses to the bar—buying time to get himself under control. I waited, looking out at the sea over the heads of early diners. The sun was sinking, orange now, and there wasn't a wisp of fog on the horizon. It would be beautiful at Touchstone tonight: daffodils and wildflowers blooming in the meadow that sloped to the cliff, the sunset gilding the pines. I hadn't been up there since early in March, and I was anxious to get back and begin putting the final touches to the new home Hy and I had built. . . .

Kelby Lincoln returned with fresh drinks. He'd taken off his dark glasses and without them his eyes looked deeply shadowed and vulnerable. He rubbed them before he replaced the lenses and said, "I'm sorry for unloading on you like that."

"No problem. Sometimes it's easier to confide your problems to a total stranger."

"Perhaps. Anyway, I was about to tell you about Econium Measures. It doesn't actually do anything except act as a clearinghouse for investors' funds, and its accounts can contain anywhere from a few dollars to eight figures; the amounts fluctuate weekly. Tessa handles every transaction herself, doesn't even have a staff."

"Isn't that unusual?"

"I wouldn't know. As I indicated, I don't really understand how she operates. But I do feel a certain responsibility to oversee things in her . . . absence, so a week after she disappeared I checked the account balances; they were huge, a total slightly over twenty-two million dollars. Her administrative assistant at the Remington Group, Steffi Robertson, explained that the week before she vanished Tessa had received a large influx of cash from the limited partners in three of her funds. It was sitting there, and the firms she was funding were waiting for her to disburse it."

"And as CEO, you can't do that?"

"No. The documents I sign have to be countersigned by my wife."

"So the funds're still in the accounts, and the companies're still waiting."

"The companies are still waiting. *InSite* magazine is on the verge of bankruptcy. But . . ."

"Yes?"

"The funds are gone. Apparently Steffi Robertson became worried that I might help myself to them. Somehow she obtained Tessa's passwords, and has been monitoring the balances. This morning she came to my home and accused me of looting the accounts over the weekend."

"Twenty-two million dollars, gone? How?"

"Electronically."

"Are you sure this Steffi Robertson isn't responsible?"

"I doubt it. She's one of those people with few aspirations of their own. And she's been with Tessa since she first formed the Remington Group. Besides, she immediately brought in a technician who so far has been unable to trace the funds, and she wanted to go to the police."

"I gather you persuaded her not to."

"Yes. Given her extreme loyalty to my wife, it hadn't occurred to her that Tessa herself may have emptied the accounts. When I mentioned that, she agreed to wait until the technician had exhausted all hope of tracing the funds."

"And how long will that take?"

"A few days, anyway."

I studied Kelby Lincoln; he looked weary and dejected—a man who had lost even his passion for his music. Not a man who could, or would, pull off a twenty-two-million-dollar scam.

"Tell me," I said, "do you have any reason to believe your wife disappeared voluntarily and has now moved those funds?"

He was silent for quite some time, toying with his empty

glass. "I have reason to believe," he finally replied, "that when it comes to money, my wife is capable of anything."

A chilling assessment from one's husband. But, as he'd said, Remington was a woman who required her creature comforts. Twenty-two million dollars was enough money to live well for several lifetimes. Or one lifetime, depending on what those particular comforts were.

Kelby Lincoln added, "So you see, Ms. McCone, the other shoe has already dropped."

"About time you turned your phone on, McCone." Adah Joslyn, sounding mightily irritated. "I've been trying to get you all afternoon."

"It was off?" I could have sworn that I'd left it on after I checked my office machine for messages while still parked in the lot at the Beach Chalet.

"Damn right it was off."

Not good. At some point I must've unconsciously silenced the cell. I resisted it, a birthday gift from my staff that I interpreted as their attempt to tether me. "Sorry," I told Adah.

"No skin off my pretty nose. But I finally got hold of Deputy Gil Martini at SFSD—he's handling this end of the Smith investigation. You can call him any time."

"Thanks. By the way, do you know anything about the Tessa Remington disappearance?"

"Officially that's in Missing Persons' bailiwick, but Homicide's keeping an eye on it. Why?"

"I just talked with her husband in connection with a job I'm doing for Glenn Solomon. Any chance Lincoln's responsible?"

"Doubtful. I read the reports, and he sounded pretty

straightforward. Admitted the marriage wasn't all it should've been, even offered to take a lie-detector test."

"Well, if you hear of any new developments, will you let me know?"

"If it's something I can give out, yes."

"By the way, how're you getting along with your star boarder?"

"What?"

"How're you getting along with Ted?"

"Don't mention that name to me. Just don't you mention it."

Adah hung up.

Now what was that about?

I continued driving along Fulton Street, Golden Gate Park to my right and the tidy expanse of the Outer Richmond to my left. I'd wait till I was back at the apartment to phone the local sheriff's deputy. Then I'd plan the evening's course of action—

The phone buzzed again. Damn tether. I glared at it before I answered.

"Sharon, it's Glenn. Where are you?"

"In my car, on the way back to where I'm staying. Why—?"

"Give me the address, and I'll meet you there."

His tone was urgent; I gave it to him without any questions.

"I'll be there in half an hour. Don't talk with anyone till I arrive." The line went dead.

More trouble. Of that I could be certain.

* * *

Glenn sampled the single-malt Scotch I'd set in front of him and nodded approval. "I needed that. Today has been hellish."

"You came from the Nagasawas'?"

"Yes."

"How're Margaret and Daniel bearing up?"

"In their usual stoical manner. Of course, they're caught up in making arrangements for getting proper care for Harry. Afterward, who knows? Margaret asked me to tell you they intend to call and thank you for pulling him off that cliff. And I thank you too."

"I only did what I had to. Do you know I met with Eddie earlier?"

"He told me."

"He's afraid his DNA contains a self-destructive gene."

"He mentioned that too. Thanks for reassuring him. He's a strong kid and likely to hold the family together through this. That's not what I want to discuss, however."

"What's happened?"

"A deputy from Tillamook County tracked me down at the Nagasawas'. You'd given my name as your client, and he was trying to locate you."

"Why?"

"An overnight bag with your name on it was found in an undisclosed location up there this afternoon. According to the deputy, it contained 'items that would tend to link Ms. McCone with the J.D. Smith murder.' What can you tell me about it?"

"The bag's probably mine. I dropped it outside Houston's cottage in Eagle Rock when I forced my way in. Later it was gone. I assumed Jody took it."

"You tell the sheriff's department about it?"

". . . No. So much else had happened that I forgot."

"What was inside the bag?"

"Standard overnight stuff, some notes on the case. Nothing that would make me out to be involved in the murder."

Glenn considered, sipping Scotch. "Well, something has them extremely interested in you. They wanted to fly a couple of investigators down here to question you tonight. I told them you were unavailable, but I'd have you in my office to talk with them at eleven tomorrow morning."

"Look, why don't I just call them and—"

Glenn made a staying motion with his hand. "No. I've spoken with a lot of law enforcement personnel over the course of my career, and I can tell perfunctory interest from the serious. These people are very serious, my friend. They have something major. Or are looking for something major. Besides, I don't allow my clients to meet with officials without benefit of counsel."

I nodded. Glenn had helped me out of a jam or two before. I would trust him with my life.

"In the meantime," he added, "you're to stay here. Do not go out, do not talk with anyone."

Instead of agreeing, I asked, "D'you think the press have gotten hold of this?"

"I wouldn't be surprised." He reached for the remote, flicked the TV set on. The local news was over, however, the national report just winding up. "Check the late broadcasts," he told me.

I showed him to the door, assured him I'd be at his office on time tomorrow. Then I went back to the living room and proceeded, as I'd planned, to line up the evening's activities.

* * *

Lia Chen, *InSite*'s Haven Maven, agreed to meet with me at Kodiak Rick's at seven. The billiards parlor-and-bar was on Third Street, in the shadow of the Central Skyway and near Moscone Convention Center. The large storefront had two smoky-glass windows facing the street, and each bore the neon outline of a wild-eyed, bushy-haired man in a fur parka and mukluks; a huge stuffed polar bear stood guard inside the door. When I entered the lounge—the walls of which were plastered with posters and signs for such places as Anchorage, Juneau, Barrow, and Skagway—I saw it was nearly deserted. In the silence I could hear the click of billiard balls in the adjoining room. Suzy Bivens, the bartender whom I'd interviewed last week about Roger, waved to me and pointed at a rear booth where Chen waited, nursing a beer.

"I guess," Chen said when I sat down, "you want to ask me why I was eavesdropping outside Max's office on Friday. At least that's what J.D. wanted to know when he came back into the building to get his raincoat. He sensed a story and was asking everybody questions, until Jorge chased him out of there."

"What kind of questions?"

She shrugged. "All I know is what he asked me. I told him that the employees all did plenty of eavesdropping. You had to, in order to stay on top of the situation."

"What situation?"

"Whether we'd have jobs from one day to the other. We all knew it was only a matter of time till the 'zine went under. And what I heard on Friday confirmed it."

"Jorge insisting on shutting down and Max resisting."

She nodded. "And now Jorge's had his way. He called a staff meeting Friday afternoon and laid everybody off.

They're not even going the bankruptcy route, just liquidating everything and returning what they can to the investors. Frankly, I'm glad to be out of there. It was getting way too weird."

"How so?"

"Paranoia. Infighting. Jorge paying the electric bill out of his own pocket but not really trying to rein in Max when he kept tapping the till for fancy food and drink. It was like Jorge didn't care if the operation went to hell, but he couldn't quite let go of it either." She looked around the bar and shivered as if she'd felt a sudden chill.

"What's wrong?" I asked.

"This place—it's eerie. A year ago on a Monday night it would've been packed. Now there are—what?—five other people here, including Suzy. For the past six months I've been hearing about folks who used to hang here running back to Des Moines and Omaha and Indianapolis with their tails tucked between their legs. And I'd say, 'Oh, no, not me. No way!' But now I'm thinking of heading to Modesto, moving in with my folks till I can find a position there."

"What about your book on *feng shui*? Isn't that bringing in some money?"

She laughed bitterly. "No, and it's no surprise. My target audience was the young and newly rich. But nowadays what laid-off dot-commer wants to shell out forty bucks for a coffee-table edition of something telling them how to arrange their surroundings to create greater harmony?"

"I'm sorry things have turned out badly for you."

"Thanks. I've always had lousy timing."

"About J.D.—did he ask you anything else besides the reason we saw you eavesdropping?"

"Well, he wanted to know about Kat Donovan, the head

of our research department. Apparently she said something to him outside the office after the fire alarm went off on Friday that struck him as strange, then took off without coming back to see what condition her workstation was in. I told him she'd been weird all week."

"In what way?"

"Distracted. Hyper. Normally Kat is calm and focused. She isn't a talkative person, and she very seldom brags—which is unusual in an organization where most people wave their egos like flags. But last Thursday we had lunch together and she told me she was coming into a lot of money and would be leaving the magazine. I asked if it was an inheritance, and she said no, she'd done something very clever and was soon to be handsomely rewarded."

I thought of the E-mails between Donovan and Dinah Vardon. She'd done a private research job for the Web-Potentate, but that was back in February.

"Did you ask Kat what this clever thing was?"

"Sure, but she wouldn't tell me. She just smiled coyly, shook her head, and finished her sandwich."

"You told J.D. about this conversation?"

"Yes. He was very interested."

I'd have to have a talk with the woman who called herself Sherlock.

The city of Alameda is actually an island southeast of Oakland, accessible by a tunnel running under the bay from Jack London Square. Formerly dominated by the largest military base in the Bay Area, the economy of its west end suffered when the naval air station was closed in 1997. But owing to San Francisco's high housing costs and the conversion of most of the base to private enterprise, it is gradually reviving. Trendy coffeehouses and cafés peacefully coexist with the old bars and diners along Webster Street, the west end's main shopping area; recreational facilities on the former military land attract residents from the more affluent east end, who in years past wouldn't have deigned to cross the boundary. But, as in any area undergoing transition, there are still pockets harboring poverty, crime, and danger; I was surprised to find that the address I had for Kat Donovan was in one of those.

The house was one story of faded pink stucco with a ridiculously short turret over the door—a gremlin's castle straight out of a Disney fairy tale. The front yard was surrounded by a chain-link fence and overgrown by high weeds. When I reached the gate I saw a FOR RENT sign in the front window.

The house was dark, the gate padlocked. A hedge screened it from the neighbors to the left, but on the right only a strip of driveway separated it from the lighted windows of the adjacent dwelling. Not a good place for trespass and, besides, the house looked vacant. After a moment I went next door and rang the bell.

The woman who peered through the screen was short, wearing a shapeless faded cotton dress and flip-flops. Her gray hair curled tightly, and her round face looked Southeast Asian. Filipino, I thought. My adoptive father had been a career NCO in the Navy, and from him I knew that many male citizens of the Philippines had joined up under the stewards' program, which guaranteed them not only steady employment but the opportunity to apply for U.S. citizenship. When the Navy pulled out of Alameda, many Filipino families stayed on, considering the island home.

"Yes?" the woman said.

"I'm sorry to bother you, but I'm looking for Kat Donovan. She gave me the address next door, but there's a For Rent sign in the window."

"Katty's gone. Moved out this morning. Damn rental agent couldn't wait to put up the sign."

"Do you know where she went?"

"Home to visit her folks, she said, then someplace warm. Didn't know where yet, told me she'd send a card when she got settled."

"You were friends, then?"

"Good neighbors. You know—we'd talk over the fence, stuff like that."

"Did she say why she was moving?"

"Got her notice from that magazine she worked for. They had a fire or some damn thing in their office Friday morning, and they decided to close down. What with the rotten job market here, Katty thought she'd do better someplace else."

"Do you know where her folks live?"

The woman shook her head. "Like I said, we was neighbors, that's all. I don't think she'll even bother to send me the postcard. That's just the kinda thing people say when they're leaving for good."

"Is there anyone in the neighborhood she was friends with?"

The woman shook her head. "Katty didn't have friends, not really. Took the bus in to the city, came home, and when she wasn't sleeping she was watching TV or running her errands. No boyfriends, no girlfriends, nobody." She hesitated, frowning. "Guess that's why I was surprised to see the blonde in the fancy car there on Saturday."

"A blond woman?"

"Uh-huh. Saturday night, she came in a fancy white sports car."

"What kind?"

"Do I look like somebody who knows fancy from fancy?"

"Can you describe the woman?"

"Blond, is all. My eyesight's pretty bad."

"What time did she arrive?"

"Around six. I thought she was an overnight guest, on account of she went in carrying this little suitcase, but she came out maybe ten minutes later, and she didn't have the case with her."

A blond woman in an expensive car delivering a small suitcase to another woman who was expecting to come into a lot of money. Most of the females involved in my investigation had dark hair.

Except for one: Tessa Remington.

Tessa Remington, who had disappeared and this weekend may have removed enough money from her company's accounts to fill many suitcases.

Dinah Vardon lived in a small cottage on Potrero Hill's Vermont Street, otherwise known as "the second most crooked street in the world"—the first being the block of Lombard between Hyde and Leavenworth on Russian Hill. Although tourists flock to Lombard, few of them know about Vermont; tonight the series of steeply sloping switchbacks was deserted. I coasted along and parked close to a concrete retaining wall bordering the dark, wooded park on the downside of the hill. As I got out of the car I heard rustlings in the underbrush that were not necessarily animal, and farther below the sound of a siren approaching S.F. General Hospital.

I crossed the pavement, climbed the steps of Vardon's cottage, and rang the bell. No answer, no lights in any of the windows. I would have liked to draw out Vardon about the research Kat Donovan had done for her, as well as Donovan's relationship with Tessa Remington, but that would have to wait for another time. And maybe it was just as well: I'd arrived here before coming up with a strategy that wouldn't involve telling her about Roger's "Project 'Zine."

Come to think of it, when *had* he retrieved the office E-mails in that file? The staff at the magazine worked long hours, and the tech department was always on call. As I'd seen last night, the process was not a quick or easy one. Roger would have needed access to the premises at times when no one was likely to be there, as well as a convincing excuse for his own presence.

I reached into the zipper compartment of my bag, found the keys I'd taken from the crimson bowl in his kitchen. Yes, the larger of the two could be to the double doors at *InSite*'s building. There was also a security system requiring a code, but if Sue Hollister was at home, I had an excellent resource in that department. The magazine had suspended publication; the offices would be deserted tonight.

At least till I arrived there.

At nine-thirty Dogpatch slumbered under the white glow of the new moon. I parked my MG a couple of blocks away from *InSite*'s building, in front of an apartment house that was being torn down. The balconies of the small units had already been removed, and the interiors of what had once been people's homes were nakedly exposed. The tenants must have fought their eviction, because someone had spray-painted on the facade, "Your time here is over. Move on!" I felt a sudden stab of sympathy for those with no place to go in an expensive and often inhospitable city.

As I walked along the street, broken glass crunched under my feet and figures moved silently in the shadows. The area had been reclaimed by the night people, and they were carrying on all sorts of clandestine activities mere yards away, but as long as I didn't bother them, they wouldn't be interested in me. Still, I clutched my keys firmly, points out—a useful weapon in lieu of the .357 Magnum that for the most part I keep in my office safe.

It was impossible to tell if anyone was inside the converted sewing factory; the only windows I'd noticed on Friday faced the rear alley and had been painted over. I slipped onto the loading dock and moved along slowly, shining my small flashlight at the logical places a system box would be located. Near the front entrance I spotted it; the installer's sticker read BARBARY COAST SECURITY, a small local firm. I dug out my cell and called Sue, whom I had contacted before driving over here and who was expecting to hear from me.

"It's one of Barbary Coast's installs," I told her.

"That makes it easy. I used to work for them. There should be a number on the box."

I peered up at it. "Nine-three-two-A."

"I use that model myself on some of my residential jobs. In fact, it's what I installed on your friend Paige Tallman's apartment. But first let me ask you: is this a B and E?"

"Not really. I have a key, but not the alarm code."

"And the key was given you by . . . ?"

"An employee." In a way.

"With the employer's authorization?"

". . . No."

"I'm not at all comfortable with this, Shar."

"Sue, it's got to do with J.D.'s murder."

That gave her pause. She'd dated him for a few months after he did a piece on her for the *Chron,* dubbing her "the first lady of S.F. security."

"In that case, I'll do it," she said. "It didn't work out with us, but we stayed friends. He was somebody you could count on. But promise me you'll keep me out of it if you get caught."

"If course."

"Okay, the key is to . . . ?"

"The front door."

"And the command panel is where?"

"Directly inside. But there's a second set of doors that you have to be buzzed through."

"Not if you're entering with a key, you don't. There's one command to turn off the alarm, then the key will work the inside door lock. What you're gonna do is override the system. I'm looking it up in my manual now, just to be sure. By the way, do you know you were mentioned on the six o'clock news?"

"The attempted suicide out at McKittridge Park?"

"Right. And there was also a teaser a while ago for the late broadcast—something about a suitcase linking you to J.D.'s murder."

"Dammit!"

"I wouldn't worry; it's probably nothing. They exaggerate to boost their ratings. Ah, here's what I'm looking for. You ready?"

"Give me a few seconds." I went to the edge of the loading dock and peered around. If anyone was watching me, it wouldn't be an upstanding citizen who would hustle to a phone and call the police. I dropped down to the pavement, went to the entrance.

"Okay," I said to Sue, "I'm ready."

"What you're gonna do is simple," she told me. "Stay cool, go slow, follow my instructions. We don't want you getting any more press than you already have."

"I'm in. Thanks, Sue."

"Don't mention it—to anyone."

"Not to worry." I broke the connection, stuffed the cell back into my bag, and waited for my eyes to adjust to the darkness. Small spotlights shone down from the vaulted ceiling above the work area, but they did little more than illuminate the girders. They were there for security reasons, but since people had come and gone at all hours, the building was probably not equipped with motion sensors that would trigger the alarm. I'd avoid passing through their beams, just to be on the safe side.

The offices were otherwise dark and silent. The work area looked much as it had on Friday, except that many of the desks were bare and white stains from the fire-retardant chemicals in the sprinkler system covered everything. The room had the muggy feel of a swamp and smelled faintly of mildew. I located my raincoat where Engstrom had draped it over the chair on Friday morning; it too was stained and spotted with the beginnings of mold. The coat was old and

I'd never much liked it anyway, so I left it there. Let the cleanup crews dispose of it.

As I passed the workstations I saw many had their drawers pulled out, and had been emptied of their contents. The laid-off staffers had made a hasty departure. I gave the desks only cursory attention before going upstairs. Vardon's office was at the end of the narrow corridor, two doors away from Engstrom's.

Desk and workstation against the side wall. Blue carpeting underfoot, still spongy. State-of-the-art computer with a huge screen—nothing but the best for the WebPotentate. Brushed chrome desk accessories, bookshelves loaded with technical manuals, Tensor desk lamp. I tried the lamp, found it hadn't shorted out in the deluge, and began going through the drawers. The desk was metal, and very little water had seeped inside.

The usual office items: pens, pencils, notepads, Post-Its. File drawer of assorted items: extra mouse pads, spare keyboard, two coffee cups, several tote bags, a pair of black high heels, a bag of Hershey's Kisses. Drawer above stuffed with papers; apparently Vardon's filing system was known only to her or nonexistent. Although I doubted she'd keep anything meaningful in such a jumble, I began going through it.

Interoffice memos, about as boring as the ones I circulated at the agency. Expense form for last month, half filled out. Flyer for a pizza restaurant, dollar-off coupon expired. Takeout menus, owner's manual for the Palm Pilot IIIxe. Fax from—

I knew that name. Barry Carver. Could it be one and the same? Yes, the address was correct. Years before, in the process of trying to add a new bathroom to my house,

Carver had practically trashed it. Now his letterhead bore a contractor's license number. My God, how had the state allowed *that* to happen?

The fax appeared to be an informal contract between Vardon and Carver, saying they mutually agreed that work on the property at 211 Water Street, scheduled to begin on March 1, be postponed until further notice. Too bad I couldn't warn her to get another contractor, but that would involve admitting that I'd broken in here and searched her office. . . .

Water Street. It sounded vaguely familiar. I had a Thomas Guide in the MG; I could pinpoint the address, drive over. Maybe Vardon had moved. But I'd have to hurry; it was now after ten, a marginally acceptable hour to drop in on someone.

No, I could see Vardon tomorrow, but I couldn't count on having the run of these offices again.

I went through all the desks on the second story and learned a few interesting facts: Jorge Amaya kept prophylactics in his upper right-hand drawer; Max Engstrom stocked enough Mylanta, Alka-Seltzer, and Beano to mix a potent cocktail; Lia Chen's publisher had turned down her proposal for a book on intimate urban gardens, and she had a drawer full of past due bills; the art director—title Leonardo da Picasso—doodled obscene caricatures of women on a scratch pad; one looked remarkably like the Money Mongrel. Interesting, but not particularly useful.

On my way out, I stopped by Kat Donovan's desk on the ground floor. All her personal effects were there. Sherlock had left town without returning to the office.

* * *

Eleven-ten. I was too keyed up to go back to the apartment, but it was late to pay Vardon a visit. Of course, my line of work gives me an excuse for appearing to have few social graces, and just showing up at odd hours puts the element of surprise on my side. Small wonder that I barely hesitated before consulting my guide and locating Water Street. It was a short block paralleling the Bay's shoreline, not far from the Islais Creek Channel on the southern waterfront. An industrial area in a very iffy part of the city. Odd place for Vardon to have bought property.

As I drove along Third Street, deep into the industrial core of the city, the pavement became crisscrossed by railroad tracks and deeply potholed. The night people were also out here, lurking in doorways of closed businesses and congregating under streetlights. They melted into the darkness as an SFPD car cruised slowly past.

I turned onto Twenty-fourth Street into an area nestled between Pier 72 and the Army Street Terminal, where shabby frame cottages stood side by side with warehouses and other business concerns. Most of the cottages appeared to be condemned, and the only lights that shone in the businesses were security spots behind the chain-link fences. A Doberman paced up and down in the yard of an auto body shop, spoiling for a reason to attack. Twenty-fourth dead-ended at Water Street, and as I turned, I recognized number 211.

It was the old Islais Creek Resort, more familiarly known as "the Last Resort" to those of us who had patronized it during its brief period of popularity. A weathered frame building that sagged above the water, it had a second-story restaurant deck and bar that had been the haunt of the more upscale clientele, and a downstairs bar and poolroom favored by the friends and associates of its owner, Tony Capello, an enterprising man who had conducted an astounding variety of illicit activities from the resort until his luck ran out and he began serving twenty-to-life at San Quentin. The main structure and several outbuildings—a boathouse where Capello had kept his cabin cruiser and the sheds that had housed ill-gotten gains—had been boarded up after his conviction, and I'd assumed they'd long ago been demolished. Now it seemed that Dinah Vardon had purchased and planned to remodel the resort.

But for what purpose? I couldn't imagine her in the role of restaurateur. And I doubted she was living there, given the building's obvious state of disrepair. All the same, I parked the MG and went exploring.

The downstairs windows were salt-caked and covered on the inside with the type of plastic that painters use to mask the glass. The door to the lower bar was chained and padlocked. A yellow plastic tape proclaiming DANGER... DANGER... DANGER... blocked the staircase to the upper deck. When I stepped over it, I realized why: many of the boards were loose or missing, and the structure wobbled under my weight. I paused, looking up, and saw that the glass door to the deck was not masked. Carefully I climbed, holding tightly to the railing.

The brightly painted tables and chairs and striped umbrellas that I remembered from past lunches there were gone from the deck; only a collapsed picnic table and empty flower boxes remained. I went to the door, took out my flashlight, and shone its beam around the interior. The bar and stools were still there, as well as a table that had blueprints spread out on it. Through an archway where batwing shutters hung, I saw a commercial cookstove.

I'd have loved to get a look at those blueprints but this door was padlocked like the one downstairs. I was good with locks, had a handcrafted assortment of picks that an informant had given me shortly before he went to prison for the third time. But idle curiosity was no justification for criminal trespass. Besides, if I wanted to know Vardon's plans for the resort, I could ask her. Its sale was a matter of public record.

I went back to the MG and decided to make another pass down the world's second most crooked street.

I was rounding the hairpin turn above Vardon's cottage when I saw a white BMW convertible pull into her driveway. Vardon was at the wheel, her head covered in a pale yellow scarf that the breeze whipped around at the nape of her neck. As the garage door rose, I pulled to the curb, got out, and hurried over there. Vardon glanced at me, registered irritated recognition, and drove inside. In a moment she came out, pulling off the scarf and stuffing it into her pocket.

"Well, Sharon McCone, supersleuth," she said, in a tone laced with sarcasm, "to what do I owe this pleasure?"

Fortunately I'd polished my cover story on my way over here. "I need to talk with you about J.D. Smith."

She frowned and tapped her foot impatiently on the pavement. "What about him?"

"Well, J.D. thought highly of you. In fact, he seemed . . . almost in awe. His landlady and I are organizing a memorial service, and I thought I might be able to persuade you to say a few words."

"You did?"

"Just a short tribute."

"And you say J.D. was 'in awe' of me."

"That's right. He was impressed by your talents. Especially impressed that you were taking on a big project like the Islais Creek Resort."

"How did he know about that?"

"Well, he was a reporter."

"Of course." She jiggled her keys, glanced at her watch. "Do you make it a habit of paying calls at almost midnight to ask people to speak at funerals?"

I widened my eyes. "Oh, no! Is it that late? To tell the truth, I was upset after the planning session with J.D.'s landlady and drove around for a while. I didn't notice the time."

"That's okay. I've been at a dinner party in Marin, and it's got me so wired that I won't sleep for hours. Let's take this inside. It's chilly out here."

Vardon led me up the steps and into the house. Its decor surprised me: velvet draperies, oriental carpets, flowered wallpaper, delicate antique furnishings. Not at all what I'd have expected of her.

She saw me looking around and said, "I didn't choose it. My former mother-in-law did. She died and left it to my ex-husband, who stuck me with it in the divorce settlement, while he kept the house on Maui that he inherited from his father." She sank onto one of the chairs, propped her booted feet on a spindly inlaid coffee table. "Look, do you want some coffee or juice? I can't offer you anything stronger; I don't drink or keep booze in the house."

I sat opposite her. "Nothing, thanks."

"So when's J.D.'s service?"

"Friday afternoon." There had been a message from Jane Harris when I'd earlier accessed my home machine.

"Where?"

"On the Marin Headlands. I'll let you know the exact spot later on."

Vardon considered, eyes coldly calculating. "I guess I could say a few words. J.D. could be a major pain in the ass and a sneaky bastard, but he also had his good points. Don't worry," she added, noting my disapproval, "I'll couch it in more flattering terms when the time comes. The two of you must've been good friends."

"For a lot of years."

"I guessed that. Otherwise you wouldn't've helped him out when he tried to get the skinny on *InSite*."

"What do you mean?"

"Come on, we both know J.D. wasn't after some puff piece on a P.I. solving a silly little manufactured mystery."

". . . Maybe."

"You can tell me about it."

I shook my head. "Confidentiality."

"Doesn't apply."

I made a show of reluctance before I said, "Okay, he suspected something was wrong at the magazine—something major that would make a good story. He was on to it when he went up to Oregon, but he didn't put anything down on paper, so I haven't a clue."

"Hmmm." Vardon looked skeptical. "Did it have to do with Tessa Remington disappearing?"

"Possibly. You're an intelligent woman; what do you think?"

"I have no opinion."

"About Ms. Remington?"

"About anything."

"You must. Even Roger Nagasawa suspected something was wrong at the magazine."

"Roger? What do you know about him?"

"For one thing, that you were involved with him."

"Oh, for God's sake, I was in high school! That was over years ago. You know, for someone who spent only a few hours on the premises you certainly know a lot about *InSite* personnel."

"It was a very fruitful few hours. When I was talking with Kat Donovan she told me she did some research for you."

Vardon frowned. "What of it? I often used Kat's services. In this case I was considering making some investments and was interested in market trends, so she put a package together for me."

"Was one of those investments the resort?"

"Yes, it was."

"And you bought it when?"

She hesitated. "In March."

Wrong. Barry Carver had been scheduled to start work on March first. Why would she lie about that?

"D'you plan to reopen it?"

"Good God, no! The restaurant business is the last thing I'd involve myself in. I plan to live in the building and operate a consulting firm out of it." Vardon stood. "I think we'd better wrap this up now. I've got a long, difficult day tomorrow, clearing out my office and settling matters with Jorge and Max. To say nothing of polishing up my résumé."

And my day promised to be difficult too—beginning with the interview with the detectives from Tillamook County. I told Vardon goodnight and headed across town to my temporary home.

Tuesday

•

APRIL 24

Sleep wouldn't claim me. I walked the floor through the early hours of the morning. My emotions, which had been burning at a white-hot pitch for two weeks, had cooled. I felt in control, levelheaded—and in the grip of obsession.

The object of my obsession was a familiar one: the truth.

I moved about the apartment slowly, taking in small details of the rooms, concentrating for minutes at a time on the weave of a drapery, the texture of the plaster, the pattern of the bricks of the fireplace.

Emotion, I thought, is fast and hot—and deadly to you. Obsession is slow and cold—and deadly to others.

I often felt this way when the facts began to dovetail with my theories. Today, I sensed, I would uncover the truth and recognize it for what it was.

The Tillamook County sheriff's investigators were already at Glenn's offices when I arrived shortly before eleven. Tom Scanlon and Dave Parsons. A matched pair in their forties who looked remarkably alike, their manner was polite and professional; their eyes sized me up shrewdly while Glenn made the introductions. We took seats around the table in his conference room, Scanlon set up a recorder, and we began.

Parsons produced my travel bag from under the table, and I identified it. He asked, "Will you tell us how it came to be out of your possession?"

I explained about dropping it outside Houston's cottage on Friday night. Parsons then asked me about its contents, and I described them.

"You flew to Portland, Ms. McCone?"

"Yes, on the eight o'clock shuttle."

"And rented a car?"

"From National." Of course they would already have checked with the airline and rental-car company.

"When did you return to San Francisco?"

"Late Saturday afternoon, the four o'clock flight."

Glenn said, "Gentlemen, may I ask why you're questioning my client about her travel arrangements?"

Scanlon said, "We're trying to establish a time line."

"To prove what?"

I said, "Glenn, I don't mind answering their questions."

He shot me an exasperated look, but didn't say anything else.

Scanlon took over the questioning now. "There's a four-hour period between the time our department finished taking your statement and when you caught your flight home. What did you do during that period?"

"An officer drove me from Tillamook to Eagle Rock, where I'd left my rental car. That took . . . well, you'd know better than I. Then I drove to Portland, which took over two and a half hours because of heavy traffic. I dropped off the car, arranged for my flight, and went straight to the gate."

"No stops? Snack bar? Ladies' room?"

Glenn said, "Detective Scanlon, is this necessary?"

I said, "No stops. I didn't want to miss my flight."

"Now"—Glenn's voice overrode the beginning of Scanlon's next question—"Ms. McCone's been forthcoming with you. It's your turn to be forthcoming with us."

The two exchanged glances. Parsons nodded. "Fair enough. This bag was recovered from a trash receptacle in one of the ladies' rooms at the airport. According to the maintenance schedule, it was placed there sometime after noon and before midnight on Saturday."

"And its contents?"

"As Ms. McCone describes them. Except there was a knife wrapped in a bloody pair of jeans and T-shirt. The blood on the clothing and the knife is a match for J.D. Smith's."

I shut my eyes, again saw the stains on his sweater, the jagged tear. It would have been difficult to pull the knife from his chest without getting covered in blood.

I asked, "What color were the jeans and tee?"

"The jeans were pale blue," Parsons said, "the tee white."

"Not mine. Was there also a pair of black jeans and a matching tee?"

"No."

"Ms. McCone," Scanlon said, "do you own a set of kitchen knives?"

I did—a very good set of German manufacture. The last time I'd cooked they were all there, but that had been a while ago. If someone wanted to frame me for J.D.'s murder . . .

A coldness crept over me. I'd had a client who had been tried and convicted on weaker evidence than that.

Glenn said, "I'm instructing my client not to respond to that line of questioning, unless you're prepared to charge her."

With a show of reluctance, Scanlon backed down. "I would like to ask Ms. McCone to recap her statement about the investigation that took her to Oregon."

"I'm sure you would, but you have her statement on file."

"There's additional information we need—"

"Sir, that was a confidential inquiry, conducted at my request. Ms. McCone is not only my client but my employee. I'll have to ask you to limit any further questions to matters contained in her statement."

Legal privilege. How many times I'd been frustrated by it. How fully I embraced it now.

"They don't really suspect me of killing J.D., do they?" I asked Glenn.

He shook his head, biting into one of the deli sandwiches the office gofer had brought in after the detectives departed. "I know how these people think. From the remainder of their questions, I gather their theory is that Houston killed Smith, cleaned up before you arrived there. Hid the knife in her bloody clothing and took the bundle with her when she saw an opportunity to slip out of the house. She picked up your travel bag on the way, drove south. Abandoned her car where they located it down the coast in Newport, hitched a ride to the airport in Portland, dumped the bag, and flew to God-knows-where."

"So why come all the way down here to talk with me?"

"That was a fishing expedition. And they don't know you, so they have to cover all the bases. They must not have much evidence, though, if they're clutching at straws like that."

I took a bite of corned beef on rye, pushed the food aside. "So what did they hope to accomplish with me?"

"They're aware you withheld details of your investigation when you made your statement, and feel one of them may contain a potential lead. They probably hoped they could intimidate you into giving everything up. Of course, they didn't count on my forceful protection of your rights."

"I admit it shook me at first when they asked if I owned a set of knives, but when you think about it, it's not logical that I'd carry one around with me. Most likely the killer took the knife from Houston's kitchen, but they haven't been able to match it to any of the others that're there."

"You say 'the killer,' not Houston."

"She claims she didn't do it."

"And you believe her?"

"I'm not sure."

"Let me tell you, my friend, they always claim they didn't do it. That was the reality I had the most difficulty dealing with when I was new to the profession: the clients were so damned guilty and such good liars."

"And now?"

"I still have my sleepless nights." He balled up the wrapper his sandwich had come in and lobbed it at the wastebasket. It missed by a good two feet. "No, I don't think you have to worry about their question about the knife. I would, however, take an inventory of your set without delay."

"And if one is missing?"

He flashed me his wolf look. "I can't advise you on that, but I know what I'd do."

Lawyers!

My brown-shingled house looked peaceful and sleepy in the afternoon sun; there wasn't a press van or lurking reporter in sight. Still, I pulled the MG into the garage and glanced around as I hurried up the front steps. I expected the interior to feel stuffy on what had turned into a warm day, but instead a fresh breeze filtered down the hallway. Michelle Curley must've decided to air it out.

I hurried to the living room, where a tidy stack of mail and newspapers sat on the sofa. Through the archway to the kitchen I could see my knife rack; two were missing, and a loaf of sourdough that I didn't remember buying sat on a board by the sink—

In the bathroom down the back hall the toilet flushed. Water ran in the sink. I stiffened, stepped back from the arch. Listened as heavy footsteps shuffled toward the kitchen. Not Michelle or her petite mother—a man. Hy, back from the Philippines? No, not yet. An intruder . . . ?

I peered around the archway. Ted entered, looking unkempt and dejected. He went to the sink, picked up a knife from the counter, and began slicing the bread.

Relief was quickly followed by a sense of violation. I stepped into the room, hands on my hips, and demanded, "What the hell're you doing here?"

He started and turned. "Shar, you scared me!"

"Well, you scared me too, so we're even. How come you're here, and not at the office?"

"I didn't feel well, so I took the afternoon off."

"And?"

"I didn't have anyplace to go. Mick said you were away for a few days and loaned me his key."

"I take it you and Neal are still on the outs."

"Yeah. And Adah and Craig threw me out. Last night I crashed with a couple of other friends, but their place is awfully small, and I could tell I was wearing out my welcome."

He looked so hangdog that I couldn't stay angry. "Well, feel free to use the guest room here."

"Are you sure it's okay?"

"I wouldn't say so if it weren't."

He sighed and set the knife down, leaned against the counter.

I asked, "Have you talked with Neal?"

"Once. After Adah and Craig threw me out . . . D'you know I barfed on his new SUV?"

"Uh-huh."

"God, I still can't believe I did that. Anyway, the next evening I went to the apartment to patch things up with Neal. But he had some guy there—handsome guy, no less—and he told me I'd have to leave. He and the guy went into his study while I packed up some stuff. Neal came out and asked where I'd be staying, and I told him Adah and Craig's. Then I got out of there before he could ask for my key back."

"He introduce you to this guy?"

"No. He acted kind of preoccupied."

"But not angry?"

"Not really. I decided to give him some space over the weekend, then try to talk with him again. But every time

I've called the phone's been tied up, and Craig says he hasn't tried to reach me at their place."

"I can't believe he'd just move somebody else in."

"Neither can I. But if he wants to, he can; it was his apartment originally, and his name's the only one on the lease."

"What about Adah and Craig? Since you went back there, I gather the barfing incident wasn't why they threw you out."

"No, it was the thing with the cat."

"Charley? Because you're allergic to him?"

"No. I insulted him."

"How on earth can you insult a *cat*?" It certainly wasn't possible with Ralph or Alice; a creature that feels it's the center of the universe is impervious to insult.

"Actually, Adah took offense for him. When she fed him a leftover filet mignon that I'd been eyeing for my lunch the next day, I told her the cat was a pig and if she didn't stop stuffing him someday he'd choke to death and she'd find him lying facedown in his food bowl like an enormous beached whale."

With a perfectly straight face I said, "Why, you swine. You dreadful swine of a skunk."

He frowned, then burst out laughing as he realized I was making fun of his own outrageously mixed metaphor. He began making noises like Ralph does when he's trying to bring up a hairball, and I began snorting like Alice does when she gets foxtails from the neighbors' weedy yard stuck up her nose.

"Lord," he said, "if you can't laugh . . ."

"I know." I got myself under control, asked, "So d'you want me to stop by and see what's going on with Neal?"

"If you wouldn't mind."

"No problem. In the meantime, make yourself at home. The neighbor kid—"

"Michelle. I've already met her. She wants to play gin rummy later."

"Don't play for money; she's a card shark, is investing her winnings."

"Young kid like that?"

"Yes, and she tells me it's only seed money."

"Saving up for a car?"

"Real estate. She claims land is where the money's really at. By the way"—I motioned at the rack—"have you seen the midsized knife?"

"In the sink. Why?"

"Long story, and I've got to go now. Will you please rest up so you can go back to work tomorrow, before the agency falls apart?"

Before I went by Telegraph Hill to check on Neal, I wanted to stop in at the office to see what manner of chaos might be reigning there. I hadn't been flattering Ted when I'd said the agency would fall apart without him; his calm and efficient presence was essential to its functioning properly, and any number of bizarre incidents had occurred on the few occasions he was absent. Today I was pleasantly surprised to find Julia monitoring the phone lines while she studied a handbook on skip tracing, and the others working quietly at their desks.

I gathered my message slips, went to my office, and returned a few phone calls. Then I took out the scribbled piece of paper that I'd found in J.D.'s raincoat pocket—tattered now from many handlings—and studied it once again.

One of the unfamiliar notations caught my eye: Afton. The English river of song? A woman's name? A company?

I went down the catwalk to the office Mick and Charlotte shared. She'd stepped out, but he was industriously typing. I peered over his shoulder at the screen, saw he was running a property search for a low-priority investigation, and said, "Put that aside for a while, will you?"

"Gladly." He saved the information and put the computer into sleep mode. "What d'you need?"

"Afton. A-f-t-o-n. What is it?"

"Can't you give me more to go on than that? I mean, it's just a word."

"Yes, it is."

"Oh, one of those." His eyes narrowed in concentration as he began formulating a way to proceed.

I looked at my watch. "I'm on my way out. I'll check with you in an hour or so."

A slow smile spread over his face. "Your cell on?"

"Yes. Why?"

"What's it worth to you if I have the info in less than an hour?"

"You know, I'd be better off putting you on a cash-incentive program than buying you all these restaurant meals."

"I'd probably be better off too. Sweet Charlotte tells me I'm getting fat."

True enough. He *had* bulked up a bit. "So let's talk about it. Have you put together those figures on the computer forensics program yet?"

"They'll be on your desk tomorrow morning."

"We'll talk then. Be prepared to bargain hard."

* * *

Ted and Neal's apartment was in an elegant art deco building on Plum Alley, a narrow half block in the shadow of Coit Tower at the top of Tel Hill. When no one answered my knock, I took the elevator back down to the ground floor—mesmerized as always by the rippling effect of light through its glass-block enclosure—and crossed the tiled courtyard to the unit of the manager, Mona Woods. Mrs. Woods, an athletic septuagenarian who today had three pencils and a pair of reading glasses anchored in her thick, upswept white hair, welcomed me warmly.

"Perhaps you can tell me what's going on up there." She motioned toward the third floor.

"What do you mean?"

"I haven't seen Ted in days. Another young man began coming and going at all hours since last Thursday. And yesterday afternoon I saw Neal and the new one carrying in some boxes. Don't tell me he and Ted have broken up?" Mrs. Woods looked genuinely distressed; she took a personal interest in the lives of her mixed bag of tenants.

"They had a falling-out, but it isn't like Neal to simply move someone else in. Of course, he hasn't been himself since he had to give up the bookshop. D'you know where he is today?"

"He left a couple of hours ago. With the new one. Probably to get more boxes." She sniffed disdainfully.

"If you see him return, will you give me a call?"

"I certainly will, dear. No one wants to get to the bottom of this business more than I. Ted and Neal are meant to be together—even if they're both too stubborn to admit it."

* * *

When my cell rang, I was maneuvering back and forth to extricate the MG from the tiny space where I'd wedged it at the end of the alley. My foot slipped off the brake as I reached for the unit, and the front end banged into the rubber bumper of the car in front of me. Startled, I took my other foot off the clutch, which stalled the engine. Then I dropped the phone and had to double over looking for it on the passenger-side floor.

Sometimes I wondered how I could be such a klutz when answering a simple phone call in a type of vehicle I'd been driving since I was sixteen, yet fly a plane while minding the radios and other instruments in a manner Hy described as "graceful."

Mick. "Count this as one more bargaining chip in my pile."

"Show-off. What've you got?"

"Afton Development. Headquartered in Atlanta, Georgia. Isn't *InSite* magazine located in Dogpatch?"

"Right."

"Well, there's your tie-in. Afton's been buying up large and small parcels there for an office-and-residential complex, as well as a hotel. On the quiet, because they don't want to get the residents in an uproar—especially the Hell's Angels, whose clubhouse they covet."

I told him the location of *InSite*'s building. "How is it positioned relative to the properties they've already acquired?"

A pause. "Right smack in the middle."

I thought of Charlotte's statement that sometimes investors wanted a company to fail because it had valuable assets that could be sold off. Remembered Jorge Amaya telling Max Engstrom that the building was the only tangible asset they owned. Had Amaya forced the magazine into failure in order to make a lucrative deal with Afton Development?

The magazine's doors stood open, but the ground-floor work area was empty. Gone were the desks and the computers, the chairs and tables. Cardboard boxes were scattered here and there, filled with what looked to be the personal belongings of employees who had not yet bothered to remove them. I continued toward the rear and up the staircase to the loft. At first I thought nobody was there, then I heard a squeak that sounded like a chair turning in Engstrom's office.

The stocky publisher sat with his back to the door, staring out at the floor below. I cleared my throat and he swiveled to face me. He looked as if he hadn't changed his rumpled shirt and chinos in days; deeply shadowed circles bagged under his eyes. In his right hand he held a tumbler full of clear liquid, and a gin bottle stood on the desk.

"Ms. McCone. How kind of you to attend the wake."

I went over and looked down at the main floor. From here the scene was even more desolate. The stains from the fire-retardant chemicals outlined where the furnishings had stood. Trash was scattered across the floor and drifted in the corners. Without the staffers and their bustle of activity, the building was merely another abandoned factory waiting to be demolished.

"Sit," Engstrom said. "Join me in a toast to the demise of an excellent publication."

I took a chair, poured a small amount of gin into a

smudged glass. Raised it and pretended to drink. "I'm sorry things turned out this way."

Engstrom rubbed his eyes. "Ah, who am I kidding? *In-Site* was a shitty publication. All these online rags are. Short on intellectual content, long on nonsense. But why should they be otherwise? Consider the readership. God knows, in fifty years no one'll remember what a real magazine or newspaper looked like."

"I don't think it's that drastic."

"Maybe not, but the world's changing—and not for the better."

"What will you do now?"

"I haven't a clue. I do know one thing: I'm through with journalism and this city. I own a small cabin in Siskiyou County. Maybe I'll hole up there and take another stab at writing the great American novel." His lips curled mirthlessly.

"Did the fire department figure out why the sprinkler system went off?"

"Someone had tampered with it."

"Who, do you think?"

"Doesn't matter now."

"You're really through with all this, aren't you? You didn't waste any time getting rid of the furnishings and equipment."

"*Jorge* didn't waste time. He's anxious to move on."

"Where to?"

"Greener pastures. A new challenge. Who knows? Or cares?"

"And you just went along with his decision."

"I didn't have much choice, given the extent of the damage. I knew we couldn't keep going. Jorge had already been talking about suspending publication, so I struck a deal with him that will allow me to get out with my initial investment intact. It isn't much, but the cabin's paid for and the taxes on it are low. If I'm careful, I should be able to get by for some time. That's better than the other investors will do."

"Really? What about the proceeds from the sale of this building?"

"Who would want it, given its condition and environs?"

"Afton Development."

"Who're they?"

Good God, had the man been so absorbed in his own games and power trips that he hadn't realized what was going on around him? "An Atlanta firm. They're buying up most of Dogpatch for a big project."

Engstrom's face went rigid as what I'd said sank in. "They never approached me," he said, "but I'll bet Jorge knows about this. He's been telling me we'll never be able to unload this building. Part of my deal is that I sign a quit-claim on my interest in it."

"I wouldn't, if I were you."

"It's already signed. He's screwed me."

"But if you agreed because he falsely represented—"

"In private. His word against mine, and who's going to believe a broken-down old hack like me?" His hand shook as he set his glass on the desk.

"Maybe it's not that hopeless—"

"No, the son of a bitch screwed me but good." Engstrom's eyes flashed with anger, and he rose, balling his fists. "That was the plan all along—sabotage the operation, force me out with a few bucks, take the money and run. He set me up and he screwed me, but he's not gonna get away with it!"

"Max—" I stood up, put out a hand, but he was already moving across the office. By the time I caught up with him he'd reached the stairway. I grabbed his arm, but he pushed me back and started down. I went after him. He swatted at me, knocking me to the side; my hand missed the railing and I fell against the step behind me, taking its edge in the small of my back. Pain shot up to my neck, down to my knees. By the time I recovered, Engstrom was out the front door.

He was going after Amaya, of course, and in his enraged and drunken state a confrontation would be dangerous to both of them. Groaning, I pulled myself up from the steps and hobbled outside. My back felt like a white-hot knife were being driven into it, but I doubted I'd sustained any serious injury. Painkillers, which I harbored in large quantities for just such emergencies, would get me through till I could see my doctor. The important thing now was to warn Amaya.

In the car I checked the list of *InSite* employees' addresses and phone numbers. Amaya lived on the 1000 block of California Street—Nob Hill. I punched his number into my cell as I started the MG, got a busy signal. All the way across town—disobeying my own dictum against phoning and driving—I hit the Redial button, but got the same result each time.

Amaya's apartment was in a highrise that spoke of wealth and privilege, at the top of the hill near Grace Cathedral and Huntington Park. Many stories of glass and stone, with a canopied entrance, and topped by a roof garden where full-size palms swayed. Parking in that rarefied part of the city has always been problematical, and today was no exception. I finally located a hideously expensive public garage a few blocks away and walked up there, my back protesting violently with every step.

Either the building didn't have a doorman or he was on break. I dialed Amaya's apartment on the intercom, received an immediate answering buzz. Curious that he hadn't bothered to ask who was there. The elevator was a high-speed model and delivered me to the sixteenth floor in minutes. Although the thickly carpeted hallway was deserted, a door at its far end stood open, and through it I heard Amaya's agitated voice. As I approached I made out the words "liability" and "want you here when the police arrive."

I picked up the pace, ignoring the pain in my back, and stepped through the door into a granite-tiled entryway. Ahead was a large living room with French doors open to a balcony; a breeze scattered petals from a pewter vase of red roses across the gleaming surface of a grand piano. Amaya stood halfway between me and the piano, cordless receiver to his ear, and on the floor lay Max Engstrom, moaning, his head bloodied. His left arm was twisted at an odd angle.

I said to Amaya, "Hang up."

He whirled toward me. "You! What are you doing here? I thought you were the paramedics. Go away. I am having a private conversation with my attorney."

"You've already told him to get over here. Now hang up!"

He hesitated, said into the receiver, "Fifteen minutes, no later," then did as I'd told him.

I knelt beside Engstrom. He was in a twilight state, halfway between consciousness and unconsciousness. "What happened here?" I asked.

Amaya looked nervous, but he was calmer now and seemed inclined to cooperate. "I was on the phone with my broker when my houseman let Max in. He came at me, shouting that he would kill me. We struggled, I grabbed his arm. It snapped, but he kept after me. And then John—John Hernandez, my houseman—hit him with a stone bookend."

I looked around, spotted the bookend under a table next to a black leather sofa. "You called the paramedics. What about the police?"

"Not yet. I wanted to allow enough time for my attorney to arrive. Why are you here? What is your connection with Max?"

I ignored his questions. "Make sure you call the police when the paramedics get here. Where is your houseman now?"

"In his room."

"How do I find it?"

"There is no reason you should talk with him."

"Let me be the judge of that."

Engstrom moaned again; he was coming around. I put my hand on his shoulder, said, "It's going to be okay, Max. The paramedics are coming."

Amaya said, "Do you know why he tried to kill me?"

"We don't have time for this now. Look after Max, but don't move him. Head injuries can be tricky. Now, where's your houseman's room?"

Amaya's expression said he'd like to tell me to go to hell, but after a moment he relented. "Down the hall, across from the kitchen." He motioned to his right.

"Okay, I'm going to talk with him. As far as the police are concerned, I'm not here. Do you understand?"

He hesitated, then nodded.

The intercom buzzed—the paramedics, finally arriving.

Amaya said, "You owe me an explanation—"

"Not now. When the police ask to question Hernandez, you come get him. I'll wait in the kitchen. Then we'll talk."

"But—"

Another buzz. "Just let them in. He needs immediate attention."

. . . that private investigator who keeps showing up when tragic things happen—or almost happen—to people . . .

The newscaster's words echoed in my mind as I went along the hallway to the room across from the kitchen. I couldn't withstand any more of that kind of publicity, and I hoped I hadn't been wrong in trusting Amaya not to give away my presence to the police.

The door to the room stood open. I knocked on the frame, and a slender, dark-haired man looked up from the suitcase he was packing. "Not a good idea, Mr. Hernandez," I said. "The police will want to talk with you."

Hernandez's thick brows drew together in a scowl. "Who're you?"

I showed him my ID.

"Private cop? You can't keep me here."

"Where're you going to go? By now the paramedics are on their way up, and the police won't be far behind."

He threw a couple of shirts into the suitcase and slammed its lid shut. "There's a service elevator—"

"I wouldn't."

"Look, I don't trust Amaya."

"If you're concerned about being charged with assault, don't be. I'm sure Mr. Amaya will back you up."

"Maybe he will, maybe he won't. Never trust an asshole."

"Why is he an asshole?"

"Because he treats me like dirt, and I'm fuckin' fed up with it. I wouldn't put it past him to side with Engstrom."

"After you saved his life?"

"Their kind, they stick together. Engstrom's an asshole too. All Amaya's friends are. And those women of his—bitches."

"A lot of women?"

"Only two that I know of. The first, that Dinah, she looked right through me—till she wanted something, and then she'd demand, no please or thank you. One time I spilled some water on her and she tried to slap me. And Tessa, she'd stop talking as soon as I walked into the room. Had better manners than Dinah, I'll give her that, but she was one cold broad."

So Amaya had been having an affair with both Dinah Vardon and Tessa Remington. Interesting.

"How long was Mr. Amaya involved with these women?"

"Well, Dinah was around when I came to work a year ago. Then all of a sudden, in June, she was gone and the other one took her place. Tessa was married, so she wasn't here nearly as much."

So that was the reason for the barbed exchange I'd witnessed between Amaya and Dinah: they'd been lovers, and he'd broken off with her for Tessa. "You seem an observant man, Mr. Hernandez. Did you ever hear Tessa or Mr. Amaya mention a company called Afton Development?"

"Well, sure. He's on the phone to them all the time."

"You overhead any of those conversations?"

"I was *paid* not to hear them."

I took a twenty from my wallet, extended it to him.

"*Well* paid."

I added another.

"Okay," he said, "I can't give you the exact words, but I figure Amaya has a deal to sell them some property. There was front-end money put up, a lot of it, back in February. And Tessa must've been involved, because she disappeared around that time, and Amaya's been stalling them ever since. They must've pressured him pretty bad, because he's been real nervous, and last Thursday he told them he was going to wrap up the deal within a couple of weeks."

"You're sure the up-front money was put up in February?"

"Yeah, Valentine's Day. How I remember is Amaya kept me busy running out for flowers, champagne, fancy food. Tessa was coming over that night. When I got back from the last trip, he was on the phone to the Afton people, telling them to wire the money to an account at some company."

"You remember the company's name?"

"It was one of those names that sounds good, but doesn't tell you what they do. Actonium . . . Uranium . . . no—Econium. Econium Measures." Hernandez hefted the suitcase. "It's been nice gossiping with you about my ex-boss, but I got an elevator to catch."

* * *

Amaya was furious with me when he came to fetch the houseman so the police could question him—so furious that I was afraid he would give my presence away. But he left me in the kitchen and, with the help of his attorney and the stockbroker with whom he'd been talking when Engstrom attacked him, made relatively short work of satisfying the law. Afterward he summoned me to the living room, where he and his attorney, Sid Curtis, proceeded to pace around, ranting at me. I sat on the sofa, reflecting that their behavior resembled the pointless activity of caged animals.

"Gentlemen," I finally said, "what did you expect me to do—tackle Hernandez and tie him up with the bedsheets?"

Sid Curtis whirled on me, thrusting out an accusatory index finger. "You know, I'm not unfamiliar with your reputation. You've subdued larger men than Hernandez and lived to brag about it."

I studied him: a small man with curly hair that stuck out at all angles from finger-combing. I was not unfamiliar with his reputation either: he had a tendency to bully anyone who opposed him.

I said, "I do not brag. Plenty of journalists have been willing to do that for me. Besides, I wasn't here today, so how could I have subdued Hernandez?"

"What the hell does that mean?"

"I also couldn't have had a very interesting conversation with him about your client's romantic life." I glanced meaningfully at Amaya, saw his lips tighten.

Curtis turned to him. "What's she talking about?"

"She was not here today, Sid. And now, if you'll excuse us, Ms. McCone and I need to talk privately."

"You are not talking with her outside my presence."

"You forget yourself, Sid. I am the client. I say what happens and what does not happen."

"You want me to leave you in the hands of this—"

"Watch it, Sid," I said. "I've subdued larger men than you."

"What did John tell you?" Amaya demanded when his attorney had left.

"That you were having an affair with Dinah Vardon and broke it off for Tessa Remington. How did Dinah react to that?"

Amaya hesitated, probably considering a blanket denial, then shrugged. "How do you think? She is a typical vengeful woman, and she made my life difficult whenever she could."

"John also said Tessa was supposed to visit here the night she disappeared, February fourteenth."

He flushed. "Damn him!"

"She never arrived or called, did she?"

"No. She had plans with her husband and some friends, which she intended to cancel at the last minute. When she didn't arrive, I assumed she hadn't been able to beg off. But when she didn't call with an explanation, I began to worry. We were to go over the final details of a joint business venture, and then we planned to celebrate. It is not like Tessa to walk away without concluding a transaction."

"Was this venture the sale of *InSite*'s building to Afton Development?"

Amaya started, then regrouped, smiling thinly. "Ah, you are quite the detective, Ms. McCone." He sat on a chair opposite me and took a cigar from a humidor on the coffee table. His hands shook slightly as he prepared and lighted it.

"Mr. Hernandez also told me you directed Afton to deposit up-front money in one of Econium Measures' accounts."

He regarded me through a haze of smoke. "I do not have to discuss my private business dealings with you."

"No, but it would be wise, in light of Tessa's disappearance. Given the fact that you were sleeping with her, plus the fact that Max came after you because he found out about the Afton deal, the police might want to take a closer look at your recent activities."

"Are you blackmailing me, Ms. McCone?"

"Advising you, perhaps."

He hesitated, considering his options. "Very well. I will explain, so you will not misconstrue what Tessa and I were attempting to accomplish. One of my functions at *InSite* was to restrain Max from his excesses. Unfortunately, he is a headstrong and overbearing man, and I had little success in that area. The magazine was losing money, and when it became apparent it would fail, Tessa grew concerned for her limited partners and decided, in effect, to kill it."

"Not a very straightforward way to do that, having you stage incidents like the bogus fire last Friday."

No response.

"I know you were responsible for them. And I can understand your reasoning. If the company was in less than total ruins, you might have received pressure from Engstrom or the limited partners to declare bankruptcy and try to revive it. But this way, you can sell off the assets, and Tessa can close down the fund and return whatever small amount of capital that remains to her investors and then pocket the profit from the building's sale. If she went the bankruptcy route, she'd come under the scrutiny of the regulators, but individual investors wouldn't demand as rigorous an accounting; they're becoming accustomed to dot-com companies failing."

His silence confirmed my theory.

I added, "I assume you saw the plan through because of pressure from Afton Development. Do you have the authority to complete the sale of the building and withdraw funds from Econium Measures' accounts?"

"No. Both require Tessa's signature."

"Do you have reason to believe she'll surface and complete the transaction?"

"I do. A fax arrived from her last Thursday, telling me to go ahead as planned."

"Where was the fax sent from?"

"I do not know. The header was blank."

"Did she say anything else in it? When she was planning to surface, for instance?"

"No."

"That's probably because she doesn't intend to."

"What does that mean?"

"Are you aware that the account into which Afton deposited the up-front money has been cleaned out? So have other Econium Measures accounts."

He froze, cigar halfway to his lips. "That cannot be."

"But it's true. According to Kelby Lincoln, someone moved all the funds last week. Twenty-two million dollars is gone, and no one's been able to trace it."

"My God!"

"And then there's another detail: on Saturday, a woman whose description matches Tessa's was seen delivering a suitcase to the magazine's head of research, Kat Donovan. I suspect it contained payoff money."

"For what?"

"Information Kat turned up."

He flushed. "So she's the one!"

"The one who what?"

"The bitch!"

"I think you'd better tell me all of it, Mr. Amaya."

"No." He ground out his cigar and stood. "This conversation is over. If you don't leave immediately, I will call building security."

When I got back to my car I called the hospital where the paramedics had taken Engstrom, for an update on his condition; they said he had a broken arm and mild concussion, but was resting comfortably. Then I called the office for messages. Julia was still there; I wondered when she found time to spend with her son, decided that was her business. Besides, I didn't want to discourage dedication in a new employee.

"Hy called," she said. "He asked me to tell you he'll be home around noon on Friday. A Mr. Hernandez wanted to thank you for letting him catch his elevator on time, said to tell you he remembered something else. Before Remington disappeared, she and Amaya were upset because somebody had found out something damaging about him—Amaya, not Hernandez—and would have to be 'silenced.' "

I didn't like the sound of that.

Julia went on, "A Mrs. Woods says the boys have returned. And Ted phoned to ask if you'd found out anything."

"Thanks, Julia. Will you transfer me to Mick, please?"

* * *

"I was on my way out, Shar."

"Sorry, this is top priority."

"Dammit—"

"Bargaining chips—remember?"

"Okay, okay. What d'you need this time?"

"A background check on one Jorge Amaya." I gave him what details I had.

"I'll get started."

Sometimes I'm so manipulative that I'm ashamed of myself, but at least it gets the job done.

It was six o'clock now—end of a long, difficult day. All over the Bay Area people were heading home in their vehicles on the crowded streets, freeways, and bridges. They were lining up for CalTrain and BART, or rushing for the ferries, streetcars, and buses. The bars and restaurants were greeting their early customers; the athletically inclined were jumping on their mountain bikes or donning their running shoes; others were picking up groceries, lighting barbecues, or thinking fondly of pizza or Chinese takeout. Thousands of mundane, comforting rituals were going on all around me.

And I wasn't taking part in any of them.

As I sat in my costly slot in the garage on the slope of Nob Hill, a familiar yet puzzling sense of loneliness and loss washed over me. It was true that years before, without fully comprehending the consequences, I'd set out on a path that few people—particularly women, at the time—would have chosen. A path involving long hours, sleepless nights, frustration, danger, and enough resultant demons to cast an epic-length horror film. But unlike many of my colleagues, I now had resources to fall back on: Hy, my family—more family than most, even with Pa and Joey gone—and my friends. The agency, my home, my cats, Two-five-two-seven-Tango, and Touchstone.

So why this overwhelming sense of emptiness?

Well, why not? Over the years I'd seen too much violence, too many evil deeds done as the result of greed, cowardice, or just plain stupidity. In the past week I'd seen the body of a friend who had died needlessly, a near suicide, and another man badly injured. I was on overload and wanted nothing more than to stow the memories in my mental bank vault, go home, and indulge in those mundane, comforting rituals allowed to other people.

But I wasn't other people. And tonight I needed to continue searching for answers.

Parking in Ted and Neal's neighborhood is even more difficult than on Nob Hill, especially in the evening when the residents—and their cars—return. I left the MG in a pay lot on the northern Embarcadero and walked up the series of concrete stairways that scale Tel Hill to the end of Montgomery Street; by the time I reached the top the pain in my back had flared up again, and I paused to gulp down two dry aspirins.

The elevator of the building on Plum Alley was descending in its glass-block enclosure, distorting the figures of its occupants till they were long ripples of color. I stood aside while two women exited, then rode up to the third floor. Music played softly in a couple of the apartments, but no sound came from the rear unit. I pressed the bell, heard footsteps coming along the hallway.

"Shar!" Neal looked surprised to see me, then frowned. "Is something wrong? Ted—"

"Ted's okay, but he hasn't been able to reach you, so he asked me to stop by." I moved inside and along the hallway to the high-ceilinged living room. The apartments on this floor had two levels, and a small kitchen was tucked behind a spiral staircase. A man sat on a stool by its counter, sipping a glass of red wine. He was tall, blond, slender, and very young—quite the opposite of Ted. I glanced at Neal, waiting for an introduction.

Neal said, "This is Steve Box. Steve, Sharon McCone."

The man nodded and extended his hand to me. "Neal's former boss. I've been hearing about that fiasco for days now."

His easy familiarity made me bristle. I said, "Actually it was Neal's partner, Ted, who was supposed to be doing the bossing." I turned to Neal. "Don't you feel you owe Ted an explanation about this?"

"This?" His gaze followed my hand as I motioned at Steve Box and comprehension flooded his eyes. "Oh, my God, you don't think . . . ? Yeah, you do."

I waited.

"This is not what . . . Steve's been helping me . . . Maybe I better just show you." He started for the staircase, and I followed. At its top the door to his library was closed. He pushed it open. "Behold the domain of the twenty-first-century bookseller."

Inside the book-lined room, next to a handsome old partners desk, stood a new workstation. Set up on it was a Macintosh G-4 Cube computer with futuristic spherical speakers, a zip drive, a scanner, and a printer.

I stared. ". . . This is yours?"

"Mine, and Wells Fargo's—at least till I pay off my MasterCard."

"You can use it?"

"I can use it, and my stock is all online, thanks to Steve."

I thought of how I, a confirmed technophobe, had taught myself to operate the computer Hy kept at Touchstone one dismal, rainy weekend. I'd considered that an achievement of considerable proportions, but Neal had completely outstripped me. "Pretty sexy hardware," I said.

"When I fall, I fall hard."

"Amen to that." Steve's voice spoke behind him. "He's already opened an auction on E-Bay that ought to net him enough to make the next MasterCard payment."

I turned to him. "What are you—some kind of consultant?"

He nodded. "I've carved out this niche to help those who weren't born into the new technology to adapt to it. Neal's by far my most talented student."

I turned to Neal. "So it was computer equipment in those boxes Mona Woods saw the two of you carting in?"

"Computer equipment and the antiquarian books I've been keeping in a self-storage unit." He motioned at several dozen cartons piled between the desk and the window. "Mona's been spying on us, huh?"

"She was concerned that you and Ted had broken up, and . . ." I looked at Steve.

He said, "Neal's a nice guy, but I don't think my wife would approve of me moving in with him."

"You didn't tell Ted about Mona's suspicions?" Neal asked.

"No. But what about him? He's staying at my house and feels really miserable."

"You say he's tried to call?"

"Yes, but the line's always busy."

"That's because I've been online. I couldn't get the phone company to come out and install another line till next week."

"That's no excuse. You could've called him."

"I could've, but I was still pissed at him, and talking when I was in that kind of mood would've done us more harm than good. Besides, I wanted to get the business up and running first, to prove to him that I can do something right."

"So do something else right—call him."

My duty to my friends carried out—at least until the next crisis—I ransomed my car from yet another costly lot and headed down the Embarcadero to the pier. By now it was close to eight and dusk had set in, enveloping the palms along the streetcar tracks and making their swaying fronds seem like spectral arms raised in supplication. The only vehicle parked in our slots was Mick's motorcycle. He was working late, which meant he had either turned up nothing on Amaya or a great deal.

As I entered his office and he swiveled away from his workstation, his expression told me the news was good. "Your man's a piece of work," he said.

I sat down in Charlotte's chair. "How so?"

"Well, the one thing that checks out is that his family's rich. Very. But the rest of it—the degrees, the business experience—is a flat-out lie. And Jorge's youthful indiscretions make mine seem tame."

"Hard to believe. What's he done?"

"The whole nine yards. Womanizing. Drinking. Drugs. He got kicked out of three parochial schools in Costa Rica and a couple of expensive prep schools up here. When he was eighteen there was a scandal involving the wife of a highly placed government official down there, and that was when the family decided it was advisable he leave the country—with a generous allowance. He lived in New York for a few years, then tried to set himself up as a producer in Hollywood. There was a problem with him playing fast and loose with his backers' funds, which his father resolved, and then he came up here. He's been at the Nob Hill address for three years, no gainful employment till the gig with *InSite* came along last June."

A gig that Remington had arranged in order to have her lover and co-conspirator on the inside. "Classic remittance man," I commented.

"Say what?"

"Nothing you'd relate to." In spite of his father being very wealthy, Mick had always preferred to pay his own way; Ricky had even had trouble getting him to accept the downpayment on his condo. "Nice work. Go home, have a good evening."

"Thanks, boss woman. I've got to rest up for our bargaining session tomorrow."

After Mick left I went to my office and tackled the stack of paperwork in my in-box. Expense reports to approve. Client reports to read and okay. Mick's eccentrically worded and frequently misspelled reports to tone down and correct. Employee complaint: cheap coffee from

Costco sucks. Memo to Ted to buy a different brand of cheap coffee from same.

By the time I finished it was after nine. I hadn't eaten since lunch with Glenn, and then very little, but I wasn't hungry. I took J.D.'s diagram from my bag and carried it and my case file to the armchair by the window.

J.D., it seemed, had stumbled onto many of the same things I had since learned or assumed. Nearly all his scrawled notations held meaning for me now, if the relations between some of them didn't. This time I recognized the lines connecting Amaya, Vardon, and Remington as a triangle. Interesting that the one linking Amaya and Remington bisected Engstrom. The connector between Roger and Jody was firm and clear, but the lines radiating out from them to the others seemed to be nothing more than J.D.'s futile efforts to think the situation through.

And the questions: Afton? He'd found out about the developers who were buying up Dogpatch property. Econ? Econium Measures, of course. CWP? He'd gone over Remington's movements on the day she disappeared, making sure that no one at the nonprofit whose board meeting she was supposed to attend had seen or heard from her. ER? Eagle Rock, Oregon. LR? I hadn't a clue.

But then again . . .

I opened the case file, paged through it. Mick had printed out a map of the Dogpatch area, shading the properties already owned by Afton Development in orange, the properties needed to complete the parcel in yellow. A number of them extended south of Dogpatch proper, and one in particular, that hadn't yet been acquired, gave access to the bay.

I studied it, matched it to my mental map. It was the site of the old Islais Creek Resort. The Last Resort. LR.

I plan to live in that building and eventually run a consulting firm out of it.

So Dinah Vardon had claimed when I'd asked about her purchase. But if that were true, why had she put her renovations on hold indefinitely? Because she'd found out Afton Development would pay a small fortune for precious bayside land? Perhaps she was holding out on them, to maximize her profit. Good business on her part—so why lie to me?

Vardon's house on Vermont Street was dark again. I rang the bell anyway, received no answer. Next I checked the Last Resort. Dark and deserted-looking. Should I call it a night?

No. A sixth sense always kicked in when I was close to the truth. Now it told me I was very close.

I drove out of the resort's parking lot, left the MG on Third Street, and doubled back on foot. The building was obscured by mist that rose like steam off the bay. Across the street I crouched down behind an abandoned truck and studied it. No lights upstairs, no lights downstairs, no lights in any of the outbuildings.

After a minute I moved away from the truck and slipped along the street, past dark houses with barred windows and boarded doors. Where the pavement ended I crossed and approached the resort from its blind side, moving through the outbuildings. The sheds in which the former owner used to store contraband were falling down, the boathouse not in much better shape. As I neared it I saw a new-looking padlock and hasp securing the door.

I checked the padlock. So new that it was not yet corroded by the salt air. I reached into my bag for my set of picks, then thought better of it and went around the structure to the water side. The rusted metal overhead door to the boatwell was frozen partway up; there was about a two-foot clearance between it and the floor beside the well. I straddled the beams between the pilings, gritting my teeth against the pain in my back, swung around on them, and squeezed through.

Even before I took out my flashlight I made out a bulky shape next to the well. A car. I turned on the flash, shone its beam over there. White BMW convertible, the type the newspaper account said Tessa Remington had driven. When I examined the license plates I saw their number didn't match the one published. But the other night Dinah Vardon had been driving a similar car. Was this hers? I went around to look in the glove box for the registration. None there. I checked under and behind the seats. Nothing.

Car coming along Water Street.

I shut the BMW's door, listened.

Coming here.

I looked around. Other than the BMW, the boatwell was the only place to hide.

Gravel crunched under the car's tires as it stopped outside.

I rushed to the well, scrambled over its side, stifling a gasp as my feet went into the icy water. Grabbing hold of the exposed beams, I lowered myself till I was knee deep in the bay and clung there, my forehead pressed to the splintery wood.

The padlock and hasp rattled, then someone opened the door and came inside. I held my breath, hoped that the slapping of the water around me wouldn't give me away. Footsteps crossed to the rear of the BMW. Something thumped on the planks, and after a few seconds I heard a whining sound.

Electric tool of some kind. Screwdriver?

Metal clanged, the tool whined again. The person went to the front of the car and repeated the process.

Changing the license plates.

Next the footsteps went to the passenger's side of the car; its door opened. In seconds it slammed shut and the person left the boathouse, fastening the padlock. It was a few more minutes before the other car's engine started up, then faded into the distance.

I pulled myself from the boatwell and lay on my stomach on the planks. My feet and calves were numb, my jeans and athletic shoes soaked. I smelled of brine and tar and some chemical whose identity I didn't even want to speculate on. After a moment I sat up and wrung out the jeans as best I could without taking them off, rubbed my calves to restore the circulation. Took off my shoes and emptied the water from them, rubbed my feet.

After I'd put on the soggy shoes, I turned on my flash and went to take a look at the new plates on the BMW. 2 KCV 743. Tessa Remington's. On the passenger's seat lay a purse and briefcase that hadn't been there earlier. The purse contained identification and credit cards in Remington's name, as well as five hundred dollars in cash. The briefcase held files relating to the various funds managed by the Remington Group, an agenda for the February 14 board meeting of the Committee for Wireless Privacy, and a dossier on Jorge Amaya that disclosed many of the facts I already knew, plus a prior arrest for statutory rape in Los Angeles, charges subsequently dropped.

Had Remington been hiding here at the Last Resort for the past two months while she gradually transferred the funds from the Econium Measures accounts? Was she planning to make a move tonight? And if so, what was her relationship with Dinah Vardon?

The briefcase had another compartment that closed with a tiny lock—easy enough to pick. Inside was a clasp envelope. I took it out, found several sheets labeled TIMELINE. It was a schedule: of deposits into Econium Measures accounts; of transfers from same. There were no names or numbers for the accounts into which the funds had been moved. Interspersed with the deposits and transfers were various cryptic notations, among them "lose Lewis file," "disable scanner," "delete payroll," "activate fire alarm." The date for the latter was this past Friday.

The last notations were dated a week from tomorrow: final payment, Afton; final transfer, Econium.

An embezzlement scheme so elaborate and meticulously planned that Remington had felt the need to spell it out for herself. Well, no wonder: amounts were penciled in beside each financial transaction; the total of funds to be transferred—undoubtedly to a protected account outside the country—was close to a hundred million dollars.

The question was, whom did she intend to share it with? Amaya? Or Dinah Vardon?

Before I left the boathouse I took out J.D.'s diagram for what seemed like the hundredth time and held it up to the light from my flash. Jody Houston's name was heavily circled; he'd thought the answers lay with her, and maybe they did.

I went over my contacts with Houston, considered what kind of person she was. Tried to think as she would.

And realized where I might find her.

No one answered my ring at Houston's apartment, but that didn't surprise me. I let myself into the building with Roger's keys, rode the elevator to Jody's floor. Unlike him, she had only one lock on her door, and the key with the purple rubber band that I'd found in his kitchen opened it. The new alarm system panel was on the wall to my right; I overrode it as I had done the one at *InSite*'s offices.

Once inside I saw a sliver of light shining from under a closed door at the rear of the apartment. Dining area and kitchen, same as Roger's, except the archway had been turned into a solid wall. I moved toward it, my footsteps muted on the thick carpet. No sound from within, but I felt a tension that tugged at my nerve endings. I opened the door.

Paige Tallman gasped and shrank backward. "Oh, my God, how'd you get in here?"

"Take it easy. I'm not here to make trouble for you."

She glanced down at my wet jeans and shoes, wrinkled her nose. "What's happened to you?"

"That's not important. Why didn't you answer when I rang?"

"I thought that was just a warning ring."

"And that I was Jody."

"I'm sorry?"

"That's who you thought I was. She's been staying here, hasn't she?"

"Why d'you think that?"

"Educated guess. Last time she ran she went someplace familiar. You told her you'd had the alarm installed, and she figured this was the last place the police—or anyone else—would look for her."

Tallman went over to a round oak table and sat down, propping her elbows on it and burying her face in her hands. "Well, you guessed right. She's been hiding here since Sunday night."

"You let her? When she's wanted for murder?"

"Of course. Jody's my friend. She said she didn't kill that reporter, and I believe her."

"Who did, then?"

She looked up, spread her hands. "If she knows, she won't say. She came home and found him dead on the living room floor and panicked. Hid him in the closet till she could decide what to do. But before she did, you showed up."

"So she ran out and left me to deal with the situation."

"No, that's not how it was. You convinced her you really wanted to help her. But when she went upstairs to get something to show to you, she looked out the window and saw the person she thought had killed the reporter."

"But she wouldn't tell you who this person was."

"No."

"And what was this alleged person doing?"

"Picking up a suitcase that was lying on the front walk. Then they ran away with it, got into a car that was parked down the street, and drove away."

"She describe the car?"

"Dark-colored economy model. The same kind she'd rented at the airport."

Eagle Rock had certainly been infested with rental cars that night. "Then what?"

"She just ran. Drove down the coast, ditched the car. Hitched here. It took a long time and when she got here she was dead tired. She slept most of Monday, and that night when we talked, she told me what I just told you."

"And today?"

"She hung around here, really nervous. Pacing. Jumping at every little noise. Smoking a lot, even though she knows how I feel about secondhand smoke. I was working at home—I'm in insurance, had a package to put together for a big commercial account—and she really got on my nerves." Tallman flushed. "I know that sounds awful: her in big trouble, and I'm complaining because she annoyed me."

"You can't help how you feel. It's a bad situation for you, too."

"Yeah, it is. I mean, she's a fugitive, and not turning her over to the cops is a crime. But how could I do that, when she's not guilty? Anyway, she did try when I complained about the smoke. Started hanging out the airshaft window to have a cigarette because she was afraid to stand by a window where she could be seen. I offered her some Valium, thinking that would help, but she said no, she had to keep a clear head so she could think."

"She give you any indication of what she was thinking?"

"Well, when I knocked off work, we had a couple of glasses of wine, and she started talking about what she should do. She was afraid to turn herself in to the cops and take her chances. She couldn't keep running; she didn't want to live like that and, besides, she didn't have any money. She couldn't stay here indefinitely. Finally she said that if the person she saw up there in Oregon was the one who killed the reporter, she was in even more danger than before. It was a no-win situation, so she might as well risk everything."

"How?"

"I don't know. She got quiet after that, and a few minutes later she went into the bedroom to make a phone call. When she came out she told me she was going to meet with the person, strike a bargain. I said wasn't that dangerous, and she said she'd told them she'd left an insurance policy just in case."

An insurance policy—the same phrase Roger had used in his last journal entry.

"She left it here, with you?"

"No, she said it wasn't in the apartment."

"But she hadn't been out since she arrived on Sunday?"

"No."

"So how were you supposed to do something with this policy, if you didn't know what it was or where?"

"I wasn't supposed to do anything. I think she was

going to use it as leverage with the person—give it to them in exchange for money and leaving her alone."

A dangerous and foolish course of action. "What time did she leave here?"

"Around eight."

Almost two and a half hours ago. "On foot?"

"Well, she didn't call a cab."

"And that's everything?"

"Yeah. You think something's happened to her, don't you?"

"Maybe."

"If it has, I'll never forgive—"

I shook my head, held up a hand to silence her. Outside a siren wailed a counterpoint to the words and phrases that echoed in my mind.

Insurance policy . . . Eddie will look out for her . . . he'll see she has an insurance policy at her fingertips . . . important that you show her the stuff I asked you to teach me . . . he asked if he could use my computer to send an E-mail, his server was down . . . not in the apartment . . . at her fingertips . . .

I asked, "Is Jody's computer still here?"

"Yeah, but it's boxed up in the closet with the other stuff she left behind."

That wasn't it, then. Damn!

Not in the apartment . . . she started hanging out . . .

I looked around, asked Tallman, "Where's the airshaft window?"

"What's that got to do—?"

"Just show me."

"In the kitchen, next to the fridge. You can't miss it."

I hurried over there. The pebbled glass pane was on

the building's side wall, where in Roger's apartment it had been covered by cabinetry. I released its latch and leaned out into a dim space that smelled of stale cooking odors and mold.

Tallman came up behind me, asked what I was doing, but I ignored her. I felt around till my fingers touched a plastic bag taped to the frame. The tape came loose and I almost dropped the bag. That was all I'd have needed in my present state—to have to climb down the shaft after it like Spiderwoman.

I moved back from the window and held the bag to the light. Inside was a disc, smaller than a CD.

When I'd come in I'd seen that the living room was set up as an office. "Do you have a Zip drive on your computer?" I asked Tallman.

"Yes."

"Download this onto the desktop, would you?"

She led me to the workstation, booted up, fed the disc into the drive.

"Thanks," I said. "You'd better go into the other room while I look at this."

"Hey, this is my—"

"Remember what Jody told you? You're better off not knowing."

She gave a grunt of displeasure, then her footsteps moved toward the dining area.

The desktop icon for the disc had appeared. I clicked on it. The file came up on the screen, and I began scrolling through the words that Roger had typed on Jody's machine and then deleted shortly before he killed himself. Not an E-mail because his server was down, as he'd claimed to her; he'd earlier sent his final messages to his brothers on his own machine. When Jody read his journal she'd figured that out and, using the method Eddie had taught them both, retrieved and stored the document on disc.

I read on, Roger's words confirming many of the things I'd already suspected.

And telling me one thing I never would have guessed.

Almost three hours now since Jody left the apartment. She was in extreme danger, if not already dead. Call 911?

No, no real evidence of where she'd gone, and it would take too long to explain my reasoning.

Go now, by myself.

But I needed an insurance policy too. I highlighted the entire document, added a message, and sent it as an E-mail to Adah Joslyn, both at her home and SFPD addresses.

Once again I crouched behind the abandoned truck on Water Street studying the resort. The mist was thicker now, and moving inland, but I could make out faint light behind the masked first-story windows. Portions of Roger's last message kept replaying in my mind.

I never should have gone there, but by then I'd realized Dinah had been using me when she came on to me that afternoon, buying time so she could do something with the material Kat had given her. God, I was a fool to believe her when she said she still loved me. But with me, Dinah always knew what buttons to push.

I'd gone by the pier for the .357 Magnum that I normally keep in the safe there. Now it was a comforting weight in the outside pocket of my bag. I have a curious love-hate relationship with firearms: love, because I'm a good markswoman and they've saved my life on a number of occasions; hate, because I've seen—and three times been responsible for—the dreadful toll they exact on human beings.

After a few minutes I left the shelter of the truck and retraced the route I'd taken earlier. The boathouse was still padlocked, and I didn't see any other car.

She said she was meeting with her contractor at five, but when I saw the cars I realized the appointment was actually with Tessa Remington. I supposed she planned to pass along whatever information Kat had turned up, and I wanted to know what it was, so I went inside. Second mistake.

There was a plank walk on the bay side of the building. As I started along it, I saw a vehicle pulled close to the railing of the lower deck. The windows of the bar overlooked the walk, but they were also masked; still, I crouched down while passing them. Now I saw that the car was a red Pontiac Firebird, a sporty but relatively inexpensive model. The plates on it were the ones that earlier had been on the BMW. I tried its doors, but they were locked.

The railing of the stairway to the upper deck seemed more wobbly than it had before. I moved slowly, testing each board with the toe of my shoe before I put any weight on it. I wasn't sure what I'd do once I got up there. I'd take care of that when the time came.

She called after eight and said she'd taken care of everything. I was to tell no one what happened, particularly you, Jody. She said that if I did, we'd both suffer the consequences. I didn't have to ask what she meant by that.

Once upstairs, I moved through the mist to the door. No lights inside the bar or the kitchen beyond. The padlock on the door, like the one on the boathouse, was a good one, would take a long time to pick. Time I didn't have.

A window similar to the ones downstairs flanked the door on either side. I spotted some loose shingles beside the left one, pried them off. Only tar paper behind them, old and brittle; I pulled it free. Most of the insulation between the stud and the window was gone; I removed what was left and went to work on the Sheetrock with my Swiss Army knife. In minutes I'd cut loose a big enough piece to stick my arm through and release the window's latch. The rusted aluminum frame grated in protest as I eased it open.

I waited to see if the noise had alerted anyone. Apparently not. After a minute I climbed up and through to the room beyond. As I recalled, a stairway led down from here to the lower level. I felt my way along the bar to the firedoor.

Locked from the other side.

From below I now heard a voice, harsh and insistent, but I couldn't make out the words. It went on and on without interruption.

You don't know her. She's a greedy, arrogant woman who thinks the rules don't apply to her. She'll probably try to intimidate you and find out how much you know. Don't underestimate her.

I put my ear to the door, straining to hear. Now a second voice was raised in protest. Again I couldn't make out the words, but they were laced with fear. The other person interrupted with a scornful laugh.

There had to be another way down there. Maybe through the kitchen—it served both floors. They must've been able to take food downstairs without carrying it through the bar area.

I took out my flashlight and moved slowly, trying not to make noise. Cobwebs brushed at my face and hands; I knocked them away. When I pushed one of the bat-wing shutters, it nearly fell off the wall. I eased it free, laid it on top of the commercial cookstove.

There was a door set into the wall beside the stove—another firedoor, perhaps. I tugged on its handle, was hit by a blast of icy air when it opened. Walk-in freezer. But why use costly energy running it when—

A chill that had nothing to do with the temperature

took hold of me. I stepped inside, not letting the door shut all the way behind me. Shone my light around—

And moved slowly toward a stainless-steel table draped in a paint-stained canvas drop cloth under which was a conspicuous bulge. I raised the cloth, shone my flash down.

Short blond hair, sparkly with ice crystals. Waxen, sculpted features that it was impossible to believe had once been poised, self-confident, animated. Bloody gash and discoloration at the right temple.

So this was how she'd "taken care of everything." Well, not quite. Tonight she planned to finish the task.

When I went inside I heard voices yelling on the second floor. I ran up the stairs to the bar and saw they were fighting physically. Screaming at each other, something about Jorge. Tessa was getting the worst of it, and I knew firsthand how much damage Dinah could inflict, so I got between them and tried to stop them. Dinah was clawing at me, and Tessa was hanging on, using me like a shield. I turned and shoved her away and she fell and hit her head on the bar. The sound was horrifying, and I knew she was dead. So, like the true coward I am, I ran out of there, away from this terrible thing I had done.

I replaced the drop cloth over Tessa Remington's frozen face. In the kitchen I leaned against the wall, breathing hard. There it was, the evidence I needed. Call 911 and—

"No!" The shout rose from downstairs, a truncated, terrified sound.

I looked around for another door. None there. But across the kitchen was a dark, empty space. No, not empty—a wooden cage. Dumbwaiter, how they sent the food downstairs.

I exchanged my flashlight for my gun. Though it was a large industrial-size cage, it would be a tight fit. If it was even operable. I located the Down button, squeezed in there—sitting down, my back to the rear, head lowered, knees bent. Pain stabbed my back in protest. I ignored it, pressed the button.

The cage jerked and bounced. Began its descent, clanking and growling. I brought my feet up, ready to kick out, the .357 grasped firmly in both hands.

The cage stopped abruptly, dealing a jarring blow to my spine. I rammed my feet at the wooden panel in front of me. It yielded, and I heard a cry of pain as it connected with flesh and bone.

I struggled out of the cage, barely gaining my footing. Stumbled back against the wall beside it.

"Watch out!" Jody Houston's voice called.

I saw the pool cue descending just in time to duck. It swished past my head. Dinah Vardon swung the cue again, and this time it connected with my shoulder. The gun slipped from my hands; I went to my knees reaching for it. Vardon whacked me across the ass.

I scooted forward on my elbows under the pool table. My fingers touched the .357; I grasped it, rolled over, and brought it up. Vardon stood over me, the cue poised.

"Drop it, Dinah!"

She backed off but didn't lower the cue.

I edged out from under the table, got to my knees and then to my feet.

"Drop it!"

She flashed me a contemptuous look, let the cue fall to the floor. "Listen," she said, "put the gun away and we'll talk."

"No way." I motioned to Houston, who sat in a straight-backed chair, her legs bound with duct tape, her arms trussed behind her. "Cut her loose."

Vardon ignored the order. "It doesn't have to be this way, you know. I have money, a great deal of it. I'll pay you—"

"I don't want your money. Cut her loose."

"You haven't heard how much. I have twenty-two million dollars. More, when I sign Tessa's name to the sale documents for *InSite*'s building and sell this property. Still more, if I can crack the codes on her offshore accounts."

"You'll have plenty of time to work on that in jail—if they let you have your computer."

"I'm not worried about jail. Or you."

"You should be."

"I don't think so. Last chance to take me up on my offer, McCone."

"No, thanks."

"Your loss." She shrugged and smiled. "If you won't take my money, I know an excellent attorney who will."

Wednesday

•

APRIL 25

It was dead midnight when the police arrived.

I'd had no difficulty preventing Dinah Vardon from leaving—in fact, I hadn't had to try. Acting oblivious of the .357 trained on her, she'd sat herself down on the pool table, called her attorney, and insisted he meet her at the Hall of Justice, then proceeded to ignore Houston and me. Later on I reflected that she reminded me of a cat that has gotten its nose out of joint: it puts its back to you and stares haughtily into the distance, but from the flattening and swiveling of its ears you can tell it is listening to everything that goes on behind it.

And in the interim between my 911 call and the arrival of the first squad cars, there was plenty for Vardon to listen to. Jody confirmed what Eddie Nagasawa had told me, and much of what I'd theorized. She'd asked Eddie about the insurance policy Roger claimed to have left her after a call from Vardon suggesting they "get together to talk about Roger." After Eddie showed her how to retrieve Roger's files, it had taken her a while to piece them together and figure out that the so-called policy was actually on her own computer. Finally she accessed it and put it on disc, uncertain as to what to do with it.

If at all possible, she didn't want to make Roger's confession public; Remington's death had been an accident, but knowledge of his part in it would tarnish his memory in the minds of those who had cared about him. She felt for Tessa Remington's husband and friends, however, and knew they deserved to learn what had happened to her. And Vardon became insistent, calling repeatedly, the conversations taking a threatening turn. When she encountered me at Roger's apartment and realized the Nagasawas were opening an inquiry into his suicide, she decided to take the disc to his father, but Daniel's seemingly skeptical reaction made her back off. Vardon called again the next day, and Jody set up an appointment with her, but fled to Oregon instead, taking the Zip disc with her.

Most likely Vardon had known or found out about Jody's cottage in Eagle Rock and gone there with the intent of killing her. But coincidentally she met up with J.D. I'd probably never know what went on during their final confrontation. And given the lack of evidence, there was an odds-even chance she would never be charged with the murder.

She'd covered up an accidental death. Figured out Tessa Remington's passwords and looted the Econium Measures funds. Driven around in the dead woman's expensive car for two months while Tessa's corpse lay in cold storage because she—as she'd bragged to Jody—could get away with it and wanted to taste what it was like to be rich. Bribed Kat Donovan to leave the area, arriving at her house in the BMW wearing a yellow head scarf that, to a neighbor who admitted to bad eyesight, made her look like "a blonde in a fancy car." Held Jody hostage and repeatedly threatened to kill her if she didn't turn over the disc.

And if I hadn't stopped her tonight, she would have disposed of Tessa's body, along with her personal effects, by pushing her car into the sea south of the city off treacherous Devil's Slide. Jody was certain that even if she'd surrendered the Zip disc she'd have been a passenger in that car.

Arrogance is its own undoing, of course. Vardon had incriminated herself because she couldn't resist bragging to Jody. And she hadn't realized the limitations of her knowledge of forensics; given the condition of Remington's body, no coroner would have believed she and Jody had died at the same time in the same car wreck.

But those crimes were nothing compared to the enormity of J.D.'s murder. It pained me to think there might never be justice for him.

Adah Joslyn's voice spoke behind me. "Damn, McCone, you know I hardly ever check my E-mail at home."

I turned toward her. Even at this late hour she was dressed in an elegantly tailored suit, her curly hair perfectly styled. "I sent a message to your office as well. Doesn't somebody monitor what comes in when you're off duty?"

"My counterparts on the other shifts, yes. One of them read it."

"So he couldn't figure it out and get over here?"

"He's a recent hire from the Detroit PD. Your note said you were headed to the Last Resort. How the hell was he supposed to know what that is?"

"You've got a point there." I glanced at the door, where Vardon was being led out in handcuffs, then looked across the room, where a paramedic was examining Jody.

"She's one tough woman," I said. "She held Vardon off as long as humanly possible. And shouted when she heard me moving around upstairs."

"If she'd've come to us in the first place, J.D. would still be alive. And you and I both know that even if Vardon's charged with murder, some hotshot lawyer's gonna get her off on lack of evidence."

Something was nagging at me. I closed my eye, struggled to bring the memory to the surface.

"McCone? You all right?"

I pictured J.D. smiling at me when we met outside *InSite*'s building last Thursday. Heard him say, "You're still doing that."

I asked Adah, "How fast can you get a search warrant for Vardon's house?"

"Case like this, pretty quick."

"Good. This is a long shot, but I'll tell you what to look for."

"Hey, McCone!"

"Uhhh?" I was in bed in the RKI apartment, bruised and battered, and once again hiding from the press. A Vicodin-induced dream involving seahorses swimming among wildflowers still had hold of me.

"You were right," Adah's voice said. "Vardon kept the jeans and tee she wore home from Oregon after she stole your travel bag."

That made me sit up. "And?"

"The penny was in the inside pocket of the jeans, right where you said it'd be."

Again Vardon had been done in by her arrogance. No one would search *her* house. No one would connect the clothing with J.D.'s murder.

"For once," Adah added, "it's a good thing you're superstitious."

"Yeah, it is." I'd distinctly remembered finding a shiny new penny and tucking it into the inner pocket of those jeans the last time I'd worn them. It was for just such occasions that the phrase "lucky penny" was coined.

Friday

•

APRIL 27

Eventually you let go of it.

Now you know there are as many reasons as there are suicides. Often more than one cause for that final self-destructive act. And none of those reasons has anything to do with the living—with you.

I let go as I stood on the Marin Headlands, remembering.

Joey. His life, and he didn't care to share it with any of us. For some reason he'd failed to bond with his own family members, just as we'd failed to bond with him. No need to feel guilt or remorse; it happens. His death was presumably the way he'd wanted it—lonely and private.

J.D. His life, and he'd given so freely of himself to others. But there had also been a closed, secretive side to him, the side that made him an investigative reporter. Death was nothing he would have willingly sought, but on occasion he'd risked it for the sake of a good story. No need for guilt or remorse there, either. He'd died doing the thing he loved most, and in time that knowledge would ease my sadness.

Behind me I heard the voices of those who had gathered on the bluff above the Golden Gate to celebrate J.D.'s life. An Episcopalian minister who had never met him but understood how much a proper service would mean to his religious parents had officiated, coached on personal details by J.D.'s friends. Tables with food and drink had been set up and, while his mother and father remained in attendance, we reminisced somberly. But after the limo hired to return the Smiths to the city departed, the gathering took on a lighter tone. Voices were raised in humorous and frequently irreverent remembrances. Glasses were raised as favorite J.D. anecdotes were related.

When my own mood turned somber again, I walked over to the guardrail to say my private good-bye to him, while looking across the bay at the city he had loved. Peace of the sort that I hadn't experienced in many months washed over me. The city was turning golden in the late afternoon sunlight. I knew it was only makeup to hide its blemishes and scars, but I also knew that the imperfections masked an inner beauty. Good people, such as those who had gathered here for J.D., were a large part of that, as were—

Strong hands grasped my shoulders. I smiled, recognizing Hy's touch.

"Hey, you," he said. "Sorry I didn't make it on time for the service. Flight delays . . ."

"It was a good one. I spoke for both of us, told the story of the whale-watching expedition."

"I'll never forget how he kept saying, 'I can't be seasick, I'm a *reporter!* We're only allowed to get sick when we're drunk!'"

"That was J.D."

"So how're you, McCone?"

"Ready."

"For?"

"Two-five-two-seven-Tango."

"Destination?"

"Touchstone."

"I figured as much, and called North Field. She's gassed up."

I pictured the airport and the city of Oakland shrinking beneath us till they were toylike. The bay receding behind us. The thickly forested ridge turning dusky as we crossed it and turned north along the coast. The scalloped coves of Mendocino County welcoming us . . .

"Home, Ripinsky."

More
Marcia Muller!

Please turn this page
for a preview of

CYANIDE WELLS

available
wherever books are sold.

Port Regis, British Columbia
Wednesday, April 24, 2002

att Lindstrom watched the tourists struggle along the pier, laden with extra jackets, blankets, tote bags, and coolers. City people, up from California on holiday and unaccustomed to the chill temperatures and pervasive damp that characterized the northern tip of Vancouver Island at this time of year. Americans were also unaccustomed to going anywhere without a considerable collection of unnecessary possessions.

Smiling ruefully, he turned around, his gaze rising to the pine-covered slopes across the small harbor. When had he stopped identifying with the few U.S. citizens who ventured this far up-island? At first he hadn't been conscious of his waning allegiance; it had simply crept up on him until one day he was no longer one of them, yet not a Canadian either. Stuck somewhere in between, perhaps permanently, and in an odd way his otherness pleased him. No, not pleased so much as contented him, and he'd remained contented until the past Sunday evening. Since then he'd felt only discontent, and a sense of unfinished business.

"Matt?" His deckhand Johnny Crowe, stood by the transom of the *Queen Charlotte,* Matt's thirty-six-foot excursion trawler. A full-blooded Kootenay, Jimmy was a recent transplant from the Columbia River Valley. He asked, "You want me to button her up?"

"Yeah, thanks." Matt gave him a half-salute and started along the dock, past fishing boats in their slips. The tourists he'd taken out for the morning's charter were bunched around their giant Ford Expedition, trying to fit their gear among the suitcases piled in its rear compartment. They'd spent the night at Port Regis Hotel at the foot of the pier—an establishment whose accommodations one guidebook had described as "spartan but clean," and from the grumblings he'd overheard, he gathered that spartan was not their first, or even second, preference.

When he reached the end of the pier, he gave the tourists a wide berth and a curt nod and headed for the hotel. It was of weathered clapboard, oncc white but now gone to gray, and not at all imposing, with three entrances off its covered front porch: restaurant, lobby, and bar. Matt pushed through the latter into an amber-lighted room with beer signs and animal heads on the walls and rickety, unmatched tables and chairs arranged haphazardly across the warped wooden floor. The room was empty now, but a few hours before, it would have been filled with fishermen returning at what was the end of their working day.

"Hey, Millie," Matt called to the woman behind the bar.

"Hey, yourself." Millie Bertram was a frizzy-haired blonde on the far side of fifty, dressed in denim coveralls over a tie-dyed shirt. The shirt and her long beaded earrings revealed her as one who had never quite made a clean break with the sixties. When Matt moved to Port Regis ten years ago, Millie and her husband, Jed, had co-owned and operated the hotel. Two years later Jed, who fancied himself a bass player of immense if unrecognized talent, ran off with a singer from Vancouver, never to be seen again. Millie became sole proprietor of the hotel, and if the prices had gone up, so had the quality of food and service.

Now she placed a mug of coffee in front of Matt. "Early charter?"

"Only charter. Those guests of yours from San Jose."

"Ah, yes, they mentioned something about a 'boat ride.'" The set of Millie's mouth indicated she was glad to have seen the last of them. "Fishing?"

"Not their thing. Bloody Marys, except for one woman who drank mimosas. Point-and-shoot cameras and a desire to see whales."

"On a day when there's not a whale in sight."

"I pointed out two." Matt sipped coffee, burned his tongue, and grimaced.

"Let me guess," Millie said. "Bull and Bear Rocks."

"You got it."

"You're a con man, Lindstrom."

"So they're leaving happy and will tell all their friends to look me up."

Millie went to the coffee urn, poured herself some, and leaned against the backbar, looking pensive. Probably contemplating the summer months that would bring more tourists with a desire for whales, who would become drunk in her bar, look askance at her chef's plain cooking, and leave her spartan guestrooms in a shambles.

Matt toyed with the ceramic container that held packets of sugar and artificial sweetener. "Mil, you're from California, right?"

"Yeah."

"You know where Soledad County is?"

She closed her eyes, apparently conjuring a map. "Between Mendocino and Humboldt Counties, on the coast. Extends east beyond the Eel River National Forest."

"You ever hear of a place called Cyanide Wells?"

"Sure. Back when Jed-the-asshole and I

were into our environmental phase, we protested at Talbot's Mills. Lumber town. Company town. Identical little houses, except for the mansions the thieving barons built on the labor of the loggers and millworkers they exploited."

Matt made motions as if he were playing a violin.

"Okay," Millie said, "so I'm still talking the talk even though I'm not walking the walk. Anyway, Cyanide Wells is maybe thirty miles northeast of there. Former gold-mining camp. Wide spot in the road back in the seventies, but I guess it's grown some by now. I do know it's got one hell of a newspaper, the *Soledad Spectrum.* Owned and edited by a woman, Carly McGuire. About three years ago they won the Pulitzer Prize for a series on the murders of a gay couple near there. How come you asked?"

"I just found out that somebody I used to know is living near Cyanide Wells."

"Somebody?" Now Millie's tone turned sly. She was, Matt knew, frustrated and puzzled by his lack of interest in a long-term relationship with any of the women she repeatedly shoved into his path.

"Somebody," he said in a tone that precluded further discussion.

Somebody who, fourteen years ago, had put an end to his life as he'd known it.

Matt sat on the deck of his cabin, looking out at the humped mass of Bear Rock, which was backlit by the setting sun. It *did* look like a whale, and he was glad he'd given the tourists their photo op this morning. Clouds were now gathering on the horizon, bleaching the sun's brilliant colors, and a cold breeze swayed the three tall pines that over the past ten years he'd watched grow from saplings. Feeling the chill, he got up and took his bottle of beer inside.

The cabin was snug: one room with a sleeping alcove on the far wall, and a stone fireplace and galley kitchen facing each other on the side walls. A picture window and glass door overlooked the sea. The small shingled building had been in bad shape when he'd first seen it, so he'd gotten it cheap, leaving enough of the money from the sale of the Saugatuck house for the downpayment on the *Queen Charlotte*. During two years of drifting about, his life in ruins, he'd taken what odd jobs he found and scarcely touched the money.

He lighted the fire he'd earlier laid on the hearth, sat down, and watched the flames build. Dusk fell, then darkness, and he nursed his warmish beer without turning on a lamp.

Fourteen years. A way of life lost. A home gone. A career destroyed.

Then, finally, he'd found Port Regis and this cabin and the *Queen Charlotte,* and he'd created a new way of life, built another home and career. True, he was not the man he'd intended to be at thirty-nine, and this was not the life he'd expected to lead. But it was a life he'd handcrafted out of ruin and chaos. If it was as spartan as one of Milli's guestrooms, at least it was also clean. If his friends were little more than good acquaintances, so much the better; he'd learned the small worth of friendship those last two years in Minnesota. He was content here—or had been, until a late-night anonymous phone call destroyed all possibility of contentment. . . .

He wasn't aware of making a conscious decision, much less a plan. He simply turned on the table lamp and went to the closet off the sleeping alcove, where he began going through the cartons stacked in its recesses. When he located the one marked P EQUIP., he carried it to the braided rug in front of the hearth, sat down cross-legged, and opened it.

Memories rose with the dust from the carton's lid. He pushed them aside, burrowed into the bubble-wrapped contents. On top were the lenses: F2.8 wide angle, Fl.8 and F2.8 telephotos, F2.8 with 1.4x teleconverter, and even a fish-eye, which he'd bought in a fit of longing but had seldom needed. Next the camera bag, tan canvas and well used. And inside it, the camera.

It was an old Nikon F, the first camera he'd ever bought and the only one he'd kept when he sold his once-profitable photography business. Heavy and old-fashioned next to the new single-lens reflexes or digital models, the markings were worn on the f-stop band, and the surfaces where he'd so often held it were polished smooth. He stared at it, afraid to take it into his hands because if he did, it would work its old magic, and then what he now realized he'd been subconsciously considering would become a reality. . . .

Don't be ridiculous. Picking it up isn't a commitment.

And just like that, he did.

His fingers curled around the Nikon, moving to long-accustomed positions. They caressed it as he removed the lens cap, adjusted speed, f-stop, and focus. He sighted on the flames in the fireplace, saw them clearly through the F3.5 micro lens with a skylight filter. Even though the camera contained no film, he thumbed the advance lever, depressed the shutter.

The mind may forget, but not the body.

She'd said that to him the last time they made love, in a sentimental moment after being separated for two months, but he sensed that her body had already forgotten, was ready for new memories, a new man. She'd told him she needed to be free—not to wound him, but with deep regret that proved the words hurt her as well. But now, after allowing him to think her dead for fourteen years, it seemed she was alive in California, near a place called Cyanide Wells. He had no reason to doubt his anonymous caller, who had taken the trouble to track him down for some unexplained reason.

"*. . . your wife is very much alive. And very cognizant of what she put you through when she disappeared. . . .*"

Matt's fingers tightened on the Nikon.

Picking it up had been a commitment after all.